Spider Legs

TOR BOOKS BY PIERS ANTHONY

Alien Plot
Anthonology
But What of Earth?
Demons Don't Dream
Geis of the Gargoyle
Ghost
Harpy Thyme
Hasan
Hope of Earth
Isle of Woman
Letters to Jenny
Prostho Plus
Race Against Time
Roc and a Hard Place
Shade of the Tree
Shame of Man
Steppe
Triple Detente
Yon Ill Wind

WITH ROBERT E. MARGROFF

Dragon's Gold
Serpent's Silver
Chimaera's Copper
Mouvar's Magic
Orc's Opal
The E.S.P. Worm
The Ring

WITH FRANCES HALL

Pretender

WITH RICHARD GILLIAM

Tales from the Great Turtle (Anthology)

WITH ALFRED TELLA

The Willing Spirit

WITH CLIFFORD A. PICKOVER

Spider Legs

PREVIOUS WORKS BY CLIFFORD A. PICKOVER

The Alien IQ Test
Black Holes: A Traveler's Guide
Chaos in Wonderland: Visual Adventures in a Fractal World
Computers, Fractals, Chaos (Japanese)
Computers, Pattern, Chaos, and Beauty
Computers and the Imagination
Future Health: Computers and Medicine in the 21st Century
Fractal Horizons: The Future Use of Fractals
Frontiers of Scientific Visualization (with Stu Tewksbury)
Keys to Infinity
The Loom of God
Mazes for the Mind: Computers and the Unexpected
Mit den Augen des Computers
The Pattern Book: Fractals, Art, and Nature
Strange Brains and Genius
Spiral Symmetry (with Istvan Hargittai)
Time: A Traveler's Guide
Visions of the Future: Art, Technology, and Computing in the 21st Century
Visualizing Biological Information

Spider Legs

PIERS ANTHONY

AND

CLIFFORD A. PICKOVER

TOR®
A TOM DOHERTY ASSOCIATES BOOK
NEW YORK

This is a work of fiction. All the characters and events portrayed in this novel are either fictitious or are used fictitiously.

SPIDER LEGS

This book is printed on acid-free paper.

A Tor Book
Published by Tom Doherty Associates, Inc.
175 Fifth Avenue
New York, NY 10010

Tor Books on the World Wide Web:
http://www.tor.com

Design by Maura Fadden Rosenthal

Library of Congress Cataloging-in-Publication Data

Anthony, Piers.
Spider legs / Piers Anthony & Clifford A. Pickover.—1st ed.
p. cm.
"A Tom Doherty Associates book."
Includes bibliographical references.
ISBN 0-312-86465-5
I. Pickover, Clifford A. II. Title.
PS3551.N73S59 1998
813'.54—dc21 97-29854
CIP

First Edition: January 1998

Printed in the United States of America

0 9 8 7 6 5 4 3 2 1

Contents

Intro

For thousands of years it was believed that ghosts, good and bad, benevolent and malignant, weak and powerful, in some mysterious way produced all phenomena; that disease and health, happiness and misery, fortune and misfortune, peace and war, life and death, success and failure, were but arrows from the quivers of these ghosts; that shadowy phantoms rewarded and punished all mankind; that they gave prosperous voyages, allowing the brave mariner to meet his wife and child inside the harbor bar, or sent the storms, strewing the sad shores with wrecks of ships and the bodies of men. Formerly, these ghosts were believed almost innumerable. Earth, air, and water were filled with these phantom hosts. In modern times they have greatly decreased in number. The remaining ghosts, however, are supposed to perform the same office as the hosts of yore.

—Robert G. Ingersoll (1881),
The Ghosts and Other Lectures,
14th Edition. C. P. Farrell:
Washington, D.C.

PART I

Phantom Rising

The history of life is written in creatures that we've barely begun to get acquainted with—jellyfish, the sponges, starfish—creatures that are found in fossil records back, in some cases, a billion years.

—Sylvia Earle

CHAPTER 1

Pycno

IT CRAWLED ALONG the hell-black ocean floor, searching with its five large dark eyes. It was not a crab—rather it was more spiderlike in appearance with obscenely thin long legs. Its mouth was a triangular opening at the end of a sucking appendage longer than its body. So ravenous was the creature that its body was not sufficient to contain its entire stomach; it carried its digestive and reproductive organs in long branches packed like sausages inside its legs.

The early morning light began to penetrate the darkness. At its current depth in the water, the phantom creature could see clearly for perhaps thirty feet. Beyond that was just a blur of blue-green. The water attenuated the red and orange colors first, giving its environment a curious cyan sheen. Beneath its feet the ocean floor was a tangled mass of vegetation, sea sponge, and shell.

As the thing walked, a small fish swam by. The spiderlike creature was of such Olympic porportions that the small fish did not realize that this was a living, potentially dangerous entity. Suddenly the creature stood still, not because it cared about the little fish, but because it sensed the presence of a larger multitentacular intruder. It began to move with a stalking, purposeful intent and then swam toward the other animal by treading water.

About twenty feet away, a giant octopus was feeding on a spiny dogfish shark. Disdaining the skin, the octopus ripped the shark open behind its gills, in order to remove its internal organs. The spiderlike creature watched the carnage for a few seconds, and then with surprising speed it snatched at the large octopus. With a sudden contraction of its body, the octopus turned brown and jetted for safer water. Black ink billowed but did not confuse the attacker. It followed its prey.

The giant octopus was once the stuff of legends, a monster that ravaged sailing vessels and lifted horrified men from the decks like bite-sized appetizers. Now the mature 500-pound male was fleeing for its life—the last large octopus of its kind in these cold waters. Unfortunately there were relatively few octopuses left, even though the harvesting of octopuses, favored as bait by the local Newfoundland fishermen, was officially banned. This was not entirely the result of local poaching.

The spiderlike creature made a second attempt to grab the octopus, which reacted by sucking water into its baglike mantle, and expelling it though a siphon. As the octopus jetted along the sea bed, the tips of its arms sometimes brushed against the ocean floor, making a slight rustling sound like leaves scraping on asphalt.

Suddenly the huge spider-creature snatched at one of the octopus's arms—which broke off and sank to the ocean floor. Unfortunately for the sea spider, the arm was quickly snatched by a smaller octopus. Cannibalism was common in the sea. Octopuses were known to eat their own kind, and when under stress, as when confined to a small aquarium tank, some octopuses even ate their own arms, which grew back in a few months.

The giant octopus would never have time to grow another arm. The sea spider grabbed it in a muscular bracelet of death. It began feeding on the soft parts and sucking out the body juices. For a few minutes there was an undulating umbrella of

20-foot-long tentacles as the octopus struggled. Its body colors darkened. It wriggled and shook as it sensed itself being slowly absorbed by the frightful proboscis, and its primitive brain felt a little of the terror of being eaten alive, of being imbibed while struggling. Even though the octopus had a beak as hard as a parrot's and could pierce crustacea shells, it had no chance. So strong was the sea spider's body, that the octopus was a tiny toy in its pair of pincerlike chelicerae.

In one last futile escape attempt, the octopus contracted its body to a fourth of its normal diameter, distorted its pliable eyeballs, and removed one of its arms through a gap between the spider's pincers. The sea spider responded by drawing the baglike mantle of the octopus deeper into its own sucking appendage. The octopus's body took on a white hue, then a dark red. The octopus lifted its weary arms as it died of oxygen starvation. Finally, it stopped moving.

Unlike the octopus and other reclusive creatures of the sea that preferred to hide in a rocky crevice or empty shell when menacing intruders approached, the huge sea spider—the pycnogonid—never felt fear. It had no natural enemies. But while the sea spider was fearless, it was certainly not stupid. It had several large, highly developed brains and was among the most intelligent of invertebrates. The pycnogonid not only learned quickly but remembered what it learned. It also revealed behavioral repertoires resembling emotion: irritability, aggression, rage—but never fear.

The surrounding ocean was a noisy place: the creature's environment was bathed in a medley of chirping, bubbling sounds. Here sound traveled at quadruple its speed in air, and it carried much better. Lately even the deep oceans were becoming polluted with the chemicals and sounds of humans, so the creature sometimes became disoriented and sought the source of the offending stimuli. The local transgressors were broad-beamed offshore service vessels which shuttled between Newfoundland and the Hibernia oil field, 170 nautical miles east of the island. Unfortunately for the pycnogonid, all the oil in the North Atlantic was in "iceberg alley", the pycnogonid's home, where the Labrador Current pulled icebergs southward from Greenland.

Ample food supplies which once had been plentiful were now becoming scarcer. The spider began to move toward the surface in search of food. Occasionally it swatted at nearby small fish and watched them die—as if for the sheer pleasure of seeing smaller, weaker animals suffer. Again and again it thrust at nearby sea creatures, too small to serve as food.

And so, swimming with its eight gigantic legs, the psychotic, serial-killing invertebrate rose slowly in the frigid darkness. It was hungry. Its digestive organs spasmed. It wished to eat.

Like a phantom rising from the depths of a dark dream, or a ghostly submarine rising from an oceanic abyss, it quietly ascended into more fertile territory. The realm of humans.

CHAPTER 2

Friends

NATALIE SHEPPARD BLINKED. "What is that?" she murmured, surprised.

Her friend followed her gaze from the wooden dock to the dark ocean. "Something in the air, or in the water?" Garth James asked, not seeing it.

"It's gone now. It—it must have been a reflection from a wave," Natalie said. "I shouldn't have spoken. I'm so accustomed to looking for suspicious things, I must be imagining them."

He smiled. "I doubt it. You strike me as an exceptionally level-headed woman. Could it have been an iceberg fragment?"

"More like a whale. Something alive, I think. But it wasn't a whale, or anything I recognized, really. I—" She shrugged.

"You could join us on our new schooner, the *Phantom,* and we'll look for it," he suggested.

Natalie smiled. "I'd love to. But I'm on duty, and my lunch break is just about done." She looked at her watch.

"Don't let him get you alone on that boat," a new voice said cheerfully. It was a beautiful young woman. "He's a demon lover on the water."

Natalie, embarrassed by the implication, was momentarily

flustered. She did not know how to deal with pseudo-passes. For the stunning creature was Garth's wife, Kalinda. Natalie had encountered them routinely a week ago, and liked them immediately. She privately envied their easy marriage. It was obvious that they had no fears of alienation. She knew she could go out all day alone with Garth, and not only would he be a perfect gentleman, Kalinda would have no concern. Oh, to have such mutual trust!

"You promised not to tell," Garth said, smiling at his wife. "But seriously, Natalie, maybe on your day off. We'd be glad to have you."

"For sure," Kalinda agreed warmly. "There's just nothing like going out on the *Phantom.*"

Natalie was sure it was so, and not merely because of the boat or the experience. Anywhere these folk went would be pleasant for all concerned. "Maybe I will," she agreed, reluctant only because she did not wish to impose. "How much longer will you be here?"

Garth shrugged. "As long as we choose. But perhaps a week, if that's convenient for you. I need to spend a bit more time with my little sister before moving on."

"Your sister?"

"Lisa. She works at Martha's Fish Store. Do you know it?"

Natalie nodded. "Yes. I've never been inside, though. I hear that—" She hesitated.

Kalinda laughed. "It has an eerie proprietor," she said. "That's what you've heard, isn't it?"

"Yes. But I'm sure that's an exaggeration."

"No, Lisa filled us in. She wouldn't work there, except that she needs the money."

"Why? Does Martha mistreat her?"

"Not exactly," Garth said. "But she can be very strange. Lisa's always afraid that one day something truly weird will happen, and she'll have to quit. But I think it's all right. Lisa's young, and hasn't met all the strange folk she's going to."

"All she meets are men hot to get into her pants," Kalinda said. "I know the feeling."

Garth patted her bottom. "So?"

"So she doesn't know how to relate to someone who isn't hot for her."

"But Martha's a woman!"

"So?" Kalinda retorted in the same tone he had used.

He looked thoughtful. "No, I don't think Martha's of that persuasion. She's just more interested in fish of any type than in people of any type."

Natalie made a mental note: check out the interior of that store, when she had a pretext. She wanted to know just how weird the proprietor of Martha's Fish Store was. Just in case something did happen. It was always better to be prepared with accurate information before a crisis occurred.

Garth reached out and touched Natalie's forehead with a gentle knuckle. He had an easy familiarity that amazed her, because she accepted from him what would have infuriated her from anyone else. "You can just about see those criminal assessment thoughts churning in there," he said, smiling. "You'd know she's a cop even without the uniform."

"He can be so obnoxious," Kalinda remarked fondly, gazing away as if addressing a video camera. "He gets worse the longer he spends on land."

Natalie put her hands on her hips. "But you were sailing just this morning!" she said.

"All of three hours ago," Kalinda agreed. "We're approaching the danger zone for his tolerance."

"I don't see why there has to be land anyway," Garth growled. "It should all sink under the sea, and take its landlubbers with it." He smiled winningly. "Present company excepted."

Natalie laughed, which was something she did not ordinarily do in public. There was something about these people that made laughter easy, even when the interaction was routine. "Well, I shall just have to suffer through the rest of my shift," she said, rising. "Do keep an eye out; I'd certainly like to know what I saw out there, if I saw anything."

"We will," Kalinda agreed. "See you soon, Natalie."

"And bring your bikini," Garth said.

"My—" Natalie paused. He had succeeded in startling her. It was a verbal trap; if she said she didn't have one, he'd suggest nude sunning. Natalie would not care to expose her body in either fashion; she was simply too lean. But his implication that she was otherwise was unsubtly flattering despite being unwarranted. "Some other decade," she said as she walked away.

"There was a day when I was the only one you teased," she heard Kalinda say to Garth.

"But we've been married ten years!" he protested. "You're all teased out."

"*Nine* years. There's still a year to go."

That was all of their banter Natalie was able to hear. Nine years? She had not guessed it was that long, because they still acted like almost-newlyweds. Probably it was a show for others. Still, it evoked desire in her—desire for a relationship like that. But she didn't ever want to get serious about a policeman, and what other type of man would tolerate a policewoman? The hours, the crises, the occasional dangers—he would surely insist that she quit her job, and she simply wasn't ready to do that. Not for anybody. Because she liked her work. It gave her life definition.

She put that disquieting thought aside. But it was immediately replaced by another: what *had* she seen in the sea? Probably just a piece of driftwood. But for an instant it had looked almost like a giant, gross, insect leg. Impossible, of course. Yet her fleeting glimpse had been so camera certain, until her rational mind corrected it. If only someone else has seen it too, to identify it as an unusual bit of flotsam, caught at an odd angle. As it was, the foolish image remained to haunt her. She couldn't afford to start seeing things that weren't there. It could play merry hell with her job performance.

Natalie knew she'd be watching the sea again, hoping to see

the thing, and identify it, and dissipate the trick her eye had played on her. Maybe she would take Garth and Kalinda up on their offer to sail briefly, just to reassure herself that there wasn't anything fantastic out there. She didn't like foolishness, especially in herself.

CHAPTER 3

Ice

THE SMALL PLEASURE boat was dwarfed by the strangely shaped icebergs floating nearby along the Newfoundland coast. In the fractured sides and grottos of these massive chunks of ice were strange rich blues and weathered aquamarines. The ocean surged into the cavernous bellies worn at the icebergs' waterlines and exploded in steepled and gabled sprays of foam. In this part of Newfoundland icebergs frequently changed shape under the chisels of the swift Labrador Current.

From far away, the small two-masted schooner blended in perfectly with its surroundings and looked like a long thin piece of ice drifting through a chilling white mosaic on the celadon sea. Closer, an observer could easily discern the boat's name engraved in golden letters on a wooden plaque hanging on the back. The sign read: PHANTOM.

The boat's occupants looked at a map of the area which showed that Newfoundland comprised two main areas, the Island of Newfoundland and the Coast of Labrador. The Island of Newfoundland, roughly triangular shaped, was separated from the Canadian mainland by the narrow Strait of Belle Isle on the northwest, the seventy-mile-wide Cabot Strait on the southwest, and the broad Gulf of St. Lawrence on the west.

The early morning rain had stopped, but the deck was still

slippery near the engine hatch where oil had soaked into the wood. Garth James sat in the cockpit of his boat with one bare foot resting on a spoke of the wheel. In his right hand was a cup of coffee. Garth was big, fairly muscular, dark-haired and swarthy, and appeared to be in his early thirties. He wore bold-colored Hawaiian swim shorts and a denim windbreaker. As he gazed across the horizon, the boat rocked gently in the deep swells. An invigorating whiff of pungent sea air filled his nostrils.

Garth turned on the boat's engine and pointed the craft in the direction of a peculiarly shaped iceberg which contained a myriad of exotic wave-cut patterns. At one moment the crevices were filled with green water. The next moment they were throwing white, foaming water back into the ocean. For the few seconds between the inrushing and outrushing of water, the caverns displayed thousands of pieces of pointed ice like sharks' teeth—white, green, and aquamarine.

Garth's curiosity about the ocean overwhelmed him at times. At 16, he had dived for the first time, donning an old helmet, weights, and compressed air to explore a Maine river bed. While at Yale University studying marine biology, he was introduced to sophisticated scuba gear. Even after his marriage at 21 to Kalinda, and the birth of their child Alan, he kept his attention focused on diving deeper and discovering the way the oceans worked.

Kalinda came up through the hatch and handed him an apple.

"Thanks," he said. Kalinda stared at the man with her sparkling eyes and then hooked her thumb in her shirt pocket and cocked her hip. He gazed at her and took her hand.

"Like your outfit," Garth said. Kalinda wore his flannel shirt, and nothing else.

"I better get something on before I freeze to death," she said, shivering. She was a slim woman, 27 years of age, with honey-colored hair, and eyes the darkest green.

"Why don't I warm you up first," Garth said as he kissed her on the lips.

"At least the weather's a bit warmer today than yesterday," she said with a charming smile that involved her eyes as well as her mouth. Like Garth, Kalinda was interested in the sea. Three years before she had been invited to join the National Science Foundation's research vessel *Anton Bruun* for a three-week exploration of the oceans near Madagascar. Together Garth and Kalinda had gone on expeditions to the Juan Fernández islands and the Galápagos Islands. Their parents, ever supportive, took care of their four-year-old during these trips.

"You really must be cold." He patted the crease of her bottom through the shirt. "Shall I follow you into the cabin?" He drew back enough to stare at Kalinda's nipples, which rose like goose bumps from beneath her inadequate outfit.

"I better put a coat on," she said, winking.

He placed his fingers under her shirt and felt her naked buttocks. He began to stroke her. She was right: her body was cold, like the anatomy of a statue. It was an interesting experience. "Galatea," he murmured.

"But I'm no ivory statue," she said. For Galatea, in mythology, was a beautiful statue later animated by the prayer of her lover.

"That's because I'm bringing you to life," he said, massaging her projecting flesh.

"Mmmm," she purred as he followed her to the cabin.

Garth had convinced Kalinda that the ultimate in unusual vacations was the North Atlantic where they could spend some time traveling among the awesome floating mountains, the icebergs. He had explained to Kalinda that the weather was fairly mild near Newfoundland. The presence of the sea moderated the temperature in the winter. The average temperature in January was about 20 degrees Fahrenheit, and 55 degrees F weather was common in the summer. However, only the south coast was ice-free throughout the winter. At first she thought his vacation idea was crazy, but when he showed her some photographs the U.S. Coast Guard supplied of magnificent ice giants plodding through Baffin Bay, she gave into the crazy adventure. They started in Quebec, traveling along the St. Lawrence River in their schooner, and continued through the Cabot Strait into the Atlantic.

Occasionally they docked along the coast of Newfoundland where weathered bald mountains rose almost from the water. Newfoundlanders affectionately called their Island of Newfoundland "the Rock." Battered by the Atlantic Ocean at Canada's easternmost point, it sometimes seemed a harsh place—remote and watery. Until the early 19th century, fish merchant monopolies, piracy, and international rivalry fiercely discouraged permanent settlement. Recently, however, Newfoundland had both modern amenities and rural values. In the past decade the government had begun to pursue an economic policy based on forestry, fisheries, and hydroelectric power. The fisheries remained the largest resource-sector employer, providing full-time work to 20,000 fishermen.

They had come to St. John's, checked in with Garth's lovely little sister Lisa, and now were on one of their side jaunts, forging north along the east coast of the island. The wind had been wrong on prior days, and that could make a difference, but this time it was right, and they were going against the current to see the icebergs. They were in no hurry.

"Are you warm yet, Galatea?" he inquired.

"Alive, but not warm," she replied. "Maybe if you heat me from the inside . . ."

There was silence while he did his best. In due course she confessed to having been warmed throughout.

An hour after making love, Garth and Kalinda emerged from the cabin to look at the coast with its charming village ports and then back at the large floating chunks of ice. "Do you think it's such a good idea to get so close to the glacier?" Kalinda asked as she turned her head. The light caught her silky hair turning it into the color of a Hawaiian sunset.

"Nothing to worry about. We'll go slow," Garth said as he tiptoed his fingers from her calf to her knee. There was usually little danger when sailing in these seas due to the number of Coast Guard boats in the area. Ever since the steamship *Titanic* collided with an iceberg and sunk, ship lanes near Newfoundland had continued to be patrolled by one or two American Coast Guard boats during the seasons when icebergs were drifting. Several nations helped to defray the cost of this patrol service.

"There must be hundreds of icebergs!" Kalinda said. Some looked like gigantic pyramids, hummocked in places to form the frigid likenesses of yawning lions. Garth turned to Kalinda.

"The location of every iceberg in these waters is radioed to the ships in the neighborhood. We can't get lost even if we wanted to."

"Let's be careful," Kalinda said. "I'd hate to collide with an iceberg."

"You're always such a worrier," he said, smiling.

"If I didn't worry, I think you'd have killed yourself by now," she said, perhaps thinking of the time he had nearly crashed the schooner into a coral reef a year ago.

Garth nodded as he edged the two-masted, motor-powered schooner even closer to an iceberg. Even though he realized that eight times as much of the ice was under the water than above, it was hard to fully appreciate that the beautiful blue waves concealed a mass of ice much larger than the behemoth before their eyes. Flashes of sunlight began to reflect off the berg's crystalline surfaces, producing an astonishing collection of scintillating orange and blue colors.

"Magnificent," Kalinda said as she pointed to the icefields, which glimmered like mercury. "The colors remind me a little of the sparkling crystals on the chandelier in my mother's home."

"Look at that one," Garth pointed. "Those kinds of glacial ice are known as 'dry docks' because of their deep U-shaped indentations. See the sparkling ponds of water at the bottom of the U?"

"Wouldn't want to get trapped at the bottom. How much do you think it weighs?"

"Probably around two million tons."

Suddenly the iceberg broke into several huge pieces, as if someone had exploded dynamite in its icy interior. It made a noise like thunder, which could be heard for several miles.

"Grab onto something," Garth cried. Kalinda ran toward the mast as rings of large waves began to radiate from the berg in all directions. The schooner began to pitch and roll as if it were in a great storm.

"Ahh," Kalinda cried as cold particles of salt spray splashed and ran down her legs. Part of the berg began to die with a crackling and crumbling. There were such roars of agony that it sounded as if the *Phantom* were under siege by cannons. When the waves subsided Garth decided he better be the first to speak.

"Everything OK?"

"I thought you said this was safe," she said sarcastically.

"Sorry. The bergs sometimes do that. Didn't realize how powerful the effect could be." After hours of direct sunlight had melted the surface ice, internal strains in the frozen water were manifest in what Newfoundland fisherman called iceberg "foundering"—the bergs exploded into huge chunks of ice. With a horrifying roar, blocks of ice bigger than a house sometimes broke away from the ice mountain.

But as Garth and Kalinda guided their craft among the icebergs for a few hours, they grew accustomed to the cacophonous sounds and sight—even grew to love them. They learned to navigate the boat among the icebergs with the grace of a downhill skier gliding back and forth between trees.

"Most of these icebergs come from the west coast of Greenland," Garth said.

"Right, I read about that. They also drift for around three years before reaching their deathbed in the warm Gulf Stream." Occasionally Kalinda liked to remind Garth about her own knowledge in marine geology, something Garth every now and then seemed to forget when he got into his scientific lecturing mood.

Now the sea was calmer.

"Care for a drink?" Garth asked.

"No thanks."

"A nap?"

"Maybe later." Although she might be tired, Kalinda evidently didn't want to miss the wonderful sights all around her.

Garth picked up a newspaper and began to leaf through it. "It says here that there are less codfish in the seas for the fishermen to catch these days, and that the Canadian government is subsidizing the fishermen. Wonder what could cause the sudden decline of fish?"

"Maybe they simply were overfishing the limited local supply."

Garth turned the pages of the newspaper. A colorful advertisement caught his eye: it was for Martha's Fish Store, which purported to be the largest marine and freshwater aquarium store in Newfoundland. It also claimed to have a tank with over one thousand neon tetra fish. He handed the advertisement to Kalinda.

"Let's take a look at Martha's Fish Store when we get back to the land. No sense in depending on Lisa for all our information."

"I'd love that."

As they traveled along the coast, with a few dozen icebergs in sight, the frequent roar of foundering icebergs made an otherwise serene setting more exciting than a roller coaster ride. At times even the noise of their ship's six-cylinder diesel engine couldn't be heard over the thunder of the bergs.

Garth yawned.

"Why don't you let me steer for a while," Kalinda said. "You take a nap below."

"Not a bad idea." Garth got stiffly to his feet, ducked under the boom, and checked a few ropes. Then he went to the hatch. He turned to Kalinda. "Come down if there's any problem."

Below, in a small, cozy room with a soft bed, a refrigerator, and other amenities, Garth checked a few maps and a compass. Then he examined his new chart drum navigator which enabled him to use traditional paper charts with loran or Global Position Satellite navigations systems.

Garth was always amazed at how well the loran system worked for determining his vessel's position. Like radar, this electronic system for *lo*ng *ra*nge *na*vigation was a World War II development. Unlike radar, loran required no special transmission from the ship. Instead a radio receiver operating on a low frequency gave loran the capability of receiving signals at great distances. Loran transmitting stations on shore operated in pairs; one was called the master, the other the slave station. The time difference between arriving signals allowed the ship to be located on a loran chart. Loran stations throughout the world afforded extensive loran coverage, but a ship had to be within 700 miles by day and 1,400 miles at night to receive the loran signals.

Earlier in the morning he had slipped a chart of the Newfoundland waters under a plastic overlay on the chart drum navigator. The drum rotated to keep the part of the map he was using in view. A moving red bead marked his boat's current position. So far, so good. They should be back in Bonavista Bay in another few hours.

Without removing any of his clothes, except for his sandals, he dived into bed and stretched out like an old dog. Before he fell asleep he thought about the sea. In spite of its dangers, humans were always attracted to the mystery and beauty of the ocean, the challenge of its unpredictability, from placid calm to raging storm. Since prehistoric times, humans' personal relationship with the ocean had been unique, unlike ties with other natural surroundings. Perhaps long before scientists realized that the sea was the mother of life, humans intuitively realized that the salty solution, so much like the chemistry of their own blood, was the source of living things.

CHAPTER 4

Spider

THE CREATURE WAS alert as it treaded water near heart-shaped corals that grew like mold from the sea floor. A crimson blob with light splotches rose from the mud in the wake of the pycnogonid. As the sea spider swam its large eyes fixed themselves on a brilliant red nudibrach mollusk, and then the spider crushed it with one of its gigantic legs.

In recent years various pollutants were causing species to mutate at a rate faster than normal. Medical wastes containing growth hormones, bacterial plasmids, and mutagens were being consumed by the local sea species. Many organisms were entirely unaffected, while some of the primitive invertebrates produced offspring with deformities and strange new physical characteristics. Many animals died. Others survived but with size and shape alterations: there were lobsters the size of pigs and with dozens of legs, two-headed crabs, and a multitude of new worm species with bioluminescent throat appendages and eyes the size of almonds. Marine scientists were becoming aware of these mutations and changes, and concern was rising. But they did not yet appreciate the magnitude of what was happening, or guess that not all of it was either natural or by chance. They would have some strong hints, however, soon enough.

As the sea spider stepped on a reef, the reef came alive: large numbers of jelly-roll creatures fled from the crevices. Above was an iceberg. Below glided small sharks and large rays. These were routine.

Suddenly the pycnogonid sensed vibrations emanating from somewhere near the sea's surface. Something big was approaching from above. The terminal claws on the creature's front legs quivered in unison with its huge chelicerae as it decided to climb the iceberg's shelf. Two impulses drove the sea spider: its desire to eat and its innate rage.

It rose for another few minutes and hit the underside of the glacier with a big bump. *Crash!* A soft explosion of ice was set off by the sea spider. After the vibrations subsided, the pycnogonid gracefully positioned its head downward, flipped its body, and began to walk upside down on the flat underbelly of the glacier—defying gravity with the aid of buoyancy. The sea was its ceiling, the ice its floor. It didn't care. It just wanted to get where it was going, whatever way that worked. It walked along the underside of the glacier until it reached its edge.

In just a few minutes, the body of the pycnogonid broke the water's surface and scrambled up an area of the iceberg which had a relatively gradual slope. Just like its arthropod cousins, the lobsters and crabs, the huge sea spider could live for some time in the fresh air. Its gills began to work in overdrive with what moisture they still contained, sucking in life-giving oxygen from the atmosphere. As it gazed out over the water in the direction of the sound and movement, the creature saw a moving object seemingly about its own size. The fact that the object was large, that it was alien, caused the sea spider no fear. It crept down the precipices and glacial snow-fields into a glacial valley, and then reached the edge of the iceberg which touched the sea. It prepared itself to attack.

CHAPTER 5

Dream

ALTHOUGH AN ICEBERG could be as big as an entire village, any sailor would have rather been shipwrecked on land than on such ice. Aside from the cold, the sides of an iceberg were often very steep. Hidden holes, crevices, and caverns added to the danger. Even if a sailor wanted to explore an iceberg's glistening surfaces and caves, it was usually too difficult for most sailing vessels to dock alongside such a mass. The unfortunate ship that crashed into one of these islands of ice usually sank, and the water was so cold that even an Olympic swimmer would have died from exposure.

Kalinda had no intention of being shipwrecked on an iceberg and took extra care to stay clear of the mammoth chunks of ice. She carefully steered the boat into a narrow channel between two icebergs, and then in the direction of an impressive rhinoceros-shaped berg with a huge arch in the middle. It was wide enough to hold a football field. On the northern side of the berg was a huge, upward pointing prominence that reminded her of a rhinoceros's horn. From this distance it seemed that a chunk of ice was missing from an area of the rhino's face, forming a dark area which composed the rhino's eye. Kalinda got out her new expensive sophisticated camera and snapped a few pictures. The camera had special protections against water splashed from any direction.

After a minute, she put the camera down. The dark area forming the "eye" on the iceberg seemed a bit strange, she thought, so she decided to take the boat closer for a better look. Just as people enjoyed watching clouds and finding animal and other shapes in their random patterns, sailors often looked at ice formations and imagined sea serpents and mermaids, and other more provocative patterns. She wondered if she should wake Garth up from his nap to see the berg with its pinnacles towering more than fourteen stories high. But of course it wouldn't evaporate before he got his chance.

Kalinda reached over to a radio on the bridge, turned it on, and began bobbing her head to the rhythm of the golden oldie "Please Mr. Postman" by the Marvelettes. Another few minutes passed; then a sudden wild scream startled her. It came from above. She looked up to see a large seagull circling with wings outstretched and motionless. Just a seagull.

The rhinoceros-shaped iceberg now loomed above her, more beautiful than any sculpture created by the hands of humans. The sun gave a kind of smooth brilliance to the whiteness of the iceberg hulk. Wherever there were cracks there were also veins of pale violet melt water that had flowed into the cracks and had refrozen. Again she gazed up at the ice horn pointing up at the blue sky like a hitchhiker's thumb. *But where was the dark area that formed its eye?* She looked some more. There it was, to the left.

The eye formation on the iceberg moved. Kalinda gasped. As the craft edged ever closer to the berg, her hands slipped on the wooden steering wheel. They were cold and clammy.

The eye moved again.

"Garth, wake up." There was no noise from below the hatch. She killed the engine. "Garth?" As she walked to the hatch, she felt a nervous shiver go up her spine. She poked her head inside and saw her husband motionless on their small bed. His eyelids fluttered with the rapid movement of his eyes. Garth was dreaming.

Kalinda hesitated. She was alarmed about what she had seen, but she knew it was probably some natural phenomenon that Garth would immediately explain. On the other hand, his dreams were often special. If she let him wake naturally, he would share his dream with her before it faded, and they would both be richer. For a long time she had been interested in the rich and largely untapped realm of dream symbolism. Kalinda had taught Garth certain psychological methods for momentarily awakening to report his dreams to her before he fell back to sleep to continue his dreaming. They both practiced and enjoyed remembering their dreams. The sharing of dreams had improved their understanding of themselves and brought them closer as a couple. So she stifled her probably baseless fear and waited; she knew it would not be long.

It wasn't. In a moment he opened his eyes, saw her, and immediately spoke his dream, knowing that she would remember it better than he would, because she was fully awake and rational. Freshness was everything, because the details faded like morning fog, leaving no trace if not caught early. And indeed it turned out to be worthwhile.

He had dreamed that he was a child back at his parents' house in Asbury Park, New Jersey. He had just purchased a strange new aquatic animal for his 110-gallon tropical fish tank. The tank was in the basement, already filled with a dazzling array of marine species: orange clown fish, long-snouted coralfish, powder blue surgeonfish, and wimplefish—all from the Indo-Pacific. When he dropped the newcomer into the tank, it immediately settled to the bottom. It looked a little like a tube worm with a sludge-green, chalky outer tube. When threatened, or at night, it retracted its pinky tentacles and hairlike projections, and closed the hinged lid at the top of its inch-thick tube. It seemed to eat the same prepared flake food that the other fish enjoyed—except it ate a lot more than other fish. Occasionally, he supplemented the diet with freeze-dried krill, blood worms, and brine shrimp.

So voracious was the tube worm that over the next few weeks Garth went through several cans of food. Each day the animal grew in size until one day it was so large it climbed out of the tank and waited in the corner of the room. When Garth came down to feed the fish, he saw that his hairy specimen was no longer in the tank. He looked around the room near the tank, and then a movement caught his eye. From the corner of the room, it came at him, with large saberlike teeth. Young Garth screamed and ran up the basement steps, the animal hot in pursuit. As he reached the basement door, he found to his horror it was locked. On the door was a computer keyboard and computer screen. The screen had the words:

PLEASE KEYPRESS CORRECT PASSWORD TO OPEN DOOR.

Garth typed one password after another on the keyboard, desperately, but none opened the door. The worm came closer and closer as it navigated the basement steps. Its moist body undulated along the carpet like that of a snake. It was only three steps away. Two steps away. One step away. Garth then suffered a fevered flash of inspiration and typed the password "DEATH," the door finally opened, and—

"And that's as far as it goes, right now," he concluded. "I'd better finish it." At which point he closed his eyes and returned to sleep. He'd trained himself not to fear his dreams.

This was too much. He might sleep for another hour, now, and the continuation would be lost in the welter of the following dreams. They had gotten all they could. Her concern for what was outside returned, perhaps augmented by the horror of the dream itself.

"Garth? Wake up," Kalinda called.

For a moment Garth was disoriented, trying to shake off the ashes of his weird dream, but then he realized where he was. Kalinda was heading outside the moment she saw him sit up. He stumbled after her, out of the hatch and on to the bright deck.

"What's wrong?" he asked, his attention shifting to the iceberg. "Wow, you discovered a magnificent berg."

"There was something on it that moved. It's not there any more."

"Maybe it was a chunk of ice that slipped." As Garth watched the iceberg he seemed not fully focused, and she knew he was trying to recall details of his weird dream and the atmosphere of impending doom. She would feed those details back to him as soon as this other thing was checked.

"It couldn't be," she said. "It was something dark. It looked like it was alive."

"The light plays tricks. Could still be ice."

"Garth, I thought I saw legs."

"A bear? I think most of the bears this far north are white."

"It was as big as this ship. Maybe bigger."

He looked at her. "Just which one of us was dreaming?" he asked, smiling.

She remained serious. "I got your dream. But this was no dream. It alarms me. I don't know what I saw."

"Natalie saw something in the sea," he said, remembering. "I wonder—?"

"Maybe so. She was shaken. So am I."

He did not try to joke any more, realizing that something strange was happening. She was relieved. She still hoped that he would come up with a natural explanation.

They looked around at the iceberg and the glittering water but saw and heard nothing out of the ordinary. Perhaps there was a smell of low tide and crawling things, but nothing more. Now and then long streaks of sunlight shot through the cloudy sky and glimmered on the multihued facets of ice in the surrounding sea. "Whatever it was," Garth said, "I guess we can't do too much about it now. It still could have been a trick of the light."

They sat in silence for a few minutes listening to the strong tonal contrasts of the sea and the gulls. In the distance they saw a few men riding on 16-foot-long fiberglass boats. The sleek crafts resembled outrigger canoes. One of the men pushed and pulled on the boat's sweep oar and moved his feet as if he were pedaling a bicycle to move the craft forward. Garth changed the subject.

"How about we get something to eat?"

"OK, would you like a tuna sandwich?" Kalinda asked. There was obviously no point in worrying further about what she might have imagined.

"Sounds great."

"Onions, paprika, mayonnaise?"

"Perfect." Even though he had had a late breakfast of eggs, bacon, homefries, and buttered toast, the cool fresh air had an invigorating effect which made him particularly hungry. She had seen it before. After such a cholesterol-rich meal, she thought he should have a few fruits and vegetables.

"How about another apple?" he said, agreeing.

"Coming right up."

Kalinda suddenly started and cocked her head in the direction of one of the boat's railings. She ran toward the bow. *"What was that?"*

"What?"

"I heard a scraping noise. Sounded like scratching."

"Where?"

She slowly made her way to the aft rail. There was a creeping uneasiness at the bottom of her heart. Her emotions reminded her of the times her neighbor's dog ran after her when she was only seven years old. The dog was a large one, a German shepherd. Often Kalinda would come home crying to her mother as the dog outside barked and barked. Her mother complained to the dog's owner and finally the dog was kept inside the house when Kalinda walked home from school.

"Maybe a chunk of ice brushed against the boat," Garth said. Kalinda feared she was beginning to give him the jitters, instead of being reassured by him. He looked all around. His tension seemed to rise a few percentage points. Still nothing unusual. But she didn't like this at all.

Boom. Boom. The scratching noises turned to dull thuds

which grew in volume. Now there was no doubt at all that something was up. She tried to suppress her wildest and most unreasonable fears, with little success.

"Maybe we should stay in the cabin and shut the door," Kalinda said.

"I think it will be OK. It's probably a baby whale. Won't hurt us."

Then a strange expression crossed his face. He was staring at her, or beyond her, eyes wide, jaw slack. "What is it, Garth?" she asked, feeling a tight knot of panic.

The ship began to rock back and forth. Water splashed onto the deck. Garth's mouth worked without producing sound as he looked around the ship. It was as if he had a pressing need to confirm he was on his own boat, that the universe had not just swiveled into some insane new dimension. He gazed at the familiar rails, gleaming deck, weathered ropes, as if willing some horror to go away. But whatever it was remained.

"Garth—" she said, clinging to a semblance of equilibrium. "What's *happening?*"

One quarter of the vessel's railing disappeared off the side of the ship, as if torn away by some colossal hand.

"Get away from the rail," Garth cried. She stepped away from it, then slowly turned. Before she looked back, Kalinda suddenly felt numb, as if her feelings were paralyzed. What could possibly be there? She forced her eyes to focus.

Slowly, a huge jointed leg appeared from the water near the lost rail. When she turned toward the rail, trying to make sense of this phantom, she saw the leg lift high, coming toward her.

Kalinda threw back her head and screamed a guttural cry of terror. She pirouetted back toward Garth but slipped on the wet deck. Now two more legs appeared as the monster tried to clamor onto the deck. There was a brittle crack of weathered wood, as the engine was torn off the boat. So sharp was the chitinous exoskeleton of the sea spider, that it left inch-deep scratch marks on the planking.

For that was what it was, she realized. An impossibly enormous spider in the sea, a creature vaguely like that of Garth's dream, only much bigger and more horrible in form. Now she saw its awful snout emerging from the water, coming over the deck, dripping sea water or saliva. She saw its gangly body heaving up. This was worse than any nightmare!

Kalinda crawled away. The sea spider came closer. It loomed over her. Ice-cold water ran off the crevices in its body onto her—water so cold that it felt like an electric shock to her skin. She dragged her body forward a few steps, but was seconds too slow. The sea spider's leg came down on her foot with a tremendous force and tore half of it off with a crunching sound. She didn't even feel the pain, just heard the crunching as she wrenched her leg away. She looked back as if mesmerized. The multilegged attacker used it chelicerae for seizing and carrying Kalinda's half-foot to its mouth. There didn't seem to be much bleeding, oddly.

"Gaah," Kalinda choked and shoved her fist into her mouth. She did not yet go into shock but continued to struggle, desperate to squeeze herself behind one of the large wooden boat masts, determined to place the mast between her and the monster. She held onto the mast with all her strength, only partially aware of the stinging pain in her fingers when she tore her thumbnails.

The sea spider continued to suck on her foot, and then, without warning, cracked the mast into two pieces. Blood oozed from the stump of her foot as she tried to tear a piece of her shirt to make a tourniquet. But the shirt would not tear. Kalinda felt as if her eyes had become as sunken as the eyes of a cadaver.

A vile ammonia odor filled the ship. Garth threw a fire extinguisher at the alien creature, but it continued to come toward Kalinda. It did not hesitate or seem concerned by Garth's movements.

"I'm coming," Garth said as he stepped closer to grab her. But the spider was too close to Kalinda to allow him to reach her without himself being trampled into human hamburger. The ammonia smell burned their nasal passages, made their eyes tear. Ridiculously Garth ran to the monster and gave a swift, vicious kick to one of its legs.

"Look out!" Kalinda screamed as the leg responded by shoving Garth into a piece of the mast. His eyes were flecked with pain as he toppled sideways. A spine on one of the legs ripped into him, so devastating that he dropped to the deck, surely feeling pain like nothing he had ever known. As he lay there stunned for a few seconds his mouth worked, and she heard him speak, as from a distance.

"Oh, Kalinda," he gasped. "I love you, and I will protect you! You can't die, you aren't going to die . . ."

Tears came through her horror as she struggled to her feet, ignoring the lancing pain from her mutilated foot. In the face of this dreadful threat, all he was thinking of was her!

The creature came swiflty up from behind Kalinda. She stepped to one side to let the creature pass and almost blacked out with pain as one of its leg spikes skewered her, its tan and white tip slicing red hot into the flesh of her chest, scraping along her sternum like fingernails on a blackboard and emerging five inches from the point of entry. She twisted with the force of the blow, taking the spine with her. A pain shot like lightning from her chest to her skull. At the same time she reacted instinctively, smashing the knuckles of her stiffened right hand into a softer area right at the creature's leg joint. The spider seemed surprised, but that was about all. It rose slowly above her, its huge black expressionless eyes staring into her own. There was no doubt it intended to consume her.

Garth screamed. Having no weapons aboard the *Phantom* to protect himself and Kalinda, it seemed likely that the monster would succeed in making Kalinda its next meal.

Now the cold water and air was beginning to have an anesthetizing effect on Kalinda. The sea water splashed on her by the spider left her with a fraction of her sense of touch. Her face was numb. She saw Garth look at her, and knew that she seemed more like an apparition, unreal, lost, already on the threshold of death.

Kalinda's heartbeat accelerated as she looked back and up at the creature's multiple bulging eyes. It loomed over her like a giant hideous balloon in a Thanksgiving parade. The balloon resemblance, however, was only superficial: vile black liquid oozed from the creature's pores and several lesions of decay. Kalinda smelled its fetid body as it edged ever closer. Its eyes looked her over with the compassionless, hungry practicality of a vulture. Yet she remained aware of peripheral things. From overhead, gulls swooped in large arcs across a sky filled with vague perpetual clouds.

"Garth—" She ended in a gargle of blood and collapsed to the deck as she began to choke. She could no longer move or talk, yet she remained conscious, able to see and hear. It was as if she had entered another realm, as a nonparticipant. She was aware of what her husband was doing. She wanted to cry to him to get away, to hide in the cabin, to radio for help. She was done for; she knew that. But maybe while the spider consumed her, Garth would have time to save himself.

Garth licked his lips. She knew he had tasted his own blood and realized he had bitten into his tongue. Somehow he managed to get to his feet, dragging his battered body backward. He stood frozen for a moment but then must have remembered that there was a large pole downstairs in the hatch. Perhaps he could wedge this into the pycnogonid's sucking appendage or stab at one of its eyes with it.

She heard him get up and stumble toward the hatch. He grabbed the doorknob, but the hatch door was jammed. "Open, damn you," he cried. He banged on it. He tugged again, and the door sprang free. He barged in.

Now Kalinda moaned, hoping that Garth could not hear her. She didn't want him to be distracted as he fought to save his own life. Blood was pulsing past the sharp bony spine in her chest. What remained of her shirt was soaked, and she could feel the sticky warmth spreading. She began to feel totally disoriented—and icy cold.

But she remained aware of Garth, hearing his footsteps,

knowing what he was doing. She knew he loved her; she loved him just as passionately, and knew his ways. She could track him by the tiniest sounds and pauses. He quickly surveyed the cabin and found the six-foot pole lying against a life preserver. She knew he was desperate, that her situation was a nightmare beyond anything he had ever encountered. She didn't want to make it worse.

So as the dreadful spider legs closed on her, she didn't even try to scream or struggle. Probably she wouldn't have been able to anyway. She played dead, knowing it was her only chance. It wasn't far from the reality. She let the legs haul her up and away in silence. She remained attuned to Garth, not because she had any further illusion that he could save her, but because his image was her best and fondest link to sanity.

He grabbed the pole and ran back toward the deck. He burst through the cabin door, his face the color of oatmeal. She knew, without seeing. He stood there on deck, trembling with fear. But Kalinda was gone. There was no movement. He looked in all directions, calling out, "Kalinda!" He looked over the rail; the surface of the tomb-deep ocean was opaque, impenetrable.

Garth reached out with his right hand toward the spot where Kalinda last stood. "Kalinda." He needed to hold her, and she wished she could oblige. "Kalinda?" The mahogany trim on the boat was splashed with blood, and the fabric of some of the sails was sodden and crimson. The desire to find her was so intense that his body began to shake. His legs became rubbery. She knew.

Reality shifted for a few seconds, so there was not even the whisper of a sound. Then the world came tumbling back into focus. There was the muted crack of icicles from the nearby glacier. Swallowing hard, Garth ran back to the cockpit, pulled the door shut, grabbed hold of a microphone attached to the radio and shouted, "Newfoundland radio—this is the schooner *Phantom!* We have no engine. Our masts are destroyed. We need help . . ."

Garth stopped suddenly, too full of sorrow and shock to continue. He heard the radio squawk a bunch of meaningless noise. After a few minutes he went back on deck, gazed into the sea, and called again: "Kalinda?"

Don't look behind the cabin, she willed him.

He heard a sound, but did not see what made it. Something flicked forward and landed on the nape of his neck. Everything went dark as he fell into the cabin below.

The last thing he heard came from above. It was the endless cries of seagulls. He was trapped on a ship in a prison of ice and sea.

But perhaps he would survive. The spider hadn't actually killed him. It might forget him by the time it was through with her.

Kalinda, suspended in the absentminded grip of the spider legs, finally let her consciousness ebb. Her one remaining regret, oddly, was that she knew she would never get to tell him the content of his dream.

PART II

Phantom Hunting

The sea sheltered ample dragons to fuel the nightmares of the entire human race.

—PETER BENCHLEY, *Beast*

CHAPTER 6

Head

ELMO SAMULES, ONE of the fisheries officers for Trinity Bay, always told visitors that the Island of Newfoundland was a rough coast to make a living on. Recently, however, offshore oil had begun to offer a promise of employment for thousands. Elmo had seen many changes to the area around Bonavista Bay since his boyhood. When he was only three years old, his parents emigrated from Milan to Canada after his father joined an unsuccessful fishing business. After that, the elder Elmo prospered in Bonavista Bay as a shingle manufacturer and later in the lumber business. The younger Elmo's formal schooling was limited to a year, followed by five years of instruction by his mother. He was an entrepreneur at age 17, leading fishing and whale watch boats in Bonavista Bay.

Elmo always loved the sea and had an early and avid interest in fish and other sea life. His interest and exploration of the nearby oceans was helped by his minimal requirement for sleep. Since his teenage days, he acquired the habit of going for long periods of time with little sleep, sometimes requiring a few hours each night to be fully refreshed. Elmo was not unlearned in science; his prodigious reading had carried him through numerous scientific and popular articles on the sea.

Today Elmo was taking Nathan Smallwood, curator of fishes

from the Harvard Museum of Comparative Zoology, on a tour of the eastern coast in a fiberglass patrol boat that hopped between wave crests like a flying fish. Smallwood was determining the extent to which oil companies' submersible catamaran drilling rigs and the huge towers of Petro-Canada drill ships were damaging the local food chain. He was also here to enjoy the beauty of Newfoundland's coasts and rivers.

Physically the two men were very different. Elmo was a large man with muscular arms wedged into a black T-shirt. He could throw a football like a cannon shot, despite an unusual configuration for his fingers. Behind the athletic facade was an encyclopedic mind, a dynamic force. Smallwood, on the other hand, was adjutant in appearance, tall, thin, quiet, swarthy. His light brown walrus mustache complemented his gray-brown hair. He wore stonewashed cotton twill trousers and a tan cotton-canvas workshirt.

They flew past trap skiffs, the traditional 25-foot Newfoundland inshore boats. Elmo waved to a group of young fishermen who hand-hauled gill nets from Trinity Bay. Orange-brown crabs clung tenaciously to the wet nets as they were pulled from the water.

"Let's go see some icebergs," Smallwood shouted to Elmo.

"Sure."

They headed out to sea. Elmo pointed upward. Above was a flock of raucous northern gannets, goose-sized birds that were themselves fantastic fishers. Occasionally a gannet plunged into the sea after prey.

Elmo turned off the engine. "You might think that Newfoundland seems a bit primeval, but it has a rich history," he said. They were now in the area of the iceberg floes. "Maritime Archaic Indians arrived 5,000 years ago to hunt seals and walruses. In 1610, the first Europeans settled on the Avalon Peninsula. Later Britain and France disputed the sovereignty of Newfoundland. I think that was in the 1700s, but today 95 percent of Newfoundland's 582,000 people trace their ancestry to Britain."

They watched the icebergs gleam intensely blue. "You really can't appreciate the beauty of the ice and snow until you see this for yourself," Smallwood said in pleased surprise.

They heard roaring and booming from some of the snowy mountains that lined the coast, punctuated by the explosive sounds that the larger icebergs made. Baffin Bay and Greenland were the factories that produced the icebergs of the North Atlantic. Ice sliding down the valleys constantly shoved the preceding ice masses out into the paleo-crystalline seas.

"It's been estimated that some of the ice may be over two hundred thousand years old, having accumulated until it is two miles deep," Elmo said. "The Labrador Current carries them down past Newfoundland where they encounter water and winds which blow them toward England. The life journey of a Greenland iceberg is about two thousand miles and lasts two years."

"Now I've seen some of Newfoundland's coast, which is fantastic," Smallwood said. "But I've had little time to explore the mainland. What's the interior of the Island of Newfoundland like?"

"Well, with the settlements clustered on the coasts, our inland areas are pretty much wilderness solitudes. Lots of nice forests. Caribou often cross our highways."

They neared Bonavista Bay and had a close encounter with two humpback whales which splashed their small craft with water as they slapped the sea with their tails. They were curious creatures and protected by Canadian law.

"That happens often," said Elmo. "They seem to take a perverse pleasure in getting us wet."

"Did you see that big scratch near its tail?"

"No, missed it."

"I wonder what could have caused it?"

"Ship propeller?"

"The cut looked too straight and narrow to have been made by a propeller."

Elmo resolved to watch more closely for tails hereafter, because his guest was right: an unusual scratch on a whale could signify something going on in the deep water, and it was his business to know about it. It was probably nothing, but he preferred to be sure. If, for example, some pleasure craft operator was experimenting with a power harpoon, something would have to be done.

They continued to travel among towering iceberg mountains of white glory. "You know, things live on those icebergs," Elmo said. "Inch-long ice worms—*Mesemchytraeus solofiugus*—feed on algae and pollen in the tiny air pockets in the ice. The worms were once thought to be mythical."

"Didn't know you were such a fine biologist, Elmo." Smallwood was obviously impressed with the big man's zoological knowledge.

"We fisheries officers study a lot," Elmo said, smiling. Both men seemed to be thoroughly enjoying their time together. They admired a reddish iceberg tinted crimson by a summer-blooming algae. Suddenly something floating nearby caught their attention.

"Look over there," Smallwood said. "It's a boat. A schooner. Looks damaged."

"Let's take a look." As they got closer they could make out the schooner's name, *Phantom.*

"What kind of name is that?" Smallwood asked.

"It does seem a bit eerie. You know what the most common boat name is?"

"Tell me."

"Serenity."

There were scratches all over the vessel. Some were just an inch long, others a foot or two in length. When they were alongside the schooner, Elmo put down an anchor, threw a rope, and jumped onto the other boat. "Anyone here?" he called.

There was no answer. "Surely not a derelict vessel?" Nathan called, smiling. "I thought those existed mainly in ghost stories."

"They do," Elmo agreed somewhat tersely. His eyes tracked grooves in the deck that led to the hatch. A wave of grayness passed over him, a kind of dark premonition. "I see a lot more scratch marks here," he yelled to Smallwood. Then he stooped to pick up a camera which rested on the wooden deck. Perhaps it held some clues as to the former occupants of the schooner.

For a few minutes there were no sounds from the schooner. Just silence. The more Elmo studied this, the less he liked it.

"Anything the matter?" Smallwood called from the patrol boat.

"Something's wrong here. Dead wrong."

"Don't keep me in suspense, Elmo. What do you see?"

But Elmo was not eager to tell what he saw. Not immediately. This was real mischief.

There was blood on the deck. The railing was torn off in places. There were signs of struggles. Heroic ones. A broken mast. A torn off engine. More blood. Something resembling an esophagus.

And there was a human head. A head with carotid arteries still dripping. The head of a woman. A head evidently torn from its missing body with incredible strength.

CHAPTER 7

Environment

MARTHA SAMULES LOOKED up as the door to Martha's Fish Store opened to admit a solid man. She was in the back, but could see the door without being readily seen, because of the shadow. This was no coincidence; she preferred to have better knowledge of her customers than they had of her, especially when they were strangers. This could make a difference, when trouble threatened.

This man was no stranger; she recognized him. Oh, no! Martha dreaded the coming encounter, for the man was her brother Elmo. They were so similar yet so different. All they ever did was quarrel, yet they couldn't let go of each other. She would have faded to the back room, leaving the store to her hireling Lisa. But Lisa wasn't due to report for another twenty minutes. Martha was stuck for it.

She stood, approaching him. She was determined to keep things positive, this one time, but knew that she would fail as she always did. She forced a smile. "What can I do for you, Elmo?"

"There's been some trouble," he said gruffly. He walked around the store, gazing at the fish tanks, as if he were a customer. By that token she knew that he was not any more comfortable with this meeting than she was. But that gave her scant comfort, because he was not a shy or evasive man. Something was really bothering him, and it was bound to bother her in a moment. "I have a meeting coming up. But that's not why I'm here. Mother's in trouble again. She may or may not make it. Will you come?"

It was just as bad as she had feared. She knew she had no reason for guilt, yet he made her feel it. "You know I won't, Elmo."

"I know how you feel, Martha. But—"

"Oh, *do* you!" She stifled the rest, clinging to her resolve.

"But she is your mother, and she is a human being. She never meant to hurt you, or knew that she was doing it. She may have allowed you to be hurt, but she was blameless in intention. I know it would please her just to see you, even if you don't say a word." But his eyes remained on the fish, not on her. "Can't you raise enough compassion to let her imagine, before she dies, that—"

"Compassion!" she snapped. She tried to hang on, but knew that she was losing control. She didn't want to make this scene. So she performed an evasive maneuver. "Do you know how many species are killed each year by humans?" Martha asked him.

The big man looked away from a tank of neon tetras and back at Martha. "No," he said, with a slightly quizzical expression on his face. She knew he was momentarily confused by her tack, not certain what she was up to, and no more eager for a confrontation than she was.

She started to lecture him. "Although it's probably impossible to know how many are killed with any accuracy, because no one knows how many species inhabit the Earth, it is clear that each year two percent of the world's rain forests are destroyed, and at this rate they will be gone in 50 years." Martha began to ramble a bit, unconcerned with the fact that her brother listened politely but neither cared nor fully understood what she was trying to say.

Since adolescence Martha had had little regard for ordinary folk, but much regard for other creatures of the planet. She saw humans overrunning the world, blithely extirpating thousands of other species, promising to render just about every other creature extinct in the next fifty years before her fellow humans finally extinguished themselves in a final orgy of pollutive destruction.

"Oh, the environment," Elmo said, recognizing the theme. "That's not—"

"Humans are destroying the planet," she yelled at him, as if he were personally responsible. "They pollute. They overpopulate their land."

"Look, Martha, we've long since agreed to disagree on this. Oky, so you feel for the animals. So do I. Who doesn't? But I believe in the wise use of the resources of the world—"

"Wise use! That's an obscenity! That's the buzzword for unfettered exploitation. It's the obliteration of every species except our own."

He shook his head. "There may be some that deserve to be obliterated, such as the malaria carrying mosquito or the parasitic blowfly. However—"

"Deserve it?" she demanded. "What can you be thinking of? Nothing deserves extinction!"

But Elmo's mouth tightened. She knew he thought she was a nut on this subject. "Something does." He said no more.

That aggravated her further. "Animal species are disappearing due to habitat destruction, pollution, and the introduction of exotic species into natural environments where they don't belong. And you think that's all right? Elmo, do you know what an exotic species is?"

"Of course. But I don't care to—"

"Didn't think so. Know how many species could be extinct in the next fifty years?" Elmo started to move away, reminding her of a rabbit with part of its nervous system removed, despite his bulk. Yet he wasn't quite ready to leave. He had never been a quitter; she could say that much for him. He wandered down the rows of tanks, as if searching for a few small fish for his own fish collection. She knew he was actually searching for some way to convince her to come to see their mother. She had to head that off.

"We just got a shipment of beautiful discus fish. Could I interest you in a few?"

"No thank you," he replied, troubled. "Martha—"

"Did you know that about twenty percent of the world's freshwater fish species are in dangerous decline?" Elmo looked back and listened. His eyes grew wide in frustration. She knew she was treating him like an idiot, considering that he was a local fishery officer who probably had such statistics memorized as a matter of business. But she couldn't stop.

Elmo looked as if he were about to bring up the matter of their mother again.

"That's why I buy my fish only from fish farms so that the natural lakes are not interfered with," Martha said, more forcefully than the subject warranted.

"Someone's coming," he said, relieved.

Martha glanced at the door. "That's only Lisa. She works for me."

Evidently giving up his mission here as a bad job, Elmo moved for the door, passing Lisa, who gave him a quick smile. Lisa thought he was a customer, and it was part of her job description to smile winningly at customers. Sometimes it made a difference in a sale, for she was a pretty girl. Of course the effort was wasted in this instance, but Martha wouldn't tell her that; she was glad he was going.

Yet her emotions were mixed as she heard the door close after him. She always fought with Elmo, and he fought with her. But they were two of a kind, for all that, and he was perhaps the one human being she cared for. Naturally she wouldn't tell him that. If only he weren't such a straightlaced conventional man. Wise use, indeed! Elmo had a fine brain, but it remained firmly in human-chauvinist channels. If only he had seen and learned what she had.

For Martha had observed, firsthand, the extinction of many species of freshwater fish in Africa and Asia, the decline in bird populations in the United States, and the rapid disappearance of the Brazilian rain forests by cutting and burning. She had watched the Brazilian fires spew out millions of tons of carbon and carbon monoxide into the air. She had clenched her fists when she had seen the great plumes traveling eastward across the Atlantic. The forests were being destroyed at the rate of a football field every second, or the size of Florida every year. Those weren't mere trees; they were a vital component of the world's system of atmospheric restoration. The rainfall pattern was changing, bringing more deserts, and the globe was warming. When it reached a certain unknown trigger point there could be a drastic change in climate, causing agricultural havoc on land and turmoil in the seas. It had happened before, from natural causes; this time it would be unnatural. The extinction of the dinosaurs had been an extreme example, though not *the* most extreme.

Her most recent trip to Cebu in the Philippines had pushed Martha over the edge. When the forest was completely logged, she found that nine out of ten bird species unique to the island were made extinct. She considered incidents like this as miniature holocausts. Like a hemorrhaging of the earth. Harvard zoologist Edward O. Wilson, her mentor and hero, estimated that the number of rain forest species doomed each year was 27,000. Each day it was 77, and each hour 3. Human actions had increased extinction between one thousand and ten thousand times over its normal background level in the rain forest.

Martha was continually depressed by the fact that the richest nations presided over the smallest and least interesting biotas, while poorest nations with exploding populations and little scientific knowledge had the largest number of animal species and incredibly intricate, vast ecosystems. If only she could make Elmo see, recruit him to her Earth-saving mission. He was just about the only person she could trust, if he were on her side. But he wasn't. He wasn't against her, exactly; he was just one of the apathetic throng who chose to believe that there wasn't a looming crisis. The absolute fool!

Now, belatedly, it occurred to her that if she had been more accommodating in the matter of their mother, her brother might have been more receptive to her own interests. She had missed a golden opportunity. Because she was just as pigheaded as he was. What a pity.

CHAPTER 8

Nathan

ST. JOHN'S, THE capital of Newfoundland, was a few miles south of Bonavista Bay. It was a port, a commercial and cultural center, and it served a population of 170,000. After Elmo and Nathan reported the grisly death on the schooner *Phantom* to the St. John's police, Elmo had the film in the camera developed.

Nathan paced back and forth around a large oak table in the corner of a mahogany-paneled police conference room. Elmo sat on a chair, resting his large arms on the table in front of him, as they both waited for a meeting with officials from St. John's police department. On the table, spread out in an array of seven photos, were large color prints made from some of the negatives in the camera they had found on the destroyed schooner.

Nathan looked at one corner of the genteel room that contained a brown-lacquered cabinet with oriental panels. "Nice furniture," he said. In another corner was an all-glass fish tank containing about fifty *Zanclus cornutus* fish, better known as Moorish Idols. On each of these marine fish were two black bars crossing a white and yellow body. Their caudal fins were black. The most prominent part of their anatomy was a long, trailing dorsal fin that protruded many inches beyond the fishes' tails. Nathan got up and wandered over to the tank.

"Beautiful fish," he said. "But isn't it kind of strange for a police department to maintain such a beautiful tank?"

"Not for Newfoundland," Elmo said. "We're all fond of fish here."

"I always wanted to have a big tank like this at home but my ex-wife always objected," said Nathan. "She said it was too much trouble. Too much money. Said we didn't have enough room in the house. Why is it that most spouses object to, or merely tolerate, the aquarium hobbies of their husbands?"

"I don't know. But I think you're right. Maybe that's why I never married."

Nathan smiled faintly, sure that the man had more substantial reasons to have missed marriage, such as the length of his fingers. But of course he wouldn't remark on that. "These Moorish Idol fish are pretty difficult to keep. They're reluctant feeders and never breed in an aquarium. Whoever is in charge of the aquarium must be pretty good with fish."

"Why thank you," said a woman who had just walked into the room.

Policewoman Natalie Sheppard and Police Chief Joseph Falow shook hands with Elmo and Nathan. Natalie had anthracite eyes and hair as black as Manchester coal. She was currently out of uniform, wearing a watermelon-colored cotton sweater dress. Nathan wished immediately that he had some pretext to get to know her better. But of course he concealed this, and turned to the other. Police Chief Falow had iron-brown eyebrows, thick sandy hair, and a lanky frame without an ounce of spare flesh. After shaking hands, they took seats around the table. Falow's thick hand pinched a cigarette. His other hand drummed the table top with a pen.

"OK, gentlemen," Falow said. "Why did you call me? What news have you got for me?" He had a masculine force about him, a great presence born of certainty.

"Take a look at these," Elmo said to Falow and Natalie. He handed the prints to the officers.

"Look like icebergs," Natalie said as she held the photos in her hands. Her voice was soft and eminently reasonable. Falow looked at the photos, but withheld judgement. He sat with the ramrod posture of a British brigadier.

"We got these from a camera we found on the *Phantom,*" Nathan said. "Take a look at the dark area at the lower left." He rose from the table and pointed at the photos.

"You shouldn't have taken the camera from the boat," Falow said with irritation. He then looked at the photos. "Looks like a crab or a spider." Falow spoke in a flat, inflectionless voice as he carefully examined an iceberg photo. "What's this have to do with the deaths on the schooner?"

Nathan said just one word: "Pycnogonid." He sat with his sneakers angled on the floor like frog's legs. There was a brooding quality about his voice.

"What's that?" asked Natalie.

"Pycnogonid," he repeated. Now there was a certain thrill of alarm in his voice. "PICK-no-GO-nid. It's a spiderlike marine animal. Pycnogonids occur in all oceans, especially the arctic. They usually dwell on the bottom."

"How big is it?" Falow asked.

"We couldn't tell just from looking at the photos," Nathan said. "So we went back out to sea to take a look at the berg first-hand to estimate the scale of the features in the photo. This sea spider is *big.*"

Natalie seemed to be listening with rapt attention. Even the air seemed to be holding its breath. Falow stripped off his jacket, and the brown leather straps of his shoulder holster stood out like large suspenders on the starched white of his shirt. They were all beginning to appreciate the magnitude of the problem.

"Today there are more than six hundred different species, and we have fossils of these creatures which demonstrate they also lived during the time of the dinosaurs." Nathan took a drink of water and continued. "They usually range in size from four millimeters in such forms as the littoral *Tanystylum* to about sixty centimeters in deep-sea species of *Colossendeis.* Little is known about the deep-sea species, but larger sizes have been hypothesized. . . ." His voice trailed away ominously.

"Don't keep us in suspense, Doctor. How big?" Falow spoke in a powerful editorial voice. He stroked his cheek with great tender fingers. Nathan didn't speak, trying to gather his words. "Get to the point," Falow said with the temperament of an underfed grizzly.

Well, he had asked for it. "This one was as big as an adult elephant," Nathan said. "It killed the people on the schooner. Tore them to shreds. We also think it was responsible for the death of an Inuit family a week ago several hundred miles north in Nain on the subarctic Labrador coast." Nathan went on, blithely ignoring the sudden silence in the room. "We think it will kill again, although there's a slim chance it will leave the coast and go out to the deep sea and leave humans alone."

"Sounds like a bunch of crap," Falow said. His cheek muscles stood out as he clenched his jaw. "Is this guy some kind of nut?" Falow turned to Natalie expecting her to say "yes," even though she knew as little about Elmo and Nathan as Falow did.

"We're not nuts," Elmo said. "Look at the photos yourself."

"Those photos are so fuzzy you could see anything you wanted in them."

"Then look at this," Nathan said. He withdrew a six-inch spine from his pocket and held it out to Falow, who did not take it. "We found this on the boat. I know it's from a pycnogonid."

"Hey, how dare you remove more evidence from the scene of a crime?" Falow got to his feet.

"What do you suggest?" asked Natalie. "Can we capture or kill it?" She turned to Falow, who was calming himself. "Whatever we do, we don't want to alarm the public, the tourists, the fishermen."

"You had better alarm someone," Nathan said. "It's fast, strong. It has a voracious appetite, and it's smart. It would *probably* be killed if someone fired enough gunshots at its head and brain. The hard part is to catch the creature in the act before it retreats back into the safety of the sea."

"What do you mean *probably* be killed?" Falow demanded.

"The nervous system of a pycnogonid is composed of a supra-esophageal brain or ganglion and a chain of six ventral ganglia," Nathan said.

"In plain English, Doctor," Falow said with a suspicious, sideways squint.

"It has more than one brain," Elmo said, a cold hard-pinched expression on his face. "Destroy one brain and the others may take control of its body."

There was a momentary silence. They were beginning to understand the nature of the problem.

"How does it attack?" Natalie asked.

"If we can extrapolate from what we know through observations of smaller specimens, the pycnogonid will grab its victim with its front legs and claws and bring the victim toward its mouth," Nathan said. "Its triangular-shaped mouth is at the end of a long sucking appendage, a proboscis. It sucks out the body fluids of its victims. It drains them alive. Like a spider."

"The question now is," Natalie said, "how should we respond?"

"How about offering a reward for its capture?" Nathan suggested.

Falow stood up and slapped his fist into his other hand with a thud. "That's the worst idea I can think of. It would cause a panic. It would turn into a media event. I can just see the posters now: $1000 Reward For Killer Sea Spider!" Falow paced back and forth for a few seconds. "Looks like we should set some traps and wait to see if it attacks again. Let's just hope the media don't get wind of this. We don't want panic in the streets."

Nathan nodded. He didn't much like the police chief, but the man was right. Panic would accomplish nothing worthwhile. So it was best to go along with Falow's dictate. But Nathan hoped that his future contacts with the police would be limited to Natalie Sheppard. She seemed reasonable as well as being attractive.

CHAPTER 9

Hospital

NOW, ON HIS way to the hospital, Elmo had time to ponder personal matters. He was sorry his sister still refused to make up with their mother, but he really couldn't blame her. He just felt obliged to keep trying, lest Mrs. Samules die without a rapprochement that he might have arranged. If she lived through this siege, he would try again next time. Martha was not a bad woman, she was just isolated from her own kind, and the most likely wedge to begin the ending of that isolation was their mother. A hopeless cause, probably, but still worth pursuing.

He had been tempted to tell Martha about the gruesome discovery on the sea, but something had held him back. Of course the news wasn't supposed to be given out yet, but Martha could keep a secret as well as anyone. Her input could have been valuable, because of her extensive knowledge of the creatures of the sea. But maybe he hadn't wanted to mix that in with the subject of their mother, lest the gruesomeness somehow be transferred. So he had tried to stay on the one matter. He had delayed his departure from the store, trying to find some avenue, but none had offered. Then he had encountered Lisa, only in passing, and—

She was beautiful, even ethereal, with a musical voice. Her eyes were somewhere between hazel and dark aquamarine, like the sea on a rainy day, and strangely soothing. She had reminded him of a lost college love—who had never known he existed, because he had known better than ever to approach her. He had learned early—very early—about the effect his appearance had on others. It had been years since he had so far forgotten himself to smile openly at any other person, and he normally kept his hands to himself, their fingers curled into loose fists. He had learned to get along.

Indeed, he had gotten along well, in every respect but socially. Others appreciated his memory and abilities. But women—however polite they were, however they masked it, they remained absolutely off-limits, emotionally. So it would be completely foolish of him to suppose that a creature like Lisa would ever see him as other than repulsive.

Yet he could dream. He had known of Lisa before, and had seen her on occasion in the shadows of the store. But this time it had been different. Her sudden lovely smile had caught him offguard, and struck through to his fancy. Cupid's dart, finding the momentary crevice in his emotional armor. He would have guarded against it, as he routinely did, had he not been distracted by his problem with his sister. Now he had been wounded in the heart. He would survive it, but it was too bad it had happened right now, when he couldn't afford to be distracted. But that was a full circle; his distraction had allowed the wound.

But perhaps there was a positive aspect to this situation. He was about to endure a negative experience. His idle fascination with a girl whom he had met, literally, in passing, might help take the edge off what was to come.

For after his meeting with officers Sheppard and Falow, Elmo was visiting his 85-year-old mother in the local hospital at Petit Forte, a few miles west of St. John's. He hated hospitals. He'd spent too much time in them as a child while doctors struggled to cope with his ulcerative colitus. Surgery had cured him, but even after all these years hospitals continued to make him feel like a nervous child.

Elmo's mother suffered from polycythemia vera, a disease in

which the bone marrow mysteriously began producing large numbers of red blood cells. As a result, her blood was unusually viscous. Elmo had personally hand-delivered requisitions to get the best blood specialist in the hospital to consult on her care.

"There's not much we can do," the doctor on call told Elmo. They stood in the white corridor outside Mrs. Samules's room. "When the red cell count skyrockets, we insert a needle into a vein and simply drain blood into a bottle on the floor. This helps a little."

Of course she was old, he reminded himself. Everybody had to die sometime, and old age was the best way to go. But he was discovering that it wasn't any more pleasant this way than when it happened to a younger acquaintance. He owed so much to her, and he didn't want her to go.

Elmo went inside the room. "How you doing, Mom?" he asked. He hid a thick swallow in his throat and turned away from all the nearby IV bottles. On the wall were some framed posters of tropical fish amidst lush freshwater vegetation: tiger barbs, cardinal tetras, and firemouth cichlids swimming among an almost comical over-abundance of duckweed, java ferns, and giant Indian water stars. Evidently the hospital administration thought these natural scenes would have a calming effect on patients. On each of the posters were the word's "Martha's Tropical Fish Store." If only Martha could have been here to see this! But of course she probably knew all about it. It wasn't that Mrs. Samules was trying to surround herself with evidences of her alienated daughter, but that the hospital had this ready source for anything relating to fish.

Martha's store—where he had met Lisa. A girl he knew almost nothing about. Except for her brilliant smile.

"Could be better. There's a pain in my left side," his mother replied. It took Elmo a moment to reorient; in the time she had taken to answer, he had suffered a lapse of proper attention. He resolved to correct that immediately.

Mrs. Samules was an unstylish, soft little woman. She leaned forward, grasping her legs just above the knees. As they talked for the next half hour, the pain got worse and she said that she felt she was going to pass out. Elmo called for the doctor.

"Mrs. Samules," the doctor called, and shook her slightly. "It's Dr. Carter; remember me?"

Mrs. Samules's eyes lifted just a little and she spoke in a whisper. "I feel lousy."

As Dr. Carter lifted her hospital gown, Elmo saw that something inside her was bulging, visibly stretching the skin of the upper abdomen.

"Am I going to die?" Mrs. Samules asked with apprehension and anxiety.

"You'll be just fine, but we have to remove your spleen." As the doctor left, Elmo followed him into the corridor and pulled him aside.

"What are her chances?" he asked.

"Unfortunately her chances of dying on the operating table are 70 percent."

"And if we choose not to operate?"

"Then she will be dead in a day." The doctor brought out a medical pamphlet on the spleen by the renowned Henry Draper, M.D. The book was illustrated with impressive daguerreotype microphotographs showing various diseases of the spleen. As Dr. Carter explained Mrs. Samules's condition to her son, most of the words simply went in one ear and out the other. The moment was filled with so much grayness and unrest. First the horror on the sea, then Lisa, and now the likely death of his mother. Elmo could not concentrate, so just shook his head as the doctor spoke.

Then he was alone in the hospital, though others were constantly going back and forth. He wished Martha had come, not merely for their mother, but for himself. His sister was one tough woman, but she would understand the ache of this awful business. As it was, unbidden mental images of his mother's wizened face alternated with those of Lisa's lovely one, and of the decapitated woman. Individually, each was disturbing; overlapping like this, they were horrible. It was as if old age illness could suddenly convert to lustrous beauty or horrible death. But his imagination refused to let the pictures go.

He had given his permission for the surgery, of course. But had he merely hastened his mother's demise? What choice had he had? Martha could have helped ease the burden of decision, had she attended. Yet suppose the two of them had differed on this, too?

Within 45 minutes Mrs. Samules was in the operating room. The doctors removed her spleen. The surgery went well, but in the recovery room she began to bleed. For the next few hours the doctors tried to stem the bleeding, but to no avail. She was slipping into a coma.

As Elmo paced back and forth in the waiting room, his attention turned to a red TV playing near the back of the room. A group of newspeople were pouring out of a dark van with WNBT CHANNEL 9 ACTION NEWS written on its side. The object of their interest was a group of witnesses standing on a stone jetty by the pounding surf. Just hours before, a group of teenagers had disappeared from the jetty at Terra Nova National Park. The group of witnesses reported supposedly seeing a huge spider.

"How can you be sure it was a spider?" a red-haired newswoman asked one of the witnesses. "Did you actually see it?"

"Yes I saw it. Actually I just saw a few of its legs. Looked like a spider or a crab. Big as an elephant!"

Local fisherman were organizing search parties for the spider. One tall man in a zip jacket with military insignias shouted into the TV camera.

"We're going to get it." He held up a rifle and waved it around like an oversized phallus. As Elmo watched the TV, he noticed an old lady in the hospital's waiting room tracked the rifle back and forth, her eyes bouncing like a metronome in a strange mixture of excitement and fear. The TV camera then panned to another member of the search party, a teenage boy in a long robe with a fractal pattern on it. He held a crystal in his hand. He gazed at it for a second, then held it up to the TV camera, and mumbled something about the end of the world and God's divine wrath. The news story ended, and a commercial with a comely actress selling shampoo blasted onto the screen. It made an odd contrast with the boy's shtick about divine wrath.

A monstrous spider? He would have laughed it off as tabloid fakery, had he not seen that woman's head. There had to be a connection.

Elmo shifted uneasily, then ran to the phone and called the police station and Nathan Smallwood. He left the hospital minutes later, thanks largely to his natural dislike of hospitals, disinfectants, corridors, and laboratories. Now at least he had a pretext.

CHAPTER 10

Call

THE PHONE RANG. Nathan picked it up. "Yes?"

"Dr. Smallwood." The voice was pleasantly familiar. "This is Officer Sheppard."

The lady policeman he had met at the meeting. "Hi, what can I do for you?" He pictured her holding the phone handset close to her windblown, sunny face. She might be wearing a cotton twill shirtdress in burnished gold, and she could have on just enough lipstick to show that her mouth was perfect. His image of her was wickedly familiar, but there were no penalties for hidden thoughts.

"I was wondering if you'd like to go for a walk downtown and discuss this sea spider problem?"

"Police business?" As if it could be anything else, in real life.

"No, personal. The whole spider incident is giving me the creeps. I also love smart men with mustaches." In his fancy she exuded a refreshingly ingenious warmth.

"Sounds good." Nathan chuckled. It seemed a long, long time since a woman called him on the phone and showed interest. Of course it was his knowledge of sea life she was really interested in, nothing else. Still . . .

Nathan had been born with a harelip, and although it had been surgically corrected, he thought the mustache enhanced his looks. Before Natalie called, Nathan was spending his Saturday in his cozy motel room by the sea trying to watch the New York Giants on TV as he read the local newspaper. As he spoke on the phone, he put down Newfoundland's weekly newspaper, *The Dispatch,* where there was a small article on mysterious deaths near the coast. The article was surrounded by a fuzzy border and below the printed matter was a drawing of a giant tarantula attacking boats. Natalie said something. Nathan listened as he fished breakfast cereal out of the box and rapidly munched the flakes.

"Where shall we meet?" he asked.

"How about we go for a walk along Main Street by the coast. Do you know where Martha's Fish Store is?"

"Yes. I'll be there." Nathan shut the football halftime show off on his TV.

"OK; see you at 7:00?"

"Sounds good." As he hung up, he marveled at this development. People met all the time to discuss business, but Natalie was perhaps the one he had most wanted to see again—and *she* had called *him.* Who said miracles didn't happen?

CHAPTER 11

Research

THE WORDS "CANTERBURY Crossing" were carved in a decorative wooden sign that hung outside by the street, floodlit from the front and backed by pine trees. Natalie Sheppard was reclining on the sofa in her attractive garden-apartment in the Canterbury complex, holding the telephone with one hand and eating a piece of raw broccoli with the other while she sat and watched *The People's Court* on the TV. A 110-gallon freshwater fish tank stood against a wall of the living room. The tank contained only a single species of fish: the tiger barb. About seventy of these two-inch-long fish swam in schools back and forth, forth and back. With their red-brown bodies fading to silver on the underside and their four distinctive black strips, they formed a moving wall of color, a magic aura of living stripes and fins.

She hung up the phone. Had she just done something foolish? She had met Nathan Smallwood only the one time, but rather liked what she had seen, and she had the impression that the feeling was mutual. His first glance at her—his pupils had dilated in seeming appreciation. Did she fit some physical image he liked? No matter; she found that she liked being liked, for whatever reason. So she had found a pretext to see him again, hoping that she wouldn't strike him as forward. It was probably an idle fancy that would soon fade, but why not play it out? Her social life here on the island was not exactly rollicking.

Meanwhile, on the horror front, things were hardly dull. A giant deadly spider ripping people apart? A creature with several brains? She definitely needed to know more.

Natalie had heard of pycnogonids, but only vaguely, so she canceled her chess class, slipped on a hip-hugging jacket in green napa leather, left her condo, and went to the local library to find out more. All around the library were trees of varied species, ages, and colors. A sparse stand of autumn-stripped maples and birches pushed their branches to the blue sky. To her left was a grove of scarecrow trees, gnarled and black, with an occasional leaf as an epitaph to warmer days of the summer. Ancient Indian laurels flanked the canted parking lot and lent a note of grace to the old building.

Some men with shovels were digging some of the soil in a nearby field. As Natalie parked her car and walked along the black slate stones to the library's entrance, she noticed the library was having its annual book fair. A local band was playing. An elderly man wearing a gray jacket approached her.

"Would you like to enter a raffle for this homemade quilt?" the man inquired as he pointed to a huge colorful quilt hanging on a wooden frame. "Only costs a dollar to enter."

"Sure," Natalie said. She didn't mind supporting the local library. The man handed her a piece of paper which read:

BENEFIT: JOHN C. HART MEMORIAL LIBRARY
WIN A HANDMADE QUILT
DRAWING: NOVEMBER (WINNER NEED NOT BE PRESENT)
DONATION: $1.00 EACH OR 6 FOR $5.00
PAY AND MAIL TO: HART LIBRARY, 1130 MAIN STREET
TWILLINGATE, NEWFOUNDLAND

Oh. It wasn't precisely local. Twillingate was a generous two hundred miles to the north by road. But their library needed support too, and the raffle was valid regardless. She'd do it.

"What's the digging all about?" Natalie said to the man.

"Do you remember the story of the German scientist who discovered the fossil tooth of a giant ape—was it at an Eskimo pharmacy where fossils were ground up for traditional medicines?"

"Yes. But that was in 1935." Since then, scientists had sporadically looked for the remains of prehistoric, giant apes that weighed 2,000 pounds and loomed 11 feet tall. Natalie thought it was a pipe dream, but who could say for sure? She would have said that a sea spider the size of an elephant was a pipe dream too, before today.

"Well, guess what they found in that field by the library?"

"You're kidding?"

"Several jawbones and more than 2,000 teeth were found of the species *Gigantopithecus.*"

"Wow, any chance they'll find an entire skeleton?"

"Several Newfoundland scientists and a paleoanthropologist from Yale are coming. They think that they'll find the remains of *Giganto* in nearby caves used to hide military supplies from German bombers. I've heard that some of them think that *Giganto* lived about three hundred thousand years ago. Ancient humans may have killed them off by hunting them or competing with them for scarce bamboo which the humans used for tools and this ancient ape used for food."

"Fascinating." But she found it hard to accept for a new reason: the climate would have had to be a lot warmer here in those days for bamboo to grow. That was possible, of course, but she would have to see more solid evidence before believing it. Natalie looked at her watch. "Got to go."

The library was fairly crowded as a result of the book fair. Natalie reached for the black and white door and noticed a few wasps hovering nearby. She stooped down to avoid them, entered the library, and approached a librarian who smiled back at her.

"Hi, I'm looking for biology books," Natalie said. One of the wasps had followed her inside and quickly headed for a window, which unfortunately was closed. She watched the wasp for a few seconds.

"Anything in particular?"

"Invertebrates. Sea spiders."

The librarian raised one of her eyebrows, then smiled, and said, "Come this way."

Natalie gazed out the library's rear windows, past the wasp that continued to dive bomb the thick pane of glass. Outside the window were motor yachts and sailboats bobbing up and down in the water alongside the harbor docks. Most of their sails were furled, their engines quiet. The library was one of her favorite hangouts, with its hardwood floors, antique Persian carpets and cream walls. It was like no library she had ever been in before, and she was happy that a good chunk of the township's taxes went to it. She didn't care if she didn't win that quilt raffle; it was for an excellent cause.

She returned her attention to the pile of books and journals at her table. Her hand moved to a nearby Tiffany lamp with its hand-blown tulip shades, and moved it closer to her reading area. She lost herself in the joy and frustration of spot research, following up several false leads for every true one.

As Nathan Smallwood had indicated at their meeting, pycnogonids lived during the Jurassic Period, about a hundred fifty million years ago. Natalie pictured monstrous sea spiders carrying on and cavorting with a tribe of brontosauruses, now called apatosauruses. No, that wouldn't work; the thunder lizards had turned out to be upland walkers, not water waders, so wouldn't have encountered the sea spiders.

Deep water species of the sea spider could be huge although tropical shallow water species could be as small as an ant. The pycnogonid's digestive and reproductive system had many branches that penetrated deeply into the creature's many legs. Most species had eight legs but some with ten or more legs were not uncommon in Antarctic regions.

The librarian came up from behind her. "I found something

else," she said to Natalie, and handed her Lockwood's *Biology of the Invertebrates* and a computer printout.

Tap, tap, tap, went the wasp on the glass.

"Thanks."

The scariest part of the creature was its proboscis, or sucking appendage, which was longer than the rest of the creature's body. The mouth looked like a triangle at the end of the long trunk of the proboscis. Natalie found very few pictures of the adult creature, but she did find several diagrams of the baby larval forms which looked nothing like the adult.

Natalie heard some high-pitched voices and looked up. Some nursery school children were leaving a room with an adult volunteer. They had just finished listening to the children's story *Ants Can't Dance*.

"How did you like it, Terrie?" one mother asked.

A beautiful little girl wearing a sweater with a golden phoenix on it replied, "Great. Can ants dance?" The girl shook her blond pony-tail with excitement.

Natalie smiled and thought that maybe someday she would get married and have a little Terrie running around her condo. Someday. She tried to return to her reading. Unfortunately the overhead bright fluorescent lights were just turned on and the white Formica surfaces of her table were a little hard on her

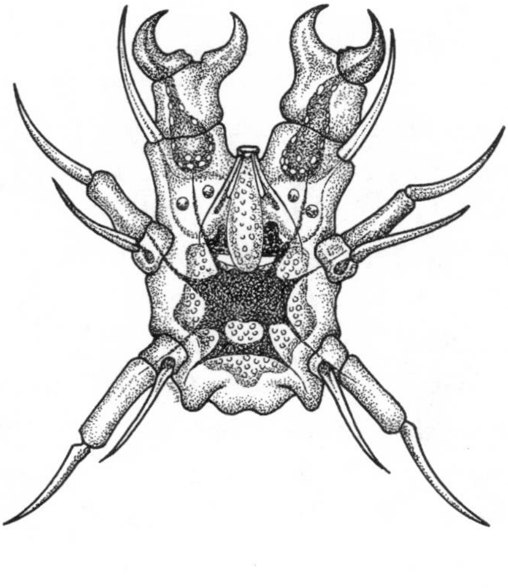

eyes, like looking into an icy arctic lake shimmering under a bright winter sun. The room was getting chillier—perhaps the librarian had reduced the heat because it was near closing time.

Tap. Tap. Tap. She really ought to get a cup and catch that wasp and take it outside.

As she read, some of the gorgeous Chinese bowls and vases that decorated the library shelves were being stored in locked cabinets for the night by a member of the custodial staff. It was almost time for her to go meet Nathan. She gazed down at her book on the table, and tried to wrap up her reading.

In some species of pycnogonid the young larvae invaded the interior of jellyfish where they lived parasitically until they emerged as sea spiders. The larval stages of *Nymphonella tapetis,* a Japanese species, lived parasitically inside the cavity of clams. But these were small spiders; what about the big ones? Surely an elephant-sized creature couldn't live in a clam, not even in larval stage.

Natalie continued to search for information on the larger species in an effort to find some clues to help them in the present predicament. Unfortunately the life cycle of the huge deep-sea species, especially members of the genus *Colossendeis,* were unknown.

This lack of knowledge by scientists was not too surprising. There was still much to learn about the marine life off the coast of Newfoundland. The submerged ice structures, the chemical and geological structure of the ocean floor, the extent and affect of pollution . . . Unfortunately, recent dumping of heavy metals and souvenir hunting had caused some depletion of fish and invertebrates off the Newfoundland coast. So not only was much of the story unknown, it might become impossible for it ever to be known, because of inadvertent extinctions.

The wasp at the window had ceased its relentless tapping on the glass and slowly crawled along the base of the window as if defeated. Its stinger undulated. Natalie was beginning to feel a little like the wasp—nervous and tired.

As she finished her reading, Natalie, like most people, was

amazed to learn of the vast marine zoo that lived beneath the ice in the Arctic. She had thought it would be a virtual desert. But marine life was plentiful. Her books and magazines showed photos of bright red shrimps filled with parasitic isopods, zebra striped amphipods, bulbous anemones with foot-long tentacles, sea fleas, football-shaped ctenophores, sea snails with iridescent shells, tiny isopods resembling daddy long legs with long, fragile forelegs to walk on silty bottoms and paddle-shaped rear legs to propel them through the water. Some of the most interesting species looked more like plants than animals: Violet holothurians—sea cucumbers—thrust out branching tentacles in search of animal prey.

She shook her head, bemused. There was just so much there, but humans knew so little. It seemed that the northernmost continental shelf of Canada covered almost a million square miles, but scientists had seen less than a few of those miles of this vast maritime estate.

As closing time loomed, Natalie had found what she was looking for in the scientific journals. She photocopied five articles, folded them, and stuck them in her purse. Then she fetched a paper cup, went to the window, and used a sheet of paper to catch the wasp in the cup. She carried it out with her, and freed it outside. The wasp hesitated for a moment on the rim of the cup as if considering how to thank her, then flew away. There was her good deed for the day.

Cheered, she walked to the car.

CHAPTER 12

Pilot

AT THE SAME time Natalie Sheppard was leaving the library, June Holland was piloting a low-flying Hercules HC-130B above a monstrous hook of ice which protruded from an iceberg floating in the sea. In the distance she saw a vast herd of caribou thunder past the shoreline. After a few minutes, she brought the plane lower and cut two of the four engines. 700 feet . . . 600 . . . 500 . . . ever closer to the ceiling of the mammoth iceberg below. Holland radioed that she was descending to 300 feet.

"OK, drop it," she shouted to her crewman.

On her signal, a young ensign hurled a soft-drink-can-sized jar full of dye down on the ice. "Got it!" he screamed to Holland.

The jar hit silently. Looking back she saw a crimson stain spreading down the canyons of the berg. To June Holland this was just another routine operation by the United States Coast Guard. They were marking the icebergs for rapid identification in studies of their drifting patterns. The dye, a mixture of calcium chloride for penetration and rhodamine-B for the crimson hue, spread a swath of color several yards in diameter across the cliffs of the ice.

Reports of all the icebergs' positions were radioed to nearby vessels at sea to help prevent collisions. Ice patrols like this dated back to 1912. The United States and 16 other maritime nations shared the cost of the ice patrol. The United Kingdom paid the largest share, but the responsibility for carrying out the assignment rested with the U.S. Coast Guard alone.

"Let's get back," Holland said. "Our fuel is low." Her gazed shifted to a small stereo system resting on the short-nap gray carpet of the cockpit's floor where there were stacks of Suzanne Vega and Peter Gabriel CDs, just the right mix of background music for a pilot flying over the sparkling ice landscapes. As she gazed out of her cockpit window at the sea and ice, her eye was caught by a motion on the windshield: a tiny brown spider crawled along the bottom of the glass and began to spin a web.

The ensign offered her a cup of hot chocolate, and she gulped down its warming contents. "Thanks," she said. "Do we have anything to eat?"

"How about a hot dog?"

"OK, slip it into the microwave oven." The small brown spider stopped for a few seconds and then began to crawl all the way to the top of the cockpit window. It raised its front legs as a thin, shiny web strand poured from the spider's bulbous abdomen. Holland saw that the spider's legs had dozens of fine hairs and that its multiple eyes never winked. It gave her the creeps.

A minute later the ensign returned with a hot dog with the works—relish, onions, mustard, ketchup, and chili. She wolfed it down. The airplane meandered back and forth over the patrol zone. It was now lighter by 4,000 gallons of fuel. The ensign made a final tabulation of iceberg sightings for dispatch by radio to the Coast Guard ships.

Holland was humming to the haunting tunes of Suzanne Vega and thinking about her dinner plans. She hadn't seen any movement outside, but the jerk of the ensign's head and the look of concern on his face was warning enough.

"What's wrong?" Holland said as she turned in her seat and looked out the left window.

"I thought I saw something moving," the ensign said. His eyes were small pools of light set in a field of dark flesh.

"Where?"

"On the iceberg."

"An animal?"

"Yes."

"How big?" She squinted through the smeared windshield.

"The size of a man."

Suddenly Holland looked down at the ocean, which was now covered by a moving crust of ice. The salt-water ice reflected the sunlight back in her eyes. Then out of the corner of her eyes she caught a movement on an iceberg. An almost-naked bleeding man was crawling on the iceberg. At least she thought he was moving. It was too far away to be sure. At first it seemed only a dream image without real substance. Something cold crawled up her back.

"What in the world?" she said to herself. Her heart beat fast as she threw herself back against her seat. The snowflake-caked windshield wiper blades left streaks of moisture on the glass through which she was trying to see.

She got out her field glasses and trained them on the ice below. She gasped, took the microphone from its mounting, and called to a nearby Coast Guard ship. She adjusted the focus of her field glasses. Was this possible? She had to make an accurate report.

Below on the ice lay a body which looked as if it were very stiff with rigor mortis. She guessed that he'd been dead for at least a day. The odd angle of his arm suggested he'd died a painful death. She brought the plane lower, keeping her eye on the fuel gauge of the plane. Moisture had accumulated on the plane's window, which she wiped away with a gloved hand, and then she looked again.

"Can't see," she whispered to herself as tendrils of ice formed on the windows of the plane. She leaned forward and let a trickle of de-icing fluid swish the frost away from the glass. She squinted and took a last look at the unpleasant sight on the ice.

The naked man moved. From the palms of each of his hands protruded a large bony spike.

June Holland swallowed deeply in a mixture of horror and a little fear. She pressed her feet to the floor of the planes' cockpit and gripped the steering lever as if she were trying to fuse her flesh with the metal alloy, because she felt as if she would fall out, straight down on the man if she did not will her body to stop trembling. She felt as if she were being dragged down a long, dark tunnel, and only now was beginning to see the horrible things at the end.

Who could he be, and how could he have gotten there? What had happened to him on the way? She doubted that the answers would be pleasant.

CHAPTER 13

Date

NATHAN SMALLWOOD TOURED Newfoundland on a rented sport-touring motorcycle. He loved the reduced nosedive and lower center of gravity. The cycle's front end transmitted braking force straight back through its massive suspension arm into a C-shaped frame near the engine. This made the bike exceptionally quiet and easy to stop, even on wet or snowy roads. As he guided the vehicle in and out of the small winding streets and coast roads, he listened to K-Newfoundland 92.1 FM from Bonavista though headphones in his helmet. He smiled, singing along with golden oldies like "California Dreaming" and "Time of the Season." It reminded him of his days in a college rock band, when he played organ for similar songs.

He arrived on Main Street at about 6:00 in the evening. Main Street was not too hard to find, and he soon guided the cycle to a small parking space. He was early, but that was fine. Because, as it turned out, so was she.

Natalie Sheppard and Nathan met on Main Street in a town with a yawning pace. A storm had passed by recently, and now the sun was breaking through the clouds with a thousand beams of golden light. The sky was amber and shimmering with a tangle of reflections like a painting by van Gogh.

"Hello, Miss Sheppard." She was wearing an orange twill dress, just about the way he had imagined her.

"Natalie." She smiled. "Good to see you again." She glanced at him with the hint of a question.

"Nathan," he said immediately.

The single traffic signal on Main Street splintered in liquid reflections beneath their feet. Martha Samules, the lady who ran the tropical fish store, was standing out on the sidewalk with hands on her large hips, looking at the couple with an expression that seemed to be equally puzzled and admiring. Nathan was aware that he and Natalie, both tall and slender, made an unusual pair. Martha's pale complexion and sharp features were enlivened by large eyes, full of interest and intelligence as she gazed at them.

"Seems like a nice town," he said. "Reminds me of that Henry Wadsworth Longfellow poem:

"Often I think of the beautiful town
That is seated by the sea;
Often in thought go up and down
The pleasant streets of that dear old town."

"I know that one," Natalie said. "I think he wrote that in 1855 and called it 'My Lost Youth.' The town used to be like the poem, although the economy has suffered a lot in recent years. But there are still many beautiful parts of town."

They walked down the wide, cobblestone street lined on both sides with a curious amalgam of restaurants, and tourist and antique shops. From somewhere in the distance came the sweet sounds of the romantic melody "Before the Next Teardrop Falls."

"Watch your step," Nathan pointed to a deep puddle. As if on cue, brief winds started to churn the puddles between the cobblestones, so they appeared to be frothing like miniature oceans, as if a subterranean volcano were melting the cobblestones from underneath.

Nathan could hear drips of water coming through nearby aluminum downspouts. "The air feels so fresh here," he said. He looked all around him, smiling. An occasional ancient evergreen poked its tall branches from the backyards of some of the stores. Large brown wooden mailboxes were conveniently nailed to the side of each shop. Many of the shops had short flagstone walks leading to their front doors.

As they walked, his thoughts turned to himself. This wasn't narcissism, but his spot self appraisal: how would he seem to this delightful woman? If she knew him better, would she be interested? He did have some assets, yet wasn't sure they were worth mentioning. Such as his writing.

He had been amazingly prolific, over the years writing over a hundred books and papers on his favorite subject: the invertebrates. His most famous papers described the shallow-water pycnogonida from the Izu Peninsula of Japan. Invertebrates, animals without backbones like worms and crabs and insects, were everywhere. He always marveled over the fact that more than 90 percent of the animal species on earth belonged to the invertebrates.

But others had quickly been bored or even repelled when he had gotten into this in the past, so maybe he had better let her ask directly for what she wanted. She had said that she wanted to know more about sea spiders, but her interest might be far more limited than his.

So what about his personal history?

Nathan's boyhood had not been an easy one, although he showed signs of genius at an early age. He was born in 1957 in the Soviet Union near Smolensk. At the age of three, he was brought to the United States by his parents and was naturalized a few years later. He taught himself to read before he was six years old, using the signs on his Brooklyn street. A couple of years later, with a little help from his mother, he taught himself to read Yiddish. When he was 8 he taught his younger sister to read. Nathan was never content to stay with his peers, and he skipped several grades, receiving a high-school diploma when he was 16.

Nathan's interest in invertebrates could be traced to his discovery of science fiction on the magazine rack at his father's store. All those wild images of huge octopi and killer squids from Planet X! At first Nathan's father objected to his interest in this fanciful subject matter, but when Nathan sold his first story at the age of 18, his father was proud. In 1982 he graduated from Harvard University with a Ph.D. in biology. And the next year he accepted a position to teach invertebrate zoology from Yale University's School of Medicine.

No she wouldn't be interested in any of that! So he would keep his mouth shut, unless he was sure she wanted information on some specific thing. That way maybe he could avoid turning her off before the hour was out.

"I understand you're interested in aquaria," Natalie said.

"Sure am." *Keep it simple, keep it safe.* "Want to get a big one for my home."

"Let's take a look in Martha's Tropical Fish Store. It's back where we started from." Natalie had a quiet air of authority and yet a rare warmth. Nathan noticed how nicely she dressed—she could have been a fashion model, he thought. He supressed his urge to take her hand as they walked.

"Great idea."

The sign hanging on the door read OPEN. They entered the store with its bubbling tanks and brightly colored fishes. A small bell jingled over their heads as they closed the door behind them. Soft light spilled in through curtains across the store front. Nathan saw a large woman was bending over one of the aquaria filled with suckermouth catfish. She looked up when the bell jingled and smiled at Natalie and Nathan. Yes, that was Martha, who had stood outside her store before.

The store was divided into four main sections: cold fresh

water, tropical fresh water, cold marine, and tropical marine. They meandered down row upon row of tanks containing bleeding heart tetras and honey gouramis. Martha came up to them.

"May I help you?" she asked. A few of her teeth were missing and the ones that were left looked rather brown in the dim light, but Nathan found the smile entirely charming. On her blouse was pinned a large blue button with red letters proclaiming: "FISH ARE FUN."

"We're just browsing, thanks," Nathan said. "We—"

Martha raised her hand to silence him. "Let me show you the latest in fish tanks. Ever hear of the super-thin tank craze?"

"Can't say that I have," Nathan replied.

"Follow me," Martha said. They came to the area of the store which had the super-thin tanks.

The aquaria reminded Nathan of the ant farm he had as a child. The colony of ants tunneled within the sand contained between two plates of plastic about a quarter inch apart from one another. The super-thin fish tanks were similar. They consisted of two plates of glass separated by a half-inch space for the water. The narrow region of water in which the fish swam essentially limited them to a two-dimensional world in which they could not turn around. The tanks were hung on the wall like a picture. Little bubbles of air were forced through the tank by a small air pump powered by what Martha assured them was an exceptionally long-lasting zinc-air battery.

"Gaah," Nathan choked. "How can they live in there like that?" He had seen many, many fish tanks during his career, but this struck him as on the verge of barbaric. Fish needed some freedom, just as people did. Many of these fish were congregating toward the right and left of the tanks because it was not so easy to swim backward.

"I agree," said Martha. "I think that once I sell these tanks I won't restock them. However, if you want to buy one of these tanks remember to place about half of the fish facing right, the others facing left. The swimming patterns look strange when all the fish face in the same direction."

"I think I would fashion turning circles at either side," he said, and was rewarded by Natalie's smile of agreement.

In one of the super-thin tanks were three-inch-long tin foil barbs. Their shiny silver bodies reflected the store lights producing a living wall of little mirrors. Natalie sighed with compassion for the confined creatures.

"OK, even if you don't want these tanks, surely there must be something for you?" Martha said. "A few discus fish?" Nathan noticed that Martha's fingers were extremely fat yet not short. He also noticed that all of the fingers were of the same length, except for the ring finger which jutted out longer than the rest. Just like Elmo's. "Are you looking at my hand?" she asked. Before Nathan could respond, Martha answered, "Don't worry, I don't shake hands. I have a condition known as ambidactyl syndrome. Nothing fatal."

"Glad to hear that. I mean I'm glad to hear it's not fatal." Suddenly his curiosity about Elmo's hands had been satisfied, and he had avoided the embarrassment of inquiring.

"I'm glad you're glad. Interested in buying a few new fighting fish?" She smiled again and this time revealed inch-long teeth in a scary grin. Her long teeth reminded Nathan of a story he had read as a child in a book called *In a Dark, Dark Room.* The old illustrated tale had scared him. He still remembered the opening lines: *I was hurrying home in the dark when I saw a man walking toward me. . . . He grinned at me. His teeth were three inches long. When I saw them, I ran.* Nathan felt a shiver run through him now as he gazed at her teeth, as long as a beaver's, but his outward countenance was cool and collected.

"Thanks again. We're just browsing. I'm thinking of starting an aquarium at home, but unfortunately any fish I bought here wouldn't survive the long trip back to Massachusetts."

"Massachusetts?" Martha's eyes seemed to grow to the size of Ping-Pong balls. "What's your occupation, if you don't mind me asking?"

"I teach at Harvard."

"A Harvard man? Oooh, policewoman, you picked a good

one this time." Martha's chuckles had a hyenalike quality—her face now had all the charm of a sawfish. Nathan suspected that she was considered by the ladies of St. John to be more than a little eccentric, and she was proving this to be the case.

"It must be difficult to run a fish store with your hand condition," Nathan said, clumsily trying to change the subject. He tried to discipline his voice, to maintain complete control.

"Not at all. I'm quite agile." With the swiftness of a great buck she plucked a hair from Nathan's head. "See?" Natalie and Nathan blinked in astonished silence.

"Good to see the inside of your store, Martha," Natalie said, evidently trying to end the conversation. She then grabbed Nathan's hand and led him away down the aisle of aquaria.

"Interesting woman," Nathan smiled slightly, not sure what to make of the situation.

"Very. I've seen her only passingly before, but I know about her reputation. It's hard to believe she has a doctorate in molecular biophysics and biochemistry. She always had tropical fish as a hobby, and after she got her Ph.D. she decided to open an aquarium store rather than go into the competitive world of academic science."

"Can she make a good living with this store?"

"I think so. They say her mail order business is thriving."

"Come on. Let's look at what else she has in her store."

"What would be your 'dream' fish tank?" Natalie asked. "Would you like to have a tank with a few large fish? Hundreds of small fish?"

"My favorites are the elephantnose fish, with their long trunk-like snouts. They're from Africa. I'd like to have a huge tribe of a hundred or more in my dream tank. That would be quite an impressive sight."

"Ah, I know those weird fish well. *Ganathonemus petersi.* You have rather bizarre tastes. They come from the Niger and Congo Rivers. Their snouts are adapted to grubbing in the bottom for worms."

They wandered over to the salt-water section of the store. Bubbles were forced through airstones to circulate the sea water. In some of the tanks were little tiny men who walked around the sand as if they were alive. "Here's a nice undulant triggerfish," Nathan said. The green body was covered with wavy orange lines. Its pelvic fins were absent, being reduced to primitive stumps. "Triggerfishes can lock their dorsal fins straight up to avoid capture. They have strong jaws and will eat invertebrates. At rest they point their heads down or lie in the sand."

He stopped, realizing that he was doing what he had resolved not to: going off the deep end about his interests. He feared that Natalie felt a bit confused as he rattled off the chain of facts, showing off his knowledge about the fish. Something special about the fish intrigued him, however.

I've encountered these fish before, was the first clear thought to come through Nathan's mind. It was déjà vu, he supposed, that false feeling that this had all happened before in his past.

He turned and looked in the next tank and saw something which was enough to give anyone the screaming meemies. His whole body tightened as he felt a whisper of terror run through him. In the tank were seven small pycnogonids resembling daddy long legs spiders. They were feeding on a severed human hand which rested on the bottom of the aquarium. One pale finger still had a gold wedding ring on it.

"Natalie, take a look at this!" Nathan screamed, almost choking. She came closer and looked into the 15-gallon aquarium.

"My God. How could the fish store not have noticed this? Let me get Martha." As she ran to Martha one of the pycnogonids used its claws to rip a piece of flesh from the thumb.

"Hoped you liked my joke," Martha said as he arrived. Her voice was light, trivial, like a rose bloom falling into silence without a sound, without any weight. Then she opened her mouth wide and started laughing. Natalie turned and stared at her. Martha's laughter stopped, as though Natalie had turned off a valve in her chest.

"Joke?" said Nathan.

"The hand," said Martha. "It's fake. Made out of compressed fish food. You should see the looks I get."

"Very funny," Natalie said.

"Where did you get the pycnogonids?" Nathan asked.

"They're all over the place now. Lots of little ones. They get trapped in all the local fishing nets these days."

There was a loud noise at the front of the store. Martha jumped quickly and ran to where the noise was coming from. Nathan and Natalie followed. Three young men stared back at them. Their heads were shaven and two of them wore black leather jackets.

"How are you today, freak?" one of the men said, leering at Martha. He wore barbaric jewelry around his neck and arms, and an ugly cloth coat fastened in front with wooden toggles. Martha said nothing but watched him closely. She looked into his protruding eyes shadowed by thick brows. Nathan was alarmed, but didn't know what to do.

Another man went to a tank of tiger barbs, placed his hand inside, and scooped up a handful, which he threw on the floor. His eyes were hard and cruel and pitiless. The three men laughed and started toward Martha.

"Why don't you get out of here," Natalie said to them. Nathan wondered whether she had her police gun with her. Surely not, because this was more like a date than a professional mission.

The fish store continued to echo with hoarse laughter. Before Natalie could intervene, Martha shifted all her weight to her left foot, tensed, and kicked out at one of the hoodlums' shoulders. The shoulder cracked with a brittle sound and the man dropped. The other two men opened their mouths in shock. So did Nathan. Had he seen what he thought he had?

"Hey freak, want to die?" one of the two uninjured gorillas barked.

"Oh, my shoulder is killing me," their friend moaned on the floor.

The two uninjured men moved toward Martha. She reacted automatically, smashing her fist into one attacker's solar plexus. With a twist of her body, she tucked in her right leg and then lashed out at the remaining goon's jaw with her foot. She kicked him hard enough to put him on an apple sauce and pudding diet for about two months, Nathan thought.

"It's time to leave," she told the three. She crouched low, her long calloused fingers rigid and extended toward them like knife blades.

Apparently the men were not convinced by her obvious fighting skills. The first one came at her again. She caught him on his fourth step, grabbing his right foot and lifting it. He landed on his side with a thud. He got up, but was very nervous now. He lunged at Martha and she hit him with a canister filter she had ripped from the tiger barb tank. His face smacked into the filter with what reminded Nathan of the satisfying sound of peanut brittle cracking.

"Son of a bitch," the man mumbled, and then all three of them ran from the store.

For a moment there was silence in the room. Martha smiled. "Did I mention I have a black belt, first Dan, in karate?" she inquired.

"No you didn't," Nathan said.

"Very helpful for those unable to accept my physical deformities."

"Yes, you were—" Natalie tried to think of the right word. "Amazing."

Nathan and Natalie looked at each other and decided to leave the store. As they reached the door, Martha pointed to a sign. It read:

I DO NOT ISSUE REFUNDS.

"Thank you very much," Natalie said to her as they walked out into the cool evening. Martha Samules stood in a slanted oblong of light from the fish store and waved goodbye.

"I knew she was weird, but I think I underestimated her," Natalie muttered as they got clear.

"Yet she knows how to take care of herself, and she had ample provocation," Nathan pointed out.

She changed the subject. "Do you think there's any relationship between the sudden rise in the pycnogonid population that Martha spoke of and the abrupt appearance of the giant pycnogonid?"

"It seems like too much of a coincidence for there not to be a correlation." But he knew that this was only conjecture, not proof of anything.

As they walked down Main Street, they passed a drugstore, chiropractor, and bakery. The bakery was having a sale on devil's food cake. A big Santa Claus kind of guy, obviously the baker, stepped outside and smiled at them. His front was draped with a whipped-cream splashed apron.

"Care for a piece of cake?"

"No thanks." Natalie smiled, as if she wouldn't have minded some on another occasion. They heard jazz music leaking out of the bakery. A few of the people in the bakery laughed excitedly.

"Please sit down," the baker insisted. In his hands were three large china plates. A raven-haired waitress came out and smiled.

"Maybe later," Nathan said. The baker's welcoming smile faded when he saw the expression on Nathan's face. *Is this whole town a little weird?* Nathan wondered.

The two of them continued down the street and looked into an antique shop. Directly behind the window were battered, charmless teapots, some marble chess sets, carved African masks, and a selection of "Ugly Stickers" from the 1960s.

"Hey, I collected Ugly Stickers when I was a kid," Nathan said. Each card contained a picture of a creature's head with a name like Joe, Sy, or Bob printed below the science-fiction physiognomies. Joe had wormlike appendages coming from his nostrils. Sy had prodigious teeth the size of cigarettes.

"How would you like to meet someone like that?" Nathan said. Natalie smiled.

They walked along Main Street, which became narrower and had fewer stores as they walked. Christmas-style lights outlined some of the roofs of the buildings. "By eight o'clock on a summer weeknight, most of Main Street is locked up as tightly as a safe," Natalie said. Bronze street lamps, governed by some master photosensor, began to throw rectangles of yellow light on the sidewalk and the fronts of old stores. *Quite romantic,* Nathan thought.

They cast tall shadows across the front of a barbershop and auto parts store. They looked into the barbershop and saw a slender gray-haired man sweeping the floor. Some of the shiny cobblestones he swept glistened like hand-finished English porcelains. Natalie waved to the man.

"Look at the apartment up there." She pointed to a small window above the barbershop. "I shared that little apartment with an older woman until she died of a stroke three years ago." Nathan nodded, not sure exactly what to say. "She had a pretty good life and enjoyed Newfoundland."

They stopped at a small truck with green twinkle lights that lent a festive sparkle to the vehicle. Inside a woman sold them ice cream cones dipped in chocolate and rolled in crushed nuts.

"Not bad," Nathan said as he licked his lips. He sniffed at the air, which became scented by roasted peanuts and popcorn. This was more like a date than ever. They hadn't even started to talk business, and he wasn't going to push it.

Suddenly he heard a noise. A big Eskimo in a hunting jacket walked past them, weaving slightly, his brown eyes fixed on the sidewalk before him. Tattooed on the back of his hands were codfish. Natalie nodded to him as he passed.

"Who was that?" Nathan asked.

"A fisherman. An out-of-work fisherman. Eskimos, known today as Inuits, used to have a cheerful view toward stress. But now alcoholism is caused by a new kind of stress—cultural upheaval."

They paused and watched a pair of inebriated Dutch-speaking dwarfs pass by, followed by a man who looked as if he had just come from a flophouse on the Bowery.

"Your town certainly is different, eclectic," Nathan remarked.

"I take it that you don't see many drunk Dutch dwarfs in the U.S.?"

"Sorry, I didn't mean to stare."

"So what did you think of those ultra-thin fish tanks of Martha's?"

"Crazy." He shook his head. "Would anyone really buy those?"

They both chuckled, and people on the streets turned to look. That made them laugh harder.

As they walked, Nathan noticed that the stores stocked tropical fruits such as lemons, but the foods were expensive—$5 for an orange—because of the high shipping costs. Some of the stores accepted payments in pelts and whale meat in addition to the common currency of the country. In this part of town many of the apartments and stores had an Italian-Mediterranean look with cream-colored stucco and Mexican tile roofs. Various hedges flanked the front walks. Malibu lights often revealed small spruce trees.

They continued to walk as the streets became more desolate. A few more inebriated Dutch dwarfs walked by, as Nathan scratched his head wondering where they were all coming from.

The two of them began to take a few steps along the slate sidewalk and looked into an alleyway where there was a small garden from which all the vegetables, with the exception of a few pumpkins and squash, had been harvested. Near the sidewalk were the dying remains of pretty chrysanthemums and cimicifuga. The heavy rain of the previous night had turned the garden into a swamp. Some squash were submerged. In the corner was a decayed doll whose face bobbed in the water. In another corner was a dead, gray Scandinavian cat. Its mouth was wide open, its teeth exposed to the rain and dirt. Lodged in its throat was an ornamental cabbage. Natalie looked a little sickened by the sight, and shivered.

"Let's keep walking," Nathan said. He found the alleyway too depressing to linger by.

"What's that?" Natalie asked as she saw something crawling through the mud. She backed away and looked at Nathan. He looked closer and smiled.

"I think we're both a bit on edge," he said. The movement in the mud was just a floating tree branch. At the far end of the alley was a fence with the graffiti:

THE SPIDER IS COMING

written in pink spray-paint.

"Looks like the town is preoccupied with the spider," Nathan said.

"Aren't we all?"

As they walked, Nathan looked uneasily at the paintless walls of abandoned stores overrun by climbing ivy. The wood was peeling from a few of the nearby balconies. The cracked windows stared back at them like the eyeless sockets of a giant skull.

Soon Main Street changed direction and ran along the coast. The mood seemed to change as sharply as the direction of the street. A cool sea breeze tickled their hair, and Natalie said, "Ah." Nathan took in a big breath of fresh air. Sand from the beaches came right up to the road, which glimmered like a great swatch of silk. On the side of the road away from the ocean there was grass.

They looked out toward the ocean and saw thousands of macaroni and chinstrap penguins congregating on a faraway iceberg. When viewed from the air the dark birds formed a pointillistic canvas on the white ice. The penguins were probably feeding on small shrimp, krill, which populated the frigid North Atlantic waters in vast swarms. Many years ago, Nathan had heard, seafarers killed millions of the penguins and boiled them, sometimes alive with wings flapping, for their oil. Babies and adults were thrown into steaming black caldrons, screaming for a few seconds, until shock and death overtook them. Today, near the top of the Newfoundland coastal food chain, the penguins' primary land-based predator was man.

"I've found that each penguin has its own personality," Natalie said as they paused to watch the noisy birds.

"You wouldn't want one as a pet."

"I know, they bray and squawk—and produce a prodigious amount of smelly guano."

"Of course, they're good to have around in Newfoundland. Did you know that the guano of chinstrap penguins fertilizes the algae, and invigorates the ecosystem?"

"You're a wealth of facts," Natalie said, sucking her mouth into a rosette. In repose, she was almost plain looking, but in animation she was beautiful. "What should we do about the giant sea spider?" she said, finally coming to the subject. "Tourism is declining. Everyone's a bit nervous. Some creeps at the north of Bonavista Bay are dropping randomly placed bombs into the sea, hoping to hit the monster. At the same time, they're destroying thousands of fish."

"I think we have to wait for it to attack again and quickly get to the scene before it gets away. Probably we should also set some traps with bait. But it would be hard to trap something that large. Maybe big cage-like traps could be constructed and set on the ocean bottom."

"Good idea. I'll make sure the police department sets up some huge spring-loaded cages with chunks of meat."

Main Street started to break up: the asphalt had potholes, and sand covered vast stretches of road. Everywhere small weeds grew through the cracks in the pavement. After another few minutes of walking they could barely perceive the road. Oh, there were a few scattered pieces of asphalt here and there, a few charred board-ends, some road-litter, and an occasional hard patch of ground that delineated the road from the sand and weeds to give the tired traveler some guidance. But an occasional chunk of asphalt did not make a road any more than a few organs made a body. It was as if the street gradually grew weary and finally gave up, ending in a small gravel path.

Mists fell across the path like steam from a bubbling kettle. It was as if the entire coastline were boiling, and whole waves were turned to steam along a volcanic beach. Their footsteps echoed hollowly through a place where children once played and tourists once traveled. A few pieces of broken colored glass twinkled in the waning light. In the faraway western hills was a panorama of golden light that filled the lowlands as far south as they could see. Nearby long fingers of land stretched into the sea. Massive black rocks roared up from the water's edge. Dusk was approaching as Nathan kicked at long strands of kelp which lay like dead worms on the gravel way.

"Look at that." Nathan pointed upward. A shimmering, gossamer curtain called the aurora borealis, or northern lights, hung above them.

"Looks like a streamer of light! The aurora!" she agreed. The name "aurora" came from the Roman goddess of the dawn, often represented as rising with rosy fingers from the saffron-colored bed of Tithonous.

"This is really beautiful. So much different than the American coast," Nathan said. He thought he saw the constellation Orion as he gazed past huge green rocks that loomed at their sides. Unusual weathering of the rocks resulted in a green web of copper tracings.

He looked toward Natalie. She smiled. Nathan's heart beat a little faster: he found himself attracted to her on several levels. She was a woman he would never find boring.

"Let me show you the forest before it gets too dark," Natalie said. The two turned slightly and walked along a trail full of pine needles. Main Street was far in the distance. Yellow birch, white birch, black spruce, white spruce, and balsam firs rose above a profusion of pink bougainvillea and yellow hibiscus. Beyond was a scrim of dark mist. The shadows looked like stalking gray cats. Daytime was dying.

After another ten minutes of walking, they saw the trees became scarce. Faint puffs of vapor hung over the sodden fields. They looked across the barren lands and bogs; the only signs of vegetation were mosses, lichens, grasses, and stunted trees.

"What animals live around here?" Nathan asked, stopping for a minute to catch his breath.

"The Island of Newfoundland teems with wildlife and freshwater fish. The chief fur-bearing animals are the otter, beaver, muskrat, fox and lynx. Game animals include hares, moose, and caribou, and black bear. I should know, I once came face to face with a black bear and had to shoot it."

A cloud reached out and grappled with the moon for possession of the night. As they walked down the forest trail, Nathan looked into a bank of snow and saw a sled dog's body preserved by the cold. Its rib cage was white, with bits of hair and flesh. "Wonder whose dog that was," he said.

"Good question."

"Let's find our way back to Main Street."

When the end of Main Street was in sight, they saw a wood bench facing the bay.

"Shall we sit for a while longer?" Natalie suggested.

"Sure." Nathan consciously strived to make himself as kind and easygoing as his father was high-strung, hoping that Natalie noticed and liked such calmness. Even though he had known her for just a few hours, Nathan liked everything he knew about Natalie, and hoped that the sentiment was being returned.

"May I make a rather personal remark?" she asked softly.

He forced a laugh. "I hope it's not that I smell bad."

"I think you are perhaps the nicest man I've met."

He was stunned. All he could manage to say was "Thank you."

Even at night the bay displayed a remarkable panoply of life. Elegant black-browed albatrosses floated in the air currents and squabbled over what was probably fish head. Arctic pigeons in dazzling brown and burgundy plumage swirled close to where Nathan and Natalie sat. Far away in the distance a group of Wilson's storm-petrels dabbled their wings in the sea as they hunted for tiny prey. Such exuberance of life, coming after months of the barren emptiness of the North Atlantic, had led early explorers to believe that the bay possessed infinite fecundity. Today, unfortunately, hundreds of gallons of diesel fuel all too often fouled beaches and destroyed wildlife.

They got up and walked closer to the sea. They looked up at the stars shining between a few wisps of clouds. On their left were long blades of Deschampsia and tufted Colobanthus. It was difficult for these plants in the winter, he was sure: temperatures often held all moisture hostage in ice. The grasses were as high as their knees, lush from recent rains. A father and his son were sitting on some large rocks with a tackle-box between them and a big yellow thermos at their feet. Occasionally the father said something to the boy as he held a rod with one hand and a cup of coffee in his other.

"Look at that yacht." Natalie pointed to a swiftly moving craft near the horizon.

"That's something." Nathan whistled.

"It's the Italian yacht *Destriero.* I read about it in the local newspapers. It's built out of light alloy and equipped with three gas turbines that drive water jets. I think it broke the world record for fastest eastbound crossing of the Atlantic Ocean. It can cruise at more than sixty-nine miles per hour."

"I wouldn't mind owning that one. But it's a little hard on a professor's salary."

They took off their shoes and socks and dug their feet into the sand, making small puddles. The water was cold and clear. Nathan wiggled his toes and felt the sand crumble slowly. The day was ending beautifully—a lovely beam of moonlight pushed through the cumulus clouds. The air stirred under a light northerly wind; the sea was calm. They walked some more, as the *Destriero* disappeared over the horizon. In the distance, Natalie saw a moose calf with its watchful mother. The mother's coat was fluffy and gray. Her hooves were scratching at the thin snow cover and soon she uncovered a meal, perhaps a lemming.

"Do you think we should go so close to the ocean with the sea spider on the loose?" Natalie asked as her feet crunched clam and scallop shells which lined the white beach.

"There's no need to worry. What's the chance that the pycnogonid would pick this time and this beach to make an attack? Near zero, I think."

Rapidly moving clouds delicately laced with snow soon blocked the moonlight. A cool sea wind whispered through the grasses and sand dunes. Occasionally a few night birds passed overhead or swooped to a nearby jetty.

Nathan wished he could put his arm around Natalie, but was wary of presuming and ruining the moment. She had complimented him, but that was perhaps because of his diffidence. Above, the celestial light fringed the moving waves in a curtain of stars. As they stood together near the gray-green gloom of the sea Nathan couldn't help hearing in his mind the words of his favorite 20th-Century poet, John Celestian. "I'd like to carry this moment of time on forever," he murmured.

She turned to him. "Pardon?"

"Sorry," he said, embarrassed. "I was remembering a poem."

She smiled. "Will you quote it for me?"

"Why certainly, if you wish," he agreed, surprised. He focused his memory, and recited:

"I'd like to carry this moment of time on forever . . .
Hanging on to joys which spring out into misty airs . . .
I must learn to stare upon your beauty without seeing,
Listen to your speech without hearing.
I must wear my protection like clothes
Never to be caught undressed again.
I must leave the silence . . . with its solitary candle,
Before my puzzle falls, leaving strange patterns upon my head."

"That's lovely," she said.

Shadows sprang up about them as if they were living creatures. Tidewater seeped into their footsteps, and they heard the sounds of water crashing on the nearby jetty. He finally made what seemed like a supreme gamble, and took her hand. She did not withdraw. The silence was broken by nothing louder than the fragile chirps of shorebirds. The only illumination came from the green and red light emitted by the bioluminescent bacteria coating the wet rocks sticking out of the sea. It was if they were standing in an ice and rock cathedral of stained glass.

It reminded him of Christmas.

PART III

Phantom Loving

The first great step towards progress is for man to cease to be the slave of man; the second to cease to be the slave of the monsters of his own creation—of the ghosts and phantoms.

—Robert G. Ingersoll,
The Ghosts and Other Lectures

CHAPTER 14

Fish Store

THE LITTLE CARD on the wall read:

The average person
sheds one-and-a-half
pounds of skin a year.

Martha Samules was fond of such curious facts and had dozens of notecards containing trivia taped to the back wall of her fish store. Another read:

If continually suckled,
a lactating woman will produce
milk for several years.

Indeed, in some primitive tribes even today women nursed their children for up to five years, and could go longer if circumstances warranted. Nursing was one reason that third world children often did better than those in "advanced" nations—until they got off the breast and started eating degraded western foods. Similarly, babies in poor regions who slept with their mothers had lower rates of sudden death than those who had to sleep alone. Wherever man interfered with nature, man suffered. But not enough for Martha's taste.

Today she was in a small, lightly soundproofed laboratory. Inside there was an array of aquarium filters, air pumps, and various tubes leading to a water-filled tank against a wall of the lab. The tank looked big enough to hold a large shark. On a dissecting table in front of her was a fist-sized pycnogonid. It lay dead on its back in a metal pan with a cork lining. The sea spider's legs were pinned to the cork to stabilize the body.

"Here goes," Martha said as she cut a small square opening in the body's hard exoskeleton using a dissecting scissor. The long legs reminded her of her own fingers. In some strange way, Martha felt that the bony sea spider was a kindred soul.

"Careful," she said to herself as she attempted to complete the cuts without damaging the underlying tissues. Finally she removed a postage-stamp-sized plate of shell from the creature's belly.

"That's interesting," she said to herself. After placing the square hatch to the side, she probed at the white, fleshy interior of the sea spider with her long finger and found a cavity, an air pocket, big enough to fit a sugar cube. Perhaps the air pocket aided in buoyancy when the animal rose to the surface of the water, she thought. Did it contain air or some other gas when the spider was submerged under the sea? Or did the body tissues simply shift into the cavity when the pressure of the sea compressed the pycnogonid's body?

This was of course not the first time she had made this discovery, but she liked to verify it in different species. She wanted to know as much about sea spiders as possible, and sometimes a routine dissection could lead to a significant breakthrough. The pycnogonid was a truly remarkable creature in its own right, and with her help it was becoming more so.

Martha Samules was born into a comfortable, happy household in a rural town in Prussian Silesia, about twenty miles south of Warsaw. She was the only daughter and third child of Ismar

Samules, a respected but somewhat eccentric Jewish distiller, innkeeper, and tropical fish hobbyist. She inherited her father's characteristics—excitability, intelligence, and deformities of the hands. At the age of six, Martha entered the local primary school, and at the age of eleven she went to the St. Maria Magdalena Humanistic Gymnasium in Breslau. Her favorite subjects were biology and Latin. She was always near the top of her class, despite the cruel teasing she suffered from the children as a result of her long fingers and teeth, and her sometimes strange behavior. At times she felt she was living with dark tormenting clouds around her. The clouds were the bullies, the teasers, and the embarrassed looks of her few friends.

There was a knock on her lab door. Irritated, Martha set down her scalpel, rinsed her hands, and went to it. There was the teenage girl whom Martha hired to work for her in the store during the week. "Lisa, I told you I don't want to be disturbed for less than an emergency," she snapped at the girl.

"The people—they—they want a refund," the girl stammered.

"Well show them the damn sign!" Martha snapped. "You know the policy. I do not give refunds."

"I—I know. But—"

Martha looked more closely at the girl. Lisa was too young and pretty for her own good, but she did have a certain talent for inducing smiles and sales, and she didn't make many mistakes. At the moment her eyes were puffy as if she'd been crying. Something was going on. Maybe she had lost a boyfriend, been foolishly distracted, and made a mistake in the store. This required a direct investigation.

Martha pushed by her and went into the store proper. There was a plump woman and a brat of a boy. "What's the problem?" Martha demanded.

"My son bought a fish here, and it ate our other pet fish and then died," the woman said.

"Where's your sales receipt?"

The woman produced it. Martha saw that it had been issued to one Brenda something or other, and that Lisa had handled it. It was for a lovely but predatory fish that had to be isolated from smaller species. An Aruana, a long silver fish resembling a snake or eel with a pair of barbels projecting from the mouth. It was cute in its fashion when small, but would quickly consume other fish and attain lengths of several feet if the aquarium was large enough. "You put this in with your others?" Martha inquired grimly.

Brenda nodded. "And it—"

"I know what it did. Weren't you warned not to do that?"

Both Brenda and her son shook their heads.

And Martha couldn't prove that Lisa had told them. The girl had probably been thinking of something else, so could have overlooked that vital detail. She was stuck for it, because she just might have been placed in the wrong.

She went to the cash register. "What was the value of the other fish you lost?"

Brenda told her. Martha dug out the money and paid for the refund and the other fish.

Brenda was evidently amazed. She surely had expected a hassle. "Well, thank you—" she started.

"Just get out of my store," Martha said tersely. "And don't come back."

"But we didn't know what would happen."

"You should have asked." Martha turned her back and stalked away.

She spied Lisa. "That will come out of your pay, you know."

Lisa gulped. "I know. I'm sorry I—"

"Don't be sorry. Just see that it never happens again." Martha went to the lab and closed the door.

The problem with Lisa was that she was typical of her generation and indeed the human kind. She just didn't think far enough ahead. As far as Martha was concerned, the whole lot of them could be dispensed with. There were just too damned many ignorant, thoughtless, garbage-generating hairless apes in the world, ruining it for all the natural creatures. She had to do business with them, because she needed money to finance her researches, but she was disgusted by the necessity.

Martha put the matter aside, and returned to her work. This was what she lived for: research, discovery, creation. It had taken her time to get here, but now she was making real progress.

After receiving her Ph.D. in molecular biophysics and biochemistry from Harvard as a result of her studies on the invertebrates in the North Atlantic oceans, Martha had been unsure where to go next. After some soul searching, she decided not to pursue an academic career with the accompanying pressure of fighting for tenure and grants. Instead she set up a small private laboratory in a rented flat near Bonavista Bay in Newfoundland. This was an incredible change of life for her, but she enjoyed it. The variety of fishes and invertebrates in the bay were a source of constant pleasure.

After a few years of research and teaching at the local high school, Martha had a touch of the entrepreneurial spirit and opened a tropical fish and aquaria store. She still maintained a small marine biology laboratory in a room in the back of the fish store where she dabbled in a variety of breeding and other small-scale research projects. Of course she kept this quite limited, because the store wasn't sufficiently private. She knew better than to risk the disaster of premature discovery. Her most significant work was scrupulously hidden elsewhere. She couldn't afford to have Lisa make a stupid mistake and let someone in there.

"Where did I put the growth hormone?" Martha whispered to herself, as she paced back and forth in the small lab like a caged tigress. This lab was an afterthought, tucked away between a bathroom and a supply closet. The shelves were covered with various scientific paraphernalia: test tubes, litmus paper, large Fluval canister filters, and worm feeders. In one fish tank were African cichlids. Another contained a vat of corrosive goo, the composition of which still eluded her. She was saving that particular challenge for an off moment, when she didn't have more important work to do.

"There it is." She grabbed a vial of green fluid and dumped it into a small aquarium filled with plants but devoid of animal life. Since Martha left Harvard she had decided to become an inventor of sorts. After some disastrous attempts to build the world's best fish tank filter, she did receive $30,000 from a prominent filter company for the rights to a canister filter which permitted mechanical, biological, and chemical filtration all in one filter medium for optimum water purification.

There was another knock at her lab door. She knew what that was for, because of the time. Martha reached for a single light bulb which hung down from the tile ceiling on a cord. She then shut the light off and left her lab, closing the door behind her. On the side of the metal door facing the fish store, stenciled in orange paint, were the words:

NO ADMITTANCE—AUTHORIZED PERSONNEL ONLY

"I'm going home now," said Lisa. Sometimes Martha wondered why she bothered with the stupid girl. But she reminded herself again that Lisa made it possible for Martha to fit in extra research sessions during slow times in the store. Still, she had been a nuisance today.

Lisa backed up when the smelled the stench of decay coming from the lab. Perhaps it was Martha herself who exuded the pungent aroma, she thought with satisfaction. She liked getting into her work, and the smell didn't bother her at all.

Lisa was the long red-haired cheerleader type. Hardly the kind one would expect to be working in a fish store, but she clearly needed the money and enjoyed the exotic sea life in the store. Those were motives Martha trusted. She would not have hired someone who could quit with impunity at any time.

"See you tomorrow." Lisa looked at Martha. There was something very fragile in her swollen eyes. That, too: Lisa was the type who could be pushed quite far without resisting. Martha did not want indepence of spirit here. Her brother had entirely too much of that, which was part of her problem with him.

"See you tomorrow," Martha said as she grinned. Martha knew that her teeth reminded Lisa of bicycle spokes. "Before you go, did you feed all the guppies?" Martha began to drool slightly as she looked at the splashes of water on Lisa's ivory linen short pants. Lisa followed her glance.

"I spilled a little water from the guppy tank on my pants," Lisa said as she gestured to herself. Then she pushed her shiny hair away from her face. Yes, she definitely was distracted today. As if she had any real concerns.

"Did you feed the guppies?" Martha asked again, stepping a little closer. Lisa opened her mouth. Closed it. Opened it.

"Stop that," Martha said. "You're beginning to look like a gold fish."

Lisa began to recover her composure and smiled a little. "Sure," she said with a quick intake of breath. "I fed them."

Martha grabbed Lisa's hand and gave it a shake. She held the hand in a clammy grasp for about five seconds. Then Martha held out one bony forefinger and tapped it on Lisa's chest for emphasis.

"Hey," Lisa said, perhaps noticing for the first time that Martha's fingernails were long and fat and almost brown. Some seemed as sharp as razors. Martha was proud of the effect. Had she had to get really rough with those punks who invaded her store the other day, those nails would have been useful.

"Be careful of the sea spiders," Martha told her. Then her voice turned cheerful and she said, "OK, have fun." Lisa scurried from the store like a rabbit fleeing a fox.

Martha started to laugh. Great big laughs. Her voice rose in intensity until it was a high-sonic stiletto. Black mollies in a nearby tank felt the vibrations of Martha's laughter and quickly retreated behind a rock. A tin foil barb floated belly up. Martha took off her "FISH ARE FUN" button and tossed it on the counter. It was closing time at Martha's Tropical Fish Store.

CHAPTER 15

Coma

ELMO'S MOTHER WAS still in a coma. Various plastic tubes in her natural and human-made orifices sustained her life like a parachute slowing the descent of a falling body. But the tubes merely delayed her descent into her oblivion; they did not stop it. She dozed in and out of near consciousness as condensation collected on tubes in her nose. Outside her window bawling winds and continuous rain imprisoned visitors and staff without umbrellas.

"Any chance she can recover?" Elmo asked Dr. Carter, as he shifted his gaze nervously from his mother, to her tubes, to the rain-spotted hospital window. He was wearing a hospital gown to protect his mother from any germs he carried on his clothing. On his head was a plastic hospital cap.

"Possible, but unlikely," Dr. Carter said. "All the signs suggest brain injury." Her pupils were dilated and did not constrict when Carter shone a light into them. She had no reflexes. "When we tried to take her off the respirator, her body made no attempt to breathe on its own."

"What does that mean?" The question was mostly rhetorical; Elmo had enough of a general notion to know that he was likely to be making funeral arrangements before long. He wished again that he could have gotten Martha to come when there had been time. Even a partial rapprochement would have been infinitely better than none.

"The contraction of the diaphragm for breathing is a primitive brain function orchestrated by cranial nerves three, four, and five. The fact that she could not breathe on her own suggests extensive neurological problems." Dr. Carter went to a light board and studied a series of head Xrays. Then he bent down again, close to Mrs. Samules's face, and began to examine her unresponsive eyes with an ophthalmoscope, checking for the telltale signs of dangerous intercranial pressure.

An EKG machine in the corner of the room started to show chaotic electrical activity in the woman's heart. The machine transmitted the electrical status of her heart to the nurses' station down the hall. Elmo tensed as he gazed at two clear bottles of fluid which hung from a rack by her bed, feeding an IV line in her right arm.

A nurse came in to take Mrs. Samules's blood pressure. "Her pressure's so damned low . . ."

"Give her some oxygen. Make it fast," Dr. Carter said.

Elmo stayed for a few hours and sometimes there were moments of hope. His mother's eyes occasionally moved from side to side, although she did not appear to be aware of her surroundings. Her diaphragm started rhythmic contractions, so she could be removed from the respirator. But her favorable progress did not continue. She drifted in a shadow world, straddling life and death like a tightrope walker.

Elmo gazed at his mother's blood, more brown than red, flowing through a clear exsanguination tube and into a vibrating bypass machine.

"It's feeding time," a nurse said. She turned on an array of halogen bulbs on the ceiling to help her see more clearly, and then she walked past Elmo and funneled liquid food through a feeding tube that ran into Mrs. Samules's stomach through her nose. The nurse then removed the urine that accumulated in a bag attached to a pole by the side of her bed. As she leaned over the woman's face, she began to apply a lubricant to her eyelids.

"What's that for?" Elmo asked the nurse.

"It prevents the eyelids from sticking together."

"Why is that a problem?" He hated this whole business, but was compelled to learn all he could about it.

"Comatose patients don't blink. They also secrete fewer tears, even when their eyes are closed."

A wave of sadness passed over Elmo like a dark swell of ocean water. He watched as the nurse filled a syringe with a cocktail of free radical scavengers and lazeroids and then injected the solution into a port in her intravenous line. Blood, heated to 99 degrees, moved with phenyl tertiary butyl nitrone though the IV lines and into her body through a vein in her arm.

The nurse dimmed the lights. Before Elmo's eyes adjusted to the reduced illumination, all he could see was the red blinking bulbs on the cardiac monitors. Mrs. Samules was almost invisible.

Elmo walked down the hallway to a coffee machine, his massive arms swinging back and forth, his eyes sandy, his bones aching. His feet were still clad in elasticized hospital slippers and they made a scraping sound. His large shoulders slumped. He walked like a slug on the cold white linoleum floor.

It seemed that this end of the hospital held a startling array of patients with strange ailments. As he passed by each room he read from explanatory cards taped to the doors. In one room was a boy with Prader-Willi syndrome. He was a short, fat, and snail-like individual whose compulsive eating had caused his parents to put a lock on the refrigerator. The syndrome had a distinct genetic cause: the boy had two chromosomes 15 from his mother, instead of one from each parent.

"What is this wing of the hospital?" Elmo whispered to himself as his depression deepened like a twilight sky. The only sounds he heard were the soft groans of the wind at the hospital windows and the loud tapping of the rain against the glass of the skylights.

In the next room was a girl with Angelman syndrome caused by two chromosomes 15 from her father. Her head was small, like a softball; her teeth were spaced inches apart; her movements were clumsy. Occasionally she laughed uncontrollably for no apparent reason. The man sharing her room seemed equally unusual. He suffered from osteogenesis imperfecta which caused an abnormality of his collagen—the main structural protein of the skin and bones. The famous painter Toulouse-Lautrec also had this disease which had made his bones fragile and stunted his growth. Elmo had to remind himself that each of these patients was more than a clinical specimen but a distinct individual loved by someone. Just as his mother was.

In fact, these people made Elmo himself seem relatively normal. All he had to worry about was keeping his mouth closed so as to conceal the length of his teeth, and keep his hands curled, and he could pass without much disturbance. Of course that wouldn't work the moment he got close to a normal woman, especially a girl like Lisa.

"It's hopeless, you dope," he muttered. "Turn it off." Yes, sure—as he might turn off his breathing. He might as well have stepped into a bullet, as into that smile of hers, unguarded. He had taken his injury, and might as well let himself dream until he recovered.

As he passed by Room P16 he heard a funny sound, and Elmo could not help but peek inside. In the room was a policeman talking to a man in bed. The dark-haired man kept repeating the words, "It was a spider. It was a spider." Each time he repeated the four words, his voice rose in pitch and intensity. As Elmo listened, a soft ripple of goose flesh traveled up his arms. He poked his head farther into the room just as a 200-pound hawk-faced policewoman approached him. Her name tag said, "Ms. Phat." She was certainly a contrast to that tall, lean Ms. Sheppard who had been at the meeting. Policewomen, like policemen, came in all types.

"Can we help you?" the policewoman said to Elmo in a voice as cold as her eyes. Both the policeman and the dark-haired patient turned and watched Ms. Phat and Elmo.

"Did he say spider?" Elmo asked.

"What's it to you?"

"I'm helping Captain Falow on a case involving what we believe to be a large sea spider," Elmo said. He saw the policeman raise his eyebrows.

"We found him naked on an iceberg," the policeman said. "He was covered with scratches and blood. Said he was attacked by a giant spider and that he was looking for his wife. Name's Garth James."

James! That was Lisa's last name. This was her brother! Suddenly this tragedy was considerably more personal than it had been. Lisa must really be broken up.

Elmo looked over to the man on the bed. He recognized him from photos he had developed from the camera found on the schooner. Never in his life had Elmo felt so confused and scared. The entire sea spider business was beyond his ability to assimilate. But he had to be sure. "Were you from the schooner *Phantom?*"

The man in the bed seemed to be drowning in a dark sea of madness. He turned his head toward Elmo and began to scream. He raised a bandaged arm with no hand above his head and started to point it to Elmo. He continued to yell.

The policeman stood up and pressed the buzzer to summon a nurse. An orderly in gray-green fatigues sprinted from the far end of the hospital corridor and into the room of the screaming man.

"It's—out—there," Garth chanted. Then he began to thrash around and then jumped out of the bed with the speed of a jackrabbit.

Ms. Phat blocked the only exit from the room with her fat body. The orderly came up from behind, grabbed Garth, and held him until the nurses came to inject a tranquilizer into his throbbing veins. Outside the rain drove against the hospital window with sudden fury.

Elmo left. He had learned something significant: that there had been a survivor. Garth James would surely have valuable information. But there was scant comfort in this discovery. Who would tell the man about the fate of his wife? What effect was it having on Lisa?

And Elmo couldn't even try to comfort her. Because she didn't know he existed.

CHAPTER 16

Restaurant

Martha Samules left her tropical fish store and walked down Main Street to her favorite restaurant, *Terrie's Place.* The outside of the restaurant looked like a graceless mausoleum, drab and cold. The only cheerful aspect of its front was a small canopy to the street which had rows of tiny red lights defining the roof line. On the door were the words:

SHRIMP NIGHT—THURSDAY, ALL YOU CAN EAT.

She ascended the soapstone steps large enough for only one person at a time to pass.

"Good evening, Miss Samules," said Gertie, a tall waitress in a slim skirt in stone wool and angora.

"Good to see you," Martha said as she walked briskly in, elegant as a knife.

"Usual table?"

"Sure." The interior of the restaurant was in vivid contrast to the stark exterior. The noise level was congenial, not annoying. An opulent carpet covered the floor in an elegant floral pattern. Around each table were overstuffed chairs strewn with needlepoint pillows. There were mirrors everywhere. After Martha sat down, Gertie handed her a large menu.

Martha studied it for a minute. "Black bean soup is our soup of the day," Gertie said.

"Thanks. I think I'll have a lobster with a small side order of linguini with mussels, scallops, and clams," Martha said to Gertie. Her voice was soft and eminently reasonable.

Suddenly Martha saw Natalie Sheppard sitting alone in the far corner of the restaurant. She got up and walked over to the policewoman.

"Natalie, good to see you here," Martha said as she smiled.

"Good to see you too," Natalie agreed reluctantly.

"I'd love you to join me at my table."

"Well—" Natalie arched her eyebrows.

"Please. I rarely get to eat with friends." Of course Martha had no friends among the human kind, but she had seen the policewoman often pass her store, keeping order in the neighborhood, and regarded her as worthwhile.

"OK."

Natalie walked with Martha to Martha's table. Gertie came over and took Natalie's order, chicken cacciatore. Martha sniffed with satisfaction at the entire arrangement. A single radiator near the table began to hiss and clank and constantly spit out a warm moist trail of vapor.

"Wish they would fix that thing," Natalie said.

"I agree."

One of the waitresses insisted on serving refreshments. Martha took a soft drink. Natalie took mineral water. When their meals finally arrived, they ate in relative silence, occasionally making small talk. Martha frequently had to pick out a piece of linguini caught between her long teeth. Natalie looked uneasy.

"How do you like this place?" Martha asked as she gestured toward the mahogany-paneled, antique-filled room.

Natalie shook her head. "This room is a bit dark for my tastes. The only reason I came was to try the food; I've heard so many good things about it." She looked around at the strange decor.

The restaurant was loaded with antiques. The table upon which they ate appeared to be a Napoléon III. The table nearest them was banded by ormolu and stood on toupie feet. Lining the shelves were beautiful 18th-Century Mandarin-pattern bowls made of porcelain.

"Watch this," Martha said as she reached into the lobster and pressed one of its nerves in the abdominal cavity. Natalie watched with curiosity. Suddenly, the lobster's claw opened and closed ever-so-slightly.

"My God," Natalie screamed. "How could you do that?"

"Anatomy, my dear. Anatomy," Martha grinned. "It's knowing just what nerves and muscles to press to get a particular response."

"Impossible! That lobster is dead and boiled."

"Actually it's broiled, not boiled. But it doesn't matter. Even the dead can move. It does, however, work better with live specimens. You just have to know the right pressure points. It's like acupuncture."

Natalie didn't seem to believe Martha. It must be some trick, she surely thought. That was of course why Martha had done it. She couldn't help showing off her bits of knowledge.

"Care for a mussel?" Martha lifted a spoon filled with some of the bivalve's tan flesh and waved it in Natalie's direction. Bright red tomato sauce dripped from the seafood and onto the amber table cloth. One piece of the flesh shot out of Martha's mouth and onto a nearby 19th-Century Italian table with an intricate marquetry inlay. Another splattered against the limestone column supporting the roof. Martha realized that she was going into one of her moods and was about to make a scene. Well, so be it.

"No thanks." Natalie looked increasingly uncomfortable.

Martha caught her own reflection in the shiny glass of a cabinet. In silhouette, in the dark light, she seemed an ominous figure, like a great vulture or dangerous vampire. She liked that. "Personally, invertebrates are my favorite foods. Mussels, squid, octopus, snails—I love them all."

"I prefer fish." Natalie's tone suggested that what she really would prefer was to be somewhere else.

"Fish have backbones. I hate those backbones. I choke on the spinal cords and ribs."

Natalie looked apprehensive about the direction the conversation was taking. She didn't seem to know whether to laugh at the absurdity of the conversation or get up and leave. Now the room seemed darker, more depressing. Rancid grease hung in the air like a wet rag. Oh, yes, this was going to be a good scene.

Martha began to point out some of the anatomical features of the food she was consuming. Natalie pretended to be more interested in the rosewood pedestals with inlaid jade in the far corner of the room. But she couldn't keep it up. She hesitated and then picked up her fork. She wanted to eat instead of listen to Martha. Well, Martha intended to see about that.

"Look at this," Martha said. "It's the clam's stomach. And this is its aortic arch." She started dissecting the various specimens on her plate. She pushed aside the shells to give Natalie a better view. Natalie put down her fork, giving up her effort to eat. She tried to swallow some of her drink, without much better success.

Martha continued as Natalie looked regretfully at her plate. Her food was getting cold, and the sauce on her chicken was congealing. She sighed. "It's been interesting Martha, but now I have to leave."

Oh, really?

Natalie started to get up.

Martha screamed. "I see parasites in my clam. Look! Hundreds of protozoa." Martha turned in the direction of their waitress. "Gertie!" she screamed in a high screech.

Gertie scurried over. "What's the matter?" she asked timidly. Gertie's father had been a tyrant, always quick to anger, always quick to subdue his wife and daughter with verbal abuse. This did little to give the waitress confidence when confronting abusive customers.

"I see parasites in my clam!" Martha repeated.

"I can't believe this is happening," Natalie said, looking ill. Gertie stared in amazement.

"Look at all these parasites," Martha yelled as she smeared

the digestive contents of the clam's stomach on the table cloth. Tomato sauce was everywhere. "Look at this. It looks like the adrenal glands of sheep and cattle." A few other people in the restaurant were staring intently at the unwholesome scene. Others were looking at their own plates with similar apprehension.

Natalie stood up.

"I'll get the manager," Gertie whispered.

"Speak up, Gertie, I can't hear you!" Martha shouted.

"I said I'll get the manager!" Gertie's mind seemed to snap and she began screaming, "I'll get the manager," over and over again at the top of her lungs as she fled.

From somewhere in the room, a diner dropped his fork. Another diner overturned her glass of water. There was something like a panic riot in the making.

Natalie slapped some money on the table and ran from the restaurant.

Martha was sorry to see her go. But once she got into one of her moods, nothing would stop it.

CHAPTER 17

Population

BACK IN THE store, Martha Samules was ashamed of herself. Not for making the scene in the restaurant, but for alienating a potential friend. Natalie Sheppard seemed like a decent sort, despite her profession. Martha seldom admitted it, even to herself, but she would have liked to have a friend or two. But somehow she never could resist the temptation to make others uncomfortable. She even did it to her brother, when she wouldn't hurt him for the world. And to their mother.

There it was. Elmo had called her and told her that Mom was in a coma after surgery. She should have gone with him to see her. Yet she couldn't. Her alienation had been too deep, too long. Even if it didn't make a lot of sense.

From the beginning, Elmo had been the ornery one. He had fought those who tried to tease him, and he had learned the art of fighting well. Let a boy say "finger" in that sneering tone, and he might soon enough feel that finger, curled with the others into a surprisingly solid fist, against his flesh. Let him curl his lip back to emulate too long a tooth, and he might find his own teeth loosened. No, boys had not teased Elmo for long! But that did not make them like him. Neither did the teachers, some of whom seemed to think he was a sending of the devil. More than one school had found pretexts to discipline him repeatedly, isolating him from his classmates. Their mother had protested, but it kept happening, and Elmo's fighting attitude didn't help his case.

She remembered the trouble when he severely hurt another boy. It didn't seem to matter that three boys, all larger than he, had jumped him and pummeled him mercilessly, and neither classmates nor the teacher had come to his rescue. He had finally, in desperation, managed to throw one clear, grab another around the waist, and heave him into the third with such force that their two heads cracked together, rendering both unconscious. That had been lucky and unlucky for him. Lucky because he hadn't been trying for anything so effective; unlucky because of the consequence. One boy had a concussion; the other wound up in the hospital for stitches. Elmo was expelled for violence.

After that Mom had tutored Elmo at home. Martha, who tended to internalize, rather than externalize in the manner of her brother, remained in school, keeping her fingers folded and her mouth closed, literally, so that her teeth didn't show. She got along despite the jeers. She didn't give anyone any concussions, though she did take some licks. And gradually her confusion and doubt congealed into the realization that she wasn't inferior, just different, and that she would never be accepted by others. All her efforts to conform, to be nice, had been wasted; she could do her very best for a century and still be a target of ridicule. Just because of her hands. Because of her teeth. Because.

Today some of her acquaintances asked her why she didn't get corrective plastic surgery. Why didn't they just mind their own business? When she was growing up, plastic surgery in her town had not been sufficiently advanced, and in any case was too costly. And although today doctors could make some improvement, Martha had an acute phobia toward dentists, hospitals, and the like. That was part of what had stopped her from going with her brother to see their mother. Even if she were to have all her teeth removed and wear dentures, her jaws would be very misaligned and would require even more surgery with no guarantee of the results. No way. All that surgery was not for her.

Martha continued to reminisce. It took her some time to make her internal adjustments, but by the time she finished school her heart had, as it were, become a crystal of ice. Only occasionally did she encounter someone with the potential to be liked, and then it always went wrong. Just as it had with Natalie Sheppard. Something in Martha just couldn't allow an artifact as dangerous as friendship to hatch from its reptilian egg. So her emotional censor cut in and broke it up before it could spread. Sheppard would avoid her like the plague, after that scene in the restaurant. Yet one faint, lonely vestige of Martha's original longing to be liked felt the pain of that necessary surgery. If only, that vestige thought, there could be just one exception. A faint thread, a tie to someone who was a friend. But the solid majority of her feelings were disciplined, knowing that in friendship was ruin. Only in complete emotional alienation from all human beings could she be what she had to be, and accomplish what she had to accomplish. Alienation from all except Elmo.

Elmo. He had thrived on the home tutoring, and learned a phenomenal amount. He had been able to keep his illusions about the decency of the human kind, because he was no longer subjected to the refutation on a daily basis. There might have been some justified bitterness in him, but it was overmatched by the constant overflowing love of their mother, who lavished her attention on him. Elmo, in withdrawing from human society physically, had been returned to it emotionally. Martha, remaining among humans, had become completely alienated from them. It was in its fashion a paradox. But it had allowed her to draw from the human society all the intellectual things she needed to accomplish her purpose.

For she, with the objectivity of alienation, had come to comprehend the fundamental problem of the world. It was being overrun by a single species. Like rabbits breeding without predation in Australia, and in England before that, humans were thoughtlessly consuming the resources needed for the future.

The notion turned her stomach, and so she had continually searched for a way to stop mankind's destruction of the environment. Wouldn't it be nice, she had thought, if she could devise some way to limit the number of humans on earth. If she could somehow craft a "Purple People" monster like that of the old humorous popular song, that did not confine its appetite to purple people. Something that liked to eat people, and could not readily be stopped. Perhaps a million or so such monsters would exert the necessary population control on human beings, particularly if they could be engineered to selectively destroy humans and invade above land for brief excursions before they had to return to the sea for their own survival.

For of course she thought in terms of the sea. That was her specialty, the home of the best the natural world had to offer. Something once confined to the sea, but freed from it so that the job could be done. Maybe she could enlist an army of ecomonsters—but no, no natural creature could be as smart as the humans were, and so any such monsters would soon be destroyed. They had to have human intelligence and know-how, and that would be possible only by having them work with selected humans, ecosoldiers, one soldier to guide each monster, perhaps through nerve and muscle stimulation. It should work if the monsters were always hungry, so they would gladly cooperate with their human hosts because they would always lead them to food—nice, fresh, raw, delightfully squealing humans.

"Mmmm," Martha moaned in pleasure at the image of armies of monsters descending on coastal cities. Even with no humans with them, they could probably kill millions of people.

Martha grinned as she fantasized. As the monsters foraged in the sea and responded to guidance from the advisors because such guidance normally led them to food, they could explore the ocean depths as no mechanical contraption might. What mechanical subs or robots could crawl through crevices and hug the ocean floor with the agility of natural creatures? She, along with a few dozen hand-picked ecosoldiers, could build dome-cities under the sea by using the monsters. The ecosoldiers could monitor sea pollution as they patrolled the sea and the coastlines and attack the offenders wherever they found them. If more than one passenger could ride a monster, each could ferry several passengers under the sea to faraway dome-cities and coasts. She supposed that the ecosoliders could also carry weapons which would protrude from tiny holes in the monsters' bodies, but too many protruding objects would give away the fact that the monsters were under human guidance. She preferred that the origin of the monsters remain a mystery.

She imagined hiding her team of ecosoldiers in Terra Nova National Park. Their monster hosts would remain in Bonavista Bay until they were summoned by the ecosoldiers in diving suits giving the proper arm signals. She and her teams would link up in the shallow waters and fan out south and west to Channel-Port aux Basques and then set up another base at Gros Morne National Park on the western coast of Newfoundland. They could perform a few test runs on the small coastal towns of Newfoundland, and by the summer they could spread south to Nova Scotia and finally her main goal: New York City, a major source of pollution, overcrowding, and environmental cruelty.

The human-monster hybrids could be unparalleled opportunity for science and humankind, but her only goal now was to destroy humans. She would continue to engineer enormous monsters that could take on humans when they entered the sea and also for short periods of time in their own technological habitats—oil drilling rigs, ships, and coastal towns.

Martha paced around her store, dreaming on. The need was great; the human population simply had to be reduced, one way or another, and there seemed to be a poetic justice to the notion of having monsters eat people, instead of people eating all other creatures. And think of the good it would do the world, getting those bunny-breeders under control at last! Because there literally wasn't room in the world for unlimited humans. Many researchers knew that, but none of them were taking the kind of action that was needed.

A fifth or more of the species of plants and animals could be made extinct by the year 2020, Martha thought, unless she personally made efforts to save them. But if she and her monsters could be ready to gobble up the surplus human population of the world—ah, then it would be different. The monsters would be a little like wolves in the woods which prevented deer and rabbits from overrunning the forest and then starving en masse. The presence of wolves was better than the alternative of uncontrolled reproduction and the ensuing pain of starvation for the deer. Humankind had no predator to stop it from overrunning the planet and starving. Unless she made one.

By the year 2002, there would be 21 "megacities" with populations of greater than 10 million or more. Of these, 18 would be in some of the poorest nations in the world. Calcutta already had 12 million people and Mexico City 20 million people. Some African cities were growing at a rate of 10 percent a year. Perhaps, whenever they were ready, the monsters could be sent to Calcutta and Mexico City to stem the rising tide of humanity.

During her summer years at Harvard, Martha had made it a point to tour some of the troubled megacities of the world. As she traveled through some African countries, such as Zaire and Egypt, she found conditions ghastly. Five-year-old children dug through clots of ox dung for undigested kernels of corn. Newborn babies were dropped into garbage bins by drug-addicted mothers. Many of the cities were kleptocracies, with looting a common occurrence.

A year after the African trip she traveled to Europe. In Upper Silesia, Poland, she discovered indiscriminate dumping of toxic wastes poisoned the water to such an extent that 10 percent of the region's newborns had birth defects. When she decided to take action and make a fuss with local officials regarding the pollution, she was jailed for a week. So much for working within the system.

Mexico City was the worst for her. The fumes of three million cars and 35,000 industries became trapped by the high ring of mountains that surrounded the city. It was then she decided that she would someday have to help the planet and somehow control the rising population and ensuing degradation of the environment.

In the early 1990s the number of people on earth was about six billion. If the birth rates remained what they were, with accompanying small declines in death rates, by 2025 the world would have nearly 11 billion people, double the number in 1992. Of course this increase in population would come at the cost of most other species. Martha hated this most of all. She cared about the animal species and the environmental disasters more than the continued poverty of most of the world. What had the burgeoning human population ever done for her, anyway?

Yet another doubling of population would take around twenty-five years. At that rate, by 2175, there would be around 700 billion people! This meant that there would be 12,000 people for every square mile of land—or 3,500 people for every square mile of Earth's surface including the oceans. Bunnies galore!

Martha sighed as she began cleaning some of the glass on nearby aquaria. Her mind continued to race with environmental facts and figures. Sometime she found it hard to stop the barrage of thoughts. She now began to think of the latest hunger estimates from Brown University. Their World Hunger Program had recently estimated that the world could permanently sustain either 5.5 billion vegetarians, 3.7 billion people who got 15 percent of their calories from animal products or 2.8 billion people who derived 25 percent of their calories from animal products, as in the wealthy countries. Of course, those snotty Americans and Canadians and most of the world's elite continued to insist upon eating animal meat. So the human population was already beyond the carrying capacity of the world. Now it was their turn to be eaten.

But she had strayed from her initial line of thought: her relationship to her brother and her mother. Elmo she could forgive, to a degree, for he was a child of the same arena she was. He was flesh of her flesh, sharing her unusual physical attributes. She still had some hope of recruiting him to her grand design. But their mother—she was of the "normal" human kind, incapable of understanding. She was expendable, along with most of the rest of her species. So it was pointless to go to see her; it would just make things more difficult. It was time for the old woman to go.

Martha shook her head. There was still some lurking emotional weakness. But if she could make it past her human mother's death, she should be secure against all else. She intended to make it.

CHAPTER 18

Come By Chance

NATALIE SHEPPARD PACED the floor of her efficiency apartment. Normally she appreciated her days off, using them to explore the neighboring countryside for special plants or simply to catch up on sleep. This time she was unsatisfied with anything she contemplated.

"What's the matter with me?" she asked herself rhetorically. It was a way she had of getting to the root of a problem, interrogating herself as if she were a suspect. "What's bugging me? The big spider? Yes, but I don't think that's it. That scene with Martha in the restaurant? That, too, but it doesn't account for this. My date with Nathan Smallwood?" She paused. "Bingo!"

Because there was no getting around it: she liked that man, and had enjoyed the time she had spent with him. She liked Nathan for the humor that glinted behind his eyes. Most of the men she met seemed rather superficial, whereas Nathan's passion for his work and his obvious kind manner had immediately attracted her to him.

Yet she had resolved not to get involved with a man that way, unless she knew him for years beforehand. Well, for months, anyway. She had met him just this week, in the middle of an ugly situation. It was way too soon to judge his real nature, and failure to do so could be as bad a mistake as not frisking a suspected assassin for weapons.

Yet again, how could she get to know him better, when he might return to Harvard at any time? She could not depend on him remaining in Newfoundland for two months just so she could study him like a species of plant and see how he blossomed. So this was a foolish fancy best dismissed.

"Damn," she muttered. "I'm going to do something I'll surely regret." She reached for the phone.

Maybe, she thought as she dialed, he wouldn't be in. The chances of catching him immediately were not great. And if he were in, he would probably be busy. He was not here, after all, on vacation. And if he was in and not busy, why would he care to spend any time with an off-duty policewoman who was neither beautiful nor eager to rush into bed with any man? She was not exactly bargain entertainment. So maybe it would be just as well if she got no answer.

She heard the emulations of the phone ringing. Three, four five. He wasn't in. Six. Time to hang up. Seven. So why wasn't she doing it? Eight. This was inane. Nine. Her hand wasn't answering to reason. Ten.

Then he picked up. "Sorry, I was in the shower. I mean, this is Nathan Smallwood."

She had to laugh. "At least put a towel on, stupid!"

He was silent a moment. Oh, no—had she ruined everything by her impulsive impertinence? This really wasn't like her. Somehow she was stumbling over her own feet when she least wanted to. Messing up like a teenage schoolgirl. "Uh, I'm sorry," she said haltingly. "I didn't mean to—uh, this is Natalie Sheppard, and—"

"Sure, Natalie, I recognized your voice. I was just putting on that towel, so as not to embarrass you further."

"You mean you *were*—?"

Then he laughed, and she laughed too, and her feeling for him surged. "This isn't business," she said after it subsided. "Not even a stupid pretext." She took a breath, gathering her nerve. "I—I liked walking with you the other day, and—" She couldn't quite say it.

"I liked it too," he agreed. "I wanted to call you, but I know you're busy."

"I have two days off now," she said quickly. "I—I was wondering whether you might—" She stalled out again.

"Are you asking me for a date?" he asked.

She felt herself blushing. "Yes."

"And to think I didn't have the nerve to ask you!" he said. "Natalie, I'd love to spend some time with you, no pretext necessary. You are the one bright spot in a somewhat trying excursion."

"Thank you." This seemed inane, but she didn't trust herself to say more.

"Shall I come to your apartment? I mean, to meet you, of course, so we can go somewhere."

"But you don't know where my apartment is," she protested.

"Yes I do. You pointed it out to me. The one you shared with the older woman, before she died."

Had she done that? Pointed it out to him? She must have. "Yes, that will be fine. You—you are free now?"

"Yes, as it happens. We are waiting for some test results, and there's not much for me to do until something new breaks. So I have time on my hands. But even if I didn't, I would try to make some for you."

The man was trying to charm her, and succeeding. "Thank you," she repeated.

Soon he was there. He was wearing jeans and jacket, evidently preferring informal wear even on a date. She liked that. She went down and out to meet him.

"Do you have anything in mind?" Nathan inquired as they came together. "I enjoyed our walk, but I think we may have seen most of the town already."

She wrestled with her discretion, and lost. "Well, normally I go out of town in my time off. I like to explore for plants, and sometimes I pick up interesting stones I might use for a rock garden. I thought we might, um, see the natural sights."

"That appeals to me," he agreed. "Where do you have in mind?"

"I have been gradually exploring outward from here," she said. "We're on the Avalon Peninsula, which I have pretty well covered in the past year. But there are some interesting formations and lakes in the main part of the Island of Newfoundland. The edge of that is about ninety miles away by road, so about as much time would be spent driving as exploring, but—"

"I'd like to see it. This entire region is far more interesting than I anticipated, and of course I'm interested in any fish there might be in those little lakes."

"There's an inlet of Trinity Bay that comes right up between Sunnyside and Come By Chance. There could be fish there."

He spread his hands. "I'm afraid you lost me. The inlet comes accidentally to where?"

She had to smile. "Small towns along the route, just north of the isthmus connecting the Avalon Peninsula to the main island. Sunnyside, and about two miles south, Come By Chance. I'm not sure how it got named."

"Oh. Come By Chance. I like it. It pretty well symbolizes our encounter."

"Between a policewoman and a specialist in fish?"

"Don't say it! I get so tired of those 'something's fishy' jokes. Between two people who ordinarily would never meet."

"Well, every encounter between people might be taken as a random event," she said. "Still, I agree, and if you don't mind the distance—"

"I am satisfied with the distance, and the company."

"Then I'll rent a car for the day," she said, gratified.

"Rent a car? Oh, I didn't realize—but I should have. Of course you would use a police car on duty, and wouldn't have a lot of use for a regular car. But you know, I have already rented a good motorcycle for the duration of my stay here. If you cared to trust my driving—"

Ride double on a sports motorcycle? Natalie had never cared to try anything that chancy. But this seemed to be a day for throwing caution to the winds. "I'd love to."

So it was they rode out on the cycle. Nathan handled it competently, and soon Natalie didn't feel as insecure as she had anticipated. In fact she was rather enjoying it. Her rump was wedged on the seat behind his, her spread thighs embracing his, and she was holding on around his torso. It was a way to be much closer to him, physically, than would have been acceptable in any other circumstance, without implying any sexual interplay. In fact, considering her present state of attraction and diffidence, it was ideal. She laid her helmeted head against his back, sheltering it from the wind of their velocity, and was marvelously content.

The road wound southwest, then west, crossing the peninsula. Then it vectored northwest, heading into the narrow connection to the "mainland." This was the bridge of land between Trinity Bay and Placentia Bay, hardly more than five miles thick. Newfoundland was a world in itself, fascinating in its convoluted detail.

It took about three hours to reach Come By Chance, because Nathan was a careful driver, not trying to push any limits. She appreciated that. In fact she appreciated just about everything about him. They passed through the town, deciding to start at a lake and work their way back. Nathan found a suitable place to pull off and park the cycle.

They dismounted. Natalie found that her legs were stiff; the ride had stretched her thighs in unaccustomed ways. As if, she thought naughtily, she had just had endless sex with a monster. The shaking of the motorcycle had also put her kidneys into gear; she had to find a bathroom. Naturally she had not considered that before guiding him here to the uninhabited countryside. They could so readily have stopped in Sunnyside.

But he understood well enough. “Let’s take a brief break,” he said. “Apart. Choose your region.”

She chose a gully with good bushes for concealment. He went somewhere else. It was a great relief.

In due course they met again at the parked motorcycle and commenced their exploration. “There should be a small lake up this way,” she said, pointing the direction. “I believe I saw it from the road once, but couldn’t pause then to explore it. I’ll look for stones and you can look for fish.”

“Fair enough.”

Natalie had an immediate problem: there were stones all over. Quartz, mica, marble—she wanted to take it all, but considering their carrying capacity on the cycle, she had to limit it to only the very smallest, choicest fragments.

Nathan saw her hungry glances. “We should have rented the car,” he said, smiling.

“No, I have to practice economy anyway,” she demurred. “I don’t want to crowd myself out of my apartment.”

“I had heard that little girls like pretty stones. I guess big girls do too.”

“It’s hard to outgrow,” she agreed, picking up the nearest stone. It was a nondescript aggregate with patches of white, brown, and yellow, weighing close to a pound. Too big to take with her, really; she could take a dozen smaller, purer, and more varied stones for that weight.

She was about to put it down when Nathan spoke. “It resembles Newfoundland. The island, I mean, as seen on a contour map, with colors denoting the elevations and lakes. See, it’s roughly in the shape of a right angled triangle. We should be about there.” He touched a spot near its southeast base. “I wonder whether we could see us, in miniature, if we had a magnifying glass?”

She looked at him, trying to keep a straight face. “I think your imagination is dangerous.” But now she found herself unable to put down the stone. It had become special. So she carried it with her despite its heft, hoping that soon she would find more suitable stones and be satisfied to exchange this for them.

They found the lake. It turned out to be too small to support fish, being hardly more than a wet weather pond. But Nathan was good natured about it. "I can survive for a day without spying a new species of fish. I'm enjoying the exploration."

But that reminded her of the way Kalinda James had teased Garth about not being able to be away from the water for more than three hours without becoming obnoxious. They had gone back out to sea—and now Kalinda was dead and Garth was raving in a hospital.

"If I said something—" he said, concerned.

"Oh, no, not your fault," she said quickly. "A chain of thought. I was talking to Kalinda James just hours before—before she died. She had spoken of her husband's need to get out to sea, as if it were an addiction, and your reference to needing to see fish—it was just a foolish connection my mind made, and it dumped me into a mire."

"I'm sorry. I had forgotten that you knew them. Of course this is a bad time for you. I shouldn't have asked you to come out here today."

She had to laugh, somewhat weakly. "*I* asked *you*, Nathan!"

"Well, I shouldn't have accepted."

"You're way too generous. I should have realized that I'd be moody and distracted, and not bothered you."

"If this is your moody and distracted phase, I'd love to know you when you're cheerful and focused!"

She looked at him, suspecting irony, but there was no evidence of it. He just seemed to be a remarkably easygoing person. She experienced a surge of awkward emotion. "Can we talk?" she asked suddenly.

"Certainly. I enjoy talking with you."

"Let's find a place to sit down."

They found a low outcropping of rocks that provided nice places to sit. They faced each other. Natalie hesitated, not sure how to begin. She held the stone in her lap, running her fingers over its contours. Nathan had the sensitivity not to prompt her. He looked entirely relaxed.

"The other night, you told me a good deal about you," she finally said.

"I may have talked too much."

"No, I found it interesting. I liked listening. And that's my problem. I—find myself getting intrigued with you in a male-female way, and it really isn't fair to continue this dialogue if—"

He smiled. "I'm interested. I'm not married. I was once, but it didn't work out. She found me too diffident about practical things, and too interested in invertebrates. I hope you aren't going to tell me that you are married."

"Not exactly. I—was. Married. And I didn't like it. It was a bad experience that I wouldn't care to repeat. So I really haven't been shopping for a man. But—am I embarrassing you?"

"You are delighting me. I think you are trying to say what I lacked the nerve to say to you."

"I'm saying that I'm not exactly virginal."

He laughed. "I should hope not! If you were once married—"

She had to smile. "I mean emotionally. The—the bloom is off. I don't know how my experience would affect my association with another man. It might doom any compatible relationship."

He nodded. "May I be impertinent, Natalie?"

"Please. I'm nervous about being too serious."

"There's a song from the musical *The King and I* that came into my head just now. It is titled, if I remember it correctly, "Shall We Dance?" and it describes how a dance can lead a couple to romance by a number of stages."

"I am familiar with it."

"It concludes 'With the clear understanding that this kind of thing can happen, shall we dance?' So the implication is that they are not going entirely blindly into the possible consequence of the event. I always liked that line." He met her gaze for a moment. "So with a similarly clear understanding, shall we talk?"

Now she had to laugh. "Yes, let's talk," she agreed gladly. He had made it easy, again.

She marshaled her memories and plunged in. "I might as well start at the beginning. Stop me when I get boring, and I'll try to cut to the chase. It—it's just not entirely comfortable getting into this particular matter."

"It would be a dull life indeed that had no discomfort. There's a Chinese curse: 'May you live in interesting times.' "

"I fear it is possible to live in boring times, and still be spoiled." She took a breath. "I was born in Ossining, New York, and moved with my family to New York City when I was eight years old. My father was a physician and chemist. My mother, the former Antonia de Paiva Pereira, was the daughter of a high ranking official in the Brazilian government." She glanced at him, but he showed no sign of boredom yet. "So it was a mixed family, of a sort, but fairly bright."

"So your intellect did not appear from nowhere," Nathan said. "I hadn't really supposed that it had."

He seemed to know just what to say! Or maybe she was primed to react positively to any remark he made. That notion made her nervous. She knew she had to get this done with soon, and suffer the worst before she allowed herself to get in any deeper emotionally.

"I was stimulated by the intellectual climate of New York City and did quite well in my school classes. When my family returned to Ossining during my high school years, I was at first depressed. But when I graduated second in my class from Ossining High School, my spirits improved, and I went on to Franklin and Marshall College in Pennsylvania where I double-majored in criminology and botany."

"And you thought this was routine?" he asked with a lifted eyebrow.

She smiled. He really did seem interested. "No. I always loved the look on friends' faces when I told them of my odd mixture of interests. Unfortunately, my father grew ill at the same time, and I had to drop out of college early to help support my family and pay the medical bills. My parents died when I was in my early twenties, at which point I was more interested in supporting myself than in returning to college. So at the age of 21 I moved to Las Vegas where I worked as a self-employed horticulturist who did work for several of the casinos."

"You majored in criminology and associated with casinos?"

"I didn't touch their business. I hate gambling. But they paid excellent money for suitable plants. It was a living, doing what I liked. But I wasn't satisfied. I'm—" She paused. "I have a great need for affection, love, and physical pleasure. I didn't like living alone. So maybe I was too ready to find romance. To convince myself."

"Aren't we all," he said.

She was glad for the pretext to delay her conclusion. "You got into something?"

"I was really too busy. But I confess that on occasion I might have wished to know one of the female students better. But who would want to share a life with a man whose passion is sea creatures without backbones?"

She had a ready answer for that, but this was not the time. "Did you ever actually inquire?"

He grinned ruefully. "Not after my first failure. I couldn't find the words, ironically. I was never at a loss for words in the classroom or on field trips, but the moment I strayed from zoology I lost my tongue. Especially in the presence of an interesting woman."

"Well, that explains why you've had no such difficulty today!"

He actually blushed. "That's not—I didn't mean—it's been so natural with you that—" He shook his head. ""I guess I put my foot in it. I apologize. I do find you—that is—" He stalled out.

She realized that he was having extreme difficulty telling her that he liked her. He really did lack ready words in this connection. She hadn't realized it before because she had pretty much carried the ball to him, so far. He wasn't short of feeling, just nerve. And—she liked that too. "No offense taken," she said, keeping her gaze on the stone. "I shouldn't have teased you." Such teasing had come so naturally to Garth and Kalinda, but obviously Natalie herself lacked the touch for it.

"I think I have just sufficiently clarified why I never married again," he said. "Or even came close to it. It was not for lack of desire. It's simply not a specialty of competence for me."

He didn't realize how attractive that made him to her. But it was best to cool it until she had said her piece. She didn't want the kind of disappointment she would otherwise risk. "At any rate, I was too eager," she continued. "I married a tall Dutch chef for the John Ebersole Restaurant in Vegas." She swallowed, then hurried on. "But the marriage ended after two years. Despite his pre-marriage promises to stop smoking and drinking, my husband continued. In fact, he began to drink more and more, and paid me less and less attention."

"What a waste," Nathan murmured.

"Maybe I was too demanding," she said, trying to be fair. "I had always been smart in school instead of popular. I simply may have expected too much of marriage."

He shook his head. "He was an alcoholic. They can be very good at placing the blame for their condition elsewhere. That marriage was surely doomed, regardless."

"Maybe so. I tried so hard, but the Dutchman seemed totally uninterested. *How could someone change so abruptly after marriage?* I wondered. I was finally happy when I had the courage to end it."

Nathan looked at her penetratingly. "I have had no personal experience with this sort of thing, but I think I ought to ask. Was he—?"

"Abusive? Yes. I didn't really understand the way of it at first. I blamed myself. And I think I am scarred."

"Emotionally," he said.

"When it started moving from the verbal to the physical, I—well, I had had training in self defense, of course. So he didn't actually beat on me. I beat on him, technically, when he tried it. But the whole thing disgusted me so much that I lost my taste for any kind of romance for some time. Now I—I would like to have a relationship with someone. With you, perhaps. But I'm just not ready for—"

"I understand," he said quickly. "I had too little; you had too much."

"But you see, if you have hopes of—of an affair—I'm probably wasting your time. I'm not saying that I wouldn't be willing to try, just that it might lead to disaster. Because of my—reactions. For example, the moment I smell liquor I get tense. Arresting drunks is fine, but I don't—don't—"

"You don't have to kiss a drunk," he said. "I well understand the aversion."

"I thought I should tell you that up-front. To free you, in case—"

"I think I am not at all like your ex-husband," he said seriously. "My problem is the opposite extreme. You need have no fear of any untoward expectations. I'm quite satisfied just to be looking for rocks and lakes with you." He considered. "But I must admit that I would like to hold your hand again."

"My hand you may have," she said, smiling. She set down the rock and put out her hand with a little flourish, and he took it. "The rest is readily told. After I left the Dutchman, I once again packed my bags. This time I took a vacation in Newfoundland—where I have been ever since. I love the land, the people, the sea, and everything. I joined the police force two years ago when I was 28. And that's my life history."

"I wasn't bored at all." He smiled ruefully. "In fact, I think this is the closest I have ever been to a woman. Emotionally. I realize that sounds odd, considering my onetime marriage, but there's the matter of rapport." He shrugged. "Perhaps I exaggerate."

"I don't think so." She considered a moment. "I was mostly satisfied, until—" She shrugged, deciding on candor. "Until Garth and Kalinda showed me how marriage could be. I was coming to understand what I had missed. Then I met you." She nerved herself again. "I have been considerably more forward with you than I ever thought I could be. If you wish to go now, please do it quickly." She glanced at the motorcycle. "Figuratively speaking. I'd rather not be stranded here physically."

Nathan laughed. "I don't think I could leave you now, literally or figuratively. I spoke too much, the other night, because somehow I just wanted you to know me. I think you wanted me to know you, similarly." He looked down, then met her gaze. "Are you repulsed by fish or invertebrates?"

"Not any more, I think. As long as they don't drink whiskey. Though some of those exhibits in Martha's Fish Store—"

"*I* was repulsed by some of that." He looked around. "Let's continue our explorations, of whatever nature."

She glanced at the sky. "That may not be wise. I see a cloud on the horizon."

"No bigger than a man's hand," he agreed. "We had better start back after all."

"Yes," she said with regret, picking up her rock. It would have to do. They walked toward the motorcycle.

CHAPTER 19

Monster

IT HAD BEEN several years ago that Martha Samules began experiments with pycnogonids in her modest lab in back of her fish store. So little was known about any species living near Newfoundland, as well as deep-sea species in general, that Martha thought she could make an interesting contribution to science, at the same time satisfying her own curiosity. She also considered the possibility that one day she might use them for her own personal purposes, the nature of which became clearer as she performed various biochemical experiments over the years.

Initially, she was simply curious about their life cycles and how they traveled so elegantly with their long, gangly legs. Subliminally she felt a connection with them on an emotional and physical level: both Martha and the sea spiders were fairly ugly and misunderstood, they both had long appendages, they both possessed a stout body and will—a will stronger than a casual observer might ever discern. Only later did she begin to formulate a plan for using the pycnogonids for her own terrible purposes: to control world population.

Each day during the cool summer, she went to Trinity and Bonavista Bay with her scuba gear, and roamed the sea floor in search of specimens. For some reason, sea spiders were more common in the cold waters of the Arctic and Antarctic seas than they were elsewhere, although they were found in all seas. This fact made the cold waters of Newfoundland a particularly nice place in which to search for the creatures. Once she spotted a sea spider, Martha slowly crept up behind it and then grabbed it with her gloved right hand. Then she tossed the writhing creature into a metallic cage. She usually came home with two or three pycnos a day for her experiments.

Back in her van, Martha submerged the cages in a large plastic vat of salt water she kept by the van's back doors. The ride from the coast to her fish store took around five minutes. The pyncos usually tried to escape by climbing the cage walls, but the cages were perfect prisons of hard metal wire. Once back at the lab she dropped them into salt-water aquaria with larger filters to keep the water clean.

Martha began to operate on the pycnos while they were still alive, after pinning them upside down on a dissecting pan. She did have reservations about cutting and probing them while they made terrible mewing sounds and waved their long proboscises, because she really didn't enjoy inflicting any pain on innocent creatures. However her need to learn more about the pycnos was greater than her hesitancy regarding any discomfort they might feel, or the ghastly sight of their writhing legs as she removed some of their shell-like exoskeletons and peeked inside.

After discovering a small air cavity at the base of the creature's abdomen, she began to probe at the muscles and nerves that lined the cavity, through the internal hatch door she had cut in the exoskeleton.

"Ooh," she squealed, as the creature's legs responded when she pressed certain pressure points inside the abdomen. What worked for lobsters worked for sea spiders too. Through the next few weeks she found that by pressing particular muscles and nerves in the abdomen, she could trigger certain specific leg motions. Through the next month a plan began to form in her mind. If she could obtain and train some specimens of the *Colossendeis* species of sea spiders, which normally could attain the size of an adult human, and somehow get them to grow to elephantine proportions, she could actually use the creatures as submarines. She could make an artificial hatch in one of the creatures' abdomens, crawl inside, and guide it under water. A crazy idea, she thought. But it might just be possible.

Although specimens of *Colossendeis* could attain sizes close to that of an adult human, Martha continued to be interested in creating even bigger versions of the animal. After reading articles by University of Maryland researchers on the use of human growth hormone in salmon to produce fish that were two to three times their normal size, she attempted to do the same with the pycnos. The process was called genetic engineering.

For starters, Martha knew of researchers who had isolated growth hormones from tiny fruit flies called *Drosophila.* When the level of the hormone was increased it had made the flies grow to three times their normal size. Since pycnogonids and fruit flies were both members of the same phylum, the arthropods, Martha hoped that the fruit fly hormones would be similar enough to have a noticeable effect on pycnos.

Starting with tiny pycno eggs, each a little larger than a grain of sand, she microinjected little pieces of microscopic bacterial DNA known as plasmids, which contained a copy of the growth hormone gene. The plasmid DNA would be acting like little drug factories, producing small amounts of the hormone in the pycno on a daily basis. Usually, hormones were naturally occurring trace substances produced by glands—they served as chemical messengers carried by the blood to various target organs. In the genetically engineered organism, the tiny plasmid DNA took the place of the glands. The plasmid DNA would integrate itself into the host animal's normal genetic sequence, and the growth hormone levels would rise.

To obtain the proper plasmids, Martha wrote to the University of Maryland and asked for a small sample of the bacteria containing the growth hormone genes. She told the researchers she wished to sequence and study the entire plasmid but not to use it in any test organism. She of course was lying.

Within a week she received a package marked

NON-HAZARDOUS BIOLOGICAL SPECIMENS

in bright red letters. A few years ago, packages of this type were marked "BIOHAZARD," but this tended to make the mail departments dangerously excited and, as a result, packages were often never shipped. In any case, the bacterial strains Martha had requested were not really considered hazardous because they did not contain any agent infectious to humans. The brown box she received contained a small plastic vial of soft agar along with the bacterium *E. coli.* containing growth hormone plasmids. The box also contained a note which reminded her it was illegal and potentially dangerous to use the plasmids in a host organism without governmental approval. The Maryland researchers also asked that their names be on any scientific papers Martha might publish as a result of her sequencing work.

"Sure." Martha chuckled when she read the last part of their letter. It read:

Of course should any patent arise from your use of our plasmids, or any commercial use of the plasmid be discovered, your legal department and ours would be expected to sign a contractual agreement.

Martha's idea to transform the sea spiders into bigger specimens depended on the theory that the growth hormones from flies should have an effect on the pycnos. Not a crazy idea, she told herself. After all, Auburn University scientists recently had shown that genetically engineered catfish containing extra copies of the human growth hormone gene grew at abnormally fast rates. And the Department of Agriculture had been experimenting with transgenic carp and succeeded in breeding fish that were twice the normal size. If it worked for catfish and carp, why not for the pycnos?

Martha scraped the contents of the vial into a glass petri dish which contained a nutrient gel on the bottom. Inside the dish, the bacteria containing the growth hormone plasmid genes would reproduce. Interestingly, the petri dish contained an agar gel that was laced with an antibiotic called ampicillin. Not only did the plasmids carry the growth hormone gene but they also contained antibiotic resistance genes, so any bacteria that grew in the disk were guaranteed to have the plasmid with the growth hormone gene. Any other bacteria that would try to grow in the dish would simply die. Martha also created huge stocks of *E. coli.* with the plasmid by growing giant bacterial colonies in gallon size flasks of liquid growth media.

After she had a significant stock, she microinjected purified DNA from the plasmids directly into fertilized pycnogonid eggs, some of which integrated the fly growth hormone genes of the plasmid into their own cellular genetic code. She carefully worked under a microscope, slowly manipulating a microneedle as it punctured an egg and allowed the new DNA to flow into the egg. If the method worked, Martha could mate the genetically engineered pycnogonids. Some of their offspring would contain the extra DNA coding for growth hormone and also grow to colossal proportions.

Normally when pycnogonids reproduced, the male fertilized the eggs as they passed out of the female. Then the male collected the eggs into masses on his smaller ovigerous legs. Glands on the femurs of these appendages formed a secretion for attaching the egg masses. It was at this point that Martha removed eggs, microinjected them, and then placed them back on the father pycno. Unfortunately, this was much easier to plan than to accomplish; the pycnos did not understand what she was doing, and were decidedly uncooperative. She could tie the spider down, and collect the eggs, and she could replace them. But when she released the creatures, they sensed the foreign nature of the eggs, and scraped them off. She got so angry once that she squashed one flat—then spent days in remorse. These were not human beings, after all; they didn't deserve to be destroyed out of hand. She had to find a way to anesthetize the rebellious spiders for long enough to let the modified eggs settle in, as it were, so that they no longer seemed foreign.

After a few months of trial and error, Martha found that genetically engineered fly growth hormone did produce pycnogonids that grew at rates much faster than normal. She estimated that if the current rates of growth continued, they would mature to elephant size in just two years. Sometimes she found it remarkable that hormones from a fly could have any effect at all on a pycno. It seemed a little like substituting water for gasoline in a car and expecting it to have a beneficial effect. However, the growth hormone molecules apparently were similar enough so that the fly molecules would have a noticeable effect on a member of this related, but different, species.

This was not to say that Martha's goal of producing huge pycnos was a simple or straightforward one. She soon found that when the pycno got very large, it had difficulty breathing, because the amount of surface area available for exchanging oxygen and carbon dioxide became smaller in proportion to the huge volume the creature now had. Not all the cells inside its body could satisfy their need for life-giving oxygen.

To solve this problem, Martha selectively bred species which contained, as infants, an unusually high level of hemocyanin, the compound which carried oxygen in the blood of pycnos. Just by chance, about 1 out of every 100 infant spiders had a slightly elevated level of hemocyanin in its blood. She bred these creatures to one another, and their offspring also had a slightly higher level of hemocyanin. The process was repeated for several generations of pycnos until the final specimens had very high levels of hemocyanin and blood corpuscles. Of course, all of this selective breathing was done with normal sized specimens to make the process quick and easy. It was with these better breathers that Martha again began her growth hormone experiments. The process of selecting these better breathers was not unlike the methods used by agriculturists to select disease-resistant plants or plants that could tolerate drought.

Martha also found it necessary to strengthen the hard outer material which served both as skin and skeleton for the creature. Unlike mammals and other higher organisms which had an internal skeleton, many creatures such as insects, lobsters and pycnogonids wore their skeleton on the outside. This outer skeleton, or exoskeleton, served several functions. It gave animals their external shape—particularly important for larger arthropods which needed rigid skeletons to retain their shape out of water. Secondly, the exoskeleton provided support for the muscles. Finally, it provided protection against predators and various forces of impact, buckling, and bending.

As a student of biochemistry in college, Martha learned that the hard bony exoskelton of arthropods was made of chitin—a long polymer, or chain, of N-acetylglucosamine molecules. Martha knew that although chitin was pretty incredible stuff, the heavy load that would be placed on the exoskeleton for an elephant-sized creature made it impossible to simply grow the pycnos to elephant size and expect them to function normally, particularly out of water. Their buoyancy in water would normally help support the weight of the creatures. The exoskeleton would simply not be able to bear the stress unless she could make it stronger or thicker.

Martha found, however, that she could produce a super-hard armorlike exoskelton by accelerating the rate at which the enzyme chitin synthase built the final chitin polymer. She also added chemical variants of the small molecule, N-acetylglucosamine, which were linked together to form the final molecular chain. This helped to further strengthen the pycnogonid's external coverings.

"Eureka," she screamed when she first hit a fist-sized pycno with a hammer and found she could not crack its exoskelton. The hammer bounced off the body as if it had struck a creature made of metal.

That had led to mischief. Her hireling Lisa, then somewhat bony and awkward, in contrast to what two years were to do for her, heard her cry and thought there had been an accident. She dashed back to the lab section, and it was all Martha could do to persuade her that there was no emergency. Fortunately the adolescent was not unduly inquisitive, and had no interest in spiders of any kind, so the secret of Martha's researches was preserved.

Unfortunately for Martha, the stronger exoskeltons were so rigid that they sometimes confined the body tissues in a vise-like prison that did not permit proper growth. Normally, during the pycno's growth, the hard exoskeleton allowed little room for expansion and so, like with other arthropods, pycnos had to shed their coverings periodically by molting to permit additional growth. A new skeleton then had to be secreted to replace the one discarded. This molting process was under hormonal control.

With the new, stronger exoskeletons, baby pycnos had great difficulty periodically shedding their skeletons. To solve this problem Martha placed the naturally occurring molt-accelerating hormones on the same bacterial plasmids as the growth hormone. The elevated levels of molting hormone did the trick, and the molting and growth process occurred fairly normally. Occasionally there were mishaps: pycnos with body tissues bursting through the joints of the exoskeletons which did not shed at the proper intervals, or animals with so much exoskeleton that they looked more like spherical lumps of marble than functioning sea spiders. But such things were part of the normal course, and were routinely selected out.

There was another type of problem. The defective things were horrible, but how could they be blamed for this? They reminded her too much of herself: freakish, compared to the common mode. Surely they would be cruelly attacked by their more normal fellows, if ever put in with them. She wished she could spare them death, but she lacked the facilities to maintain her failures, even if they should prove to be capable of survival. So after considerable and pained reflection, she gently put such misfits out of their misery by overdosing them with anesthetic, with an uncharacteristic tear in her eye.

Her last step in creating the pycnogonids of monstrous proportions was to increase the pycnos' strength so that they could move their huge bodies. To create more powerful muscles,

Martha strengthened the actin and myosin molecules which were the basis for all muscle actions in animals. As a result, the muscles were several times as strong as in normal pycnos. Naturally, these stronger muscles needed additional energy to function so Martha also increased the levels of the energy rich substances phosocreatine and the enzyme phosphocreatine kinase. Phosphocreatine supplied the energy for muscle contraction.

But before they grew to their full new size, she put the more muscly versions through their paces: stress tests, pulling objects, finally even showing them off to the girl Lisa, who was suitably appalled. Lisa had no notion of the significance of these creatures; all she knew was that spiders were horrible. She came close to freaking out more than once, and that pleased Martha. "If you ever tell anyone else about my private experiments, I'll put some in your underwear," she said, and was gratified to see the girl almost faint. Of course it was a bluff; the little pycnos couldn't survive for long out of the water yet, and would be just as freaked out by human underwear as Lisa was at the idea of having them there. But Lisa didn't know that, and anyway, a dead water spider would frighten her almost as much as a live one.

All of her biological manipulations had initially been enhancements to the pycnogonid's natural body architecture and biochemistry—and did not actually provide any new biological features. She did, however, want to make it possible for the pycno to easily see above water without having to lift its entire body out of the ocean. To do this, she had a plan to add two new functional eyes near the end of the proboscis. The process required a few months of experimentation to solve. In the end, she simply implanted pycno eye tissue under the exoskeleton of the proboscis when it was beginning to form during its embryonic stage. The additional tissue sent out biochemicals to the surrounding tissue and began a cascade of biochemical and physical events that eventually induced the formation of retina and optic nerves beneath each new eye.

The process of biochemical induction occurred normally during the course of embryonic development. One embryonic tissue had a chemical effect on a neighbor so that the developmental course of the responding tissue was drastically changed from what it would have been in the absence of the inductor. One of the classic examples of embryonic induction was the formation of the lens of the eye as a result of the inductive action of the optic cup upon the overlying tissue.

With the pycnos, nine out of ten times, the new optic nerves were able to grow and find their way back to the creature's forward brain, where they made a functional connection. Although Martha could have extended her discoveries and technologies to the implantation of new eyes in humans, she was not very concerned with humans. She didn't like humans very much. But she loved her new pycnos.

CHAPTER 20

Lisa

ELMO NEVER MADE a third trip to the hospital. A hospital clerk called him with the news that his mother was dead. "We'll need your authorization for the disposition of the body," she said with marvelous insensitivity.

"I will have to check with my sister," he said numbly. He had known this was coming, but still found himself unprepared.

"Of course," the clerk said disapprovingly.

He made his way to the store. He didn't know what Martha's reaction would be, but he had to tell her. She was in a general way alienated from the species of mankind, having suffered more rejection at a more formative age than he had, and the death of their mother might have the effect of cutting her the rest of the way free. Or it might not affect her at all, she being long since alienated from Mrs. Samules. But he had to have her okay to arrange for the cremation; she was after all the closest blood kin available.

He approached the store, paused, nerved himself, and entered. The young woman, Lisa, was behind the counter, talking to a customer. Elmo hung back, waiting for the store to clear before getting to his ugly business. "You will have to speak to Martha," she was saying.

"Well, where is she?" the man demanded.

"She's out at the moment, but I expect her back in an hour."

"I can't wait a damn hour! These are bad fish she sold me, and I want a refund now."

Bad fish? Elmo had his differences with his sister, but one thing she would never do was sell inferior fish. This had to be a confusion. But it wasn't his business.

"I'm sorry," Lisa said, evidently flustered. "I'm not allowed to give refunds. It's against store policy." Her eyes flicked to the posted sign, but the man ignored the signal. "They have to be handled by Martha herself," Lisa continued somewhat doggedly. "If you can just come back in an hour—"

"No! These are bad fish, and I want my money back now."

Lisa blinked. Elmo was surprised to see that she was evidently near tears. She was young, and innocent, and didn't know how to handle obnoxiousness. She had also suffered a recent bereavement. So he stepped forward, knowing that he would probably regret it. "Perhaps I can help," he said.

The man whirled on him. "Who the hell are you?"

"Elmo Samules, a fishery officer for Trinity Bay."

The customer didn't seem to pick up on the name, perhaps because Martha Samules seldom used any but her first name. "You got a refund?"

"No, but I do know something about fish." He looked at the plastic container the man held. "When did you buy those?"

"Two days ago. And now they're dead."

"You left them in that container throughout?"

"Yeah. Got to take them on the ferry south tomorrow. But not any more. They must have been diseased."

"No. They died from oxygen deprivation. You should have put them immediately into an aerated aquarium. Didn't Martha tell you that?"

"Of course I know fish need oxygen to survive. I opened the container every four hours. And no, Martha didn't say a thing about the fish being in a sealed container."

"She did!" Lisa interjected. "I remember. And anyway, opening the container once every four hours is far too seldom."

"Well, when I get *home,* she said. But I'm not home yet. I live in New York. So I kept them here."

Elmo shook his head. "Sir, you killed those fish. No sense waiting for Martha; she won't give you any refund. In fact, I'd advise you to be far away when she learns of this. Those are valuable fish."

"I'll say! I paid a mint for them! And I want it back. Now."

"You are out of luck," Elmo said firmly. "You should not be buying fish until you learn something about them."

"What I learned is that this is a gyp joint!" the man said, getting red in the face. He turned back to Lisa. "Now listen, you little bitch—"

Elmo reached up, gripped the man's shoulder with thumb and fingers, and squeezed. "There is no call for that kind of language. Please leave now."

"Listen, buster, you can't—" But the man broke off as Elmo increased the pressure of his grip. It was becoming apparent that there was a lot of power in that hand. Then he dropped the container, turned, and stalked out. Elmo let him go.

Lisa was already rushing to the fish container. It was stoutly constructed, and had not burst. She picked it up as if it were a baby. "Thank you, sir," she said gratefully. Then her eyes brightened with recognition as she stood, hugging the container. "Haven't we met?"

"Yes. I was just leaving the store the other day when you arrived. You smiled at me." Understatement of the decade! She had conquered him with that devastatingly innocent expression.

"Oh, yes, now I remember." She squinted. "But apart from that, you look familiar, somehow."

Elmo smiled, carefully, not parting his lips. "I should. I am Martha's brother Elmo. I have the same oddities of form she does." He held up one hand, opening it and spreading the fingers to show their unusual configuration.

"Oh, the name! Samules. I didn't make the connection." Now she smiled radiantly, as she had before. He could have sworn the whole store brightened in that moment. "I'm Lisa James. You saved me some real trouble, I think. I didn't know what to do."

"Glad to do it for a lovely damsel," he said, hoping this would come off as clever praise rather than oafish exaggeration.

She flushed, evidently taking it the right way. "I—I have to take this to the back room. If you can wait a moment."

"Gladly, Lisa." It was an unexpected pleasure to be talking with her like this. Sheer luck, but he would take any luck he had.

She carried the container to the back room. She returned in a moment, brushing back her long reddish hair with one hand. She was a breathtakingly lovely creature whom Martha probably demeaned. Martha did tend to resent pretty people. But of course Martha resented *all* people. "I really appreciate how you helped me," she said. "Now what can I do for you?"

Oh. She assumed he had come here for a reason, naturally enough. As indeed he had. He would have liked to ask her for a date, but knew better. She surely saw him as a grim older man, as he was. "I came to see Martha."

"She's not in. She—"

"I heard."

"Could I take a message for her?"

"I don't know if this is a suitable message. There has been a death in the family."

Lisa's face clouded. "Oh, I know how that is."

"You do?" he asked before he thought. Of course she did; he had known that all along.

"My brother Garth—I mean his wife Kalinda—the monster got her. She was a really nice person. She made my brother very happy."

The right woman could do that for a man, he was sure. A woman like Lisa? "You're Garth James' sister? I saw him in the hospital." It was easier not to try to explain how deeply involved in that whole business he had been.

"Yes. He—he's delirious. But what happened—it's so horrible."

Elmo wished he could put his arm around her trembling shoulders, to comfort her. But he couldn't. "I don't believe he is delirious. He's speaking the truth. There's a giant sea spider out there. Something unknown to science. It's my job to find that thing and kill it before it wreaks any more havoc."

"Oh, I hope you do, Mr. Samules! It's so awful."

"We're going to ride the ferry to where the thing struck, the day after tomorrow. We're organizing a party. We need to know more about it. Exactly what it is, where it ranges, and what is likely to stop it."

"Why not just shoot it, Mr. Samules?"

He hesitated, then gambled. "Call me Elmo, if you wish. After all, I didn't call you Miss James."

She smiled hesitantly. "All right, Mr.—Elmo."

Score one for the home team! "But as to why we won't just shoot it," he continued. "We might kill it, and it might sink out of reach, and we would never know exactly what it was. That would be a loss to science. And there might be others of its kind. We must try to immobilize it. To capture it, if that's possible. We need to come to understand it well enough to deal with any number of its species, if the occasion requires it. That's the only truly practical course."

"Oh, I see," Lisa said, her face lighting with comprehension. "Yes, of course you're right. I hope you do catch it."

Another notion occurred to him. "Perhaps you would like to join us on the ferry, when we make our search. You certainly have a personal interest in this matter."

"Oh, I do! But won't it be dangerous?"

"Yes, it may be, if we locate the creature. Of course it's more likely that we won't see anything, and it will be wasted effort. We may have to try it a number of times before we connect, if we do connect. It's likely to be a cold, nervous vigil. I shouldn't have mentioned it."

"Oh, I'm interested," she protested. "I just don't want to get in your way. I wouldn't be any help at all in a crisis, I know it. And I wouldn't know any of the people."

Was fate tempting him to overreach himself, and lose everything? He had to play it out and see. "You would know *me,* Lisa. And perhaps others we hope to have along, like Nathan Smallwood—" But she looked blank. "And Natalie Sheppard."

She brightened. "The policewoman! Yes. She's nice. But if anything happened, I'd probably just scream and grab on to the nearest person. I'm not very brave."

"I assure you that I would not mind having you grab on to me, Lisa. Not that you would want to." He held up his splayed fingers again, reminding her of his ugliness.

She looked at the fingers, visibly set back. "Do you also—the teeth—?"

"Yes," he said, not showing them. "But in other respects Martha and I are not at all alike. I don't have anything against ordinary people."

"That's nice," she said uncertainly. It was clear that she was somewhat in awe of him, and not in a wholly complimentary sense. Then she decided. "But I think I would like to go. My brother—" She clouded up again.

"I understand." It was time to leave, before he messed up this phenomenal chance. "I think I will leave my message for Martha. It is that our mother has died, and we must approve her cremation so the hospital can release the body."

"Oh. Yes. I'll tell her. She should be in soon." She looked up, meeting his gaze for a moment. "I'm sorry. For your mother."

"Thank you. I'm sorry for your brother and his wife. But I think he'll make it."

"Thank you." She tried to smile again, but didn't succeed. Her effort was touching, however.

Elmo turned resolutely and left the store. He did not want Lisa to suspect how interested he was in her, lest he turn her completely off. Probably it could come to nothing, but he would spin out the dream as long as he could. The death of his mother, the discovery of Lisa—they did offset each other, in their peculiar fashion, and that helped stabilize him.

It was a dark cloud, he thought, that lacked a silver lining. This cloud was exceedingly dark, but the lining was very pretty.

CHAPTER 21

Hatch

AFTER DONNING SCUBA gear and an oxygen tank, Martha climbed into one of the huge pycnogonids that waited for her in the shallow waters off the coast of Bonavista Bay. It did not fear her because it had become accustomed to her presence since hatching. It saw her as the source of its food, and of pleasure and pain.

To gain entry to the beast, she approached it from its front and waved her arms back and forth in a signal she had worked out so that it would recognize her. As if taking a cue from a director, the pycno squatted so that Martha could lift herself into the hatch. Inside, there was room enough for her to sit comfortably. A battery powered light on her helmet illuminated the eerie cavity, casting shadows off the glistening gray walls that surrounded her. Various fibers and muscle groups contracted along the walls as if in anticipation. The scene gave a whole new meaning to "living room." Entirely satisfied with her cozy home away from home, Martha closed the chitin hatch door.

The door to the pycno had been relatively simple for her to engineer. One day she had gone to her local department store and purchased some door hinges and knobs. Later she had cut a hatch in the sea spider using an underwater circular saw, and then screwed the hinges on one side and the doorknob hardware on the other. Before she affixed the hinges she painted them the same color as the pycno so to camouflage their presence. The pycnogonid did not move when she cut the hole, because it had become thoroughly accustomed to her constant cutting and probing since its origin.

Now that she was comfortably seated within the spider she quickly oriented herself, intimately familiar with all the bumps and ridges of the living room. First, Martha pulled out some optical fibers she had implanted in the floor of the creature. The fibers functioned as periscopes. She had mounted two such fiber optic periscopes about a month ago. They protruded ever so slightly from the beast's abdomen, so that she could get a crude image of the pycnogonid's surroundings while still inside it. If the primary periscope should break or become dirty, she could use the second as a backup.

She stuck one end of the periscope to her specially designed diving mask and with her hands began to rotate and twist the tube to see all around her. Yes, all systems seemed operative.

Finally she pressed upon the ceiling of the living room to give the pycno a signal to begin walking away from the coast and into deeper waters. As they descended, bubbles of spent air from the scuba tank began to accumulate in the internal cavity she sat in and made their way out of the spider via the small cracks between the chitin hatch door and the main body.

Training of the pycngonid to do her whims seemed like a lifetime job. Gradually, as a result of rewarding the sea spider by leading it to food within a half hour of opening its hatch, she conditioned it so that it gladly submitted to her invasion of its body. She also could stimulate some of the nerves which enervated its reproductive organs, thereby giving it a pleasurable feeling when it did as it was instructed. She also found various pain centers, which she used only seldom when the pycno misbehaved.

But then she found a more immediate way to influence it, though this had its risk. She tested it once, then saved it for the time she had need. All she required was a hypodermic and a particularly potent drug.

The cocaine shot into the pycnogonid's dorsal tubular heart in a concentrated injection from the syringe. Suddenly, the spider's plasma enzymes called cholesterases attacked the cocaine, splitting many of the molecules to render them inert. However the chemical onslaught was simply too great for the pycno's natural defenses. Within five seconds, the cocaine was coursing from the hemocoel, a blood cavity consisting of spaces between its muscle tissues, into the legs and returning to the heart by the dorsal hemocoel. The pharmacological effects of the cocaine were intense and instantaneous. The creature's tubular heart started thumping like a conga drum played by a jazz musician.

At the same time, the cocaine molecules streaked to the brain. Like a hot poker boring through an ice block, the cocaine penetrated the blood brain barrier and stimulated the primitive pleasure centers. Hundreds of neurons began to pulse their own neurotransmitters in a chemical dance of pleasure. However, the biochemical orgy lasted for a few minutes, soon to replaced by a more ominous emotion—rage.

Yes, this would do. If natural hunger did not encourage the creature enough to do what needed to be done, this should make the difference. She would keep a sufficient supply with her when she traveled with pycno.

CHAPTER 22

Storm

THE STORM DIDN'T wait. They had hardly started traveling on the motorcycle before the seemingly small cloud shoved up past the horizon and revealed itself as the leading edge of a monster. Stiff gusts of wind preceded it, becoming bad enough to make Nathan Smallwood distinctly nervous. He pulled over to the side of the road, perforce. "I'm afraid we'll be blown into a ditch," he said over the rising howl of air.

"Me too!" Natalie agreed immediately. "It was starting to feel like drunken driving."

And she would be especially sensitive to that, he realized, because of her alcoholic ex-husband. "I'm afraid my notion of using the motorcycle wasn't a good one."

"No, it was a good idea, just bad luck."

"Maybe we can find shelter close by. We're not far from Sunnyside, though I'm inclined to suspect at the moment that this name is a misnomer." He was trying to ease the tension of an event gone bad, and feared he wasn't succeeding.

"I don't remember any houses in this vicinity," she said. "We had better just wait it out."

"But we'll get soaked."

"I confess I don't relish the prospect. But I'd really rather not ride on that cycle right now."

He appreciated that; he didn't want to ride it either, in this treacherous weather. "Maybe we can take shelter under a tree."

"No way; that's the first place lightning would strike."

She was right. So they waited as the first drops of rain spattered around them. Then, having tasted earth, the storm got serious, and there was a sudden downpour. They were completely soaked in a moment.

"Damn, I'm sorry," he said miserably.

"Not your fault, Nathan. I suggested this region. If I'd been satisfied to scout around closer to home—"

"If I'd been satisfied to use a car—"

"If I'd kept an eye out for the weather, instead of talking so much—"

"I wanted to learn about you."

"We were careless, and we got soaked," she concluded. Indeed, her hair was sadly bedraggled and hung in lank black tresses across her shoulders.

"I can't think of anyone with whom I'd rather get soaked." Again he was making an effort at humor, but he realized as he spoke that he meant it literally.

She rewarded him with a wan smile. He wished he could kiss her, but of course anything like that was out of the question. So they just stood there in separate islands of discomfort.

After what seemed like an interminable time there came a lull in the storm. "Shall we risk it?" he asked her.

"Maybe we can get into Sunnyside," she agreed.

"To somewhere we can get warmed and dried."

They got on the cycle and proceeded cautiously south. But the storm, as if realizing that they might escape, revved up again, threatening to blow them away. Worse, there seemed to be nowhere to stop in Sunnyside. The sky wasn't sunny, he thought, so Sunnyside had turned its back on the world. They had to go on to Come By Chance.

And there, just as the rain got serious, he spied an inn, or the equivalent. A sign said VACANCY. He pulled in.

"I don't mind paying for a room, if there's a washer and

dryer," he said. "We could take turns getting our clothes fixed, and go on when the storm abates."

"Good idea," she agreed. "We'll go Dutch." He saw that her lips were slightly blue; his own were probably similar. They had to get dry.

He parked the cycle under cover, hoping it would survive the wetting it had already had. Then they entered the house. "Do you have a—"

"Yes," the woman said immediately. "And bathrobes you two can borrow while you're getting those things dried."

"How much—"

"Double occupancy, one night," she said, pointing to a posted sheet with the rates.

"Oh, we'll pay for it, but we aren't staying the night," he said.

"Yes you are."

"No, we just got caught by the storm. We'll be riding back to St. John's when it passes."

"And it will pass in the night," she said. "This is an eight hour storm; you can see its spread on the TV weather. You don't want to be out in it on that little cycle. Not to worry; supper and breakfast are included in the tab, and nobody's ever complained about our food."

He exchanged a glance with Natalie. They were obviously stuck for it. "Two rooms, then, please," he said.

"One room is all we have."

"But we're not married," he blurted.

The woman's glance moved from him to Natalie, apprais-ingly. "But close enough to it," she decided.

He looked helplessly at Natalie, who was now shivering. "Close enough," she agreed.

So Nathan paid for double occupancy, and the woman showed them to the room. "The washer and dryer are down the hall, there," she said. "I'll bring robes. Don't run the TV too loud, too late. Supper when you're ready."

In the room, Nathan faced Natalie, quite out of sorts. "I never anticipated—"

"I know it. Now we'll both have to strip completely, and we can take turns using the shower. We're adults, after all. Suppose we flip a coin for first shower?"

"You can have it," he said quickly. "You're shivering."

"All right. You take care of the bathrobes, meanwhile."

"Gladly." He turned to the door, resolutely facing away from her. But his imagination pictured her peeling the sodden clothing off, stepping naked into the shower. He felt guilty for not restraining it.

Soon the woman came with the robes, and he accepted them with thanks. He closed the door, but did not turn around until he heard the shower starting. Then he took the robes to the little bathroom and hung one within easy reach of the shower stall. He saw her wet jeans lying on the floor, about the only place where they wouldn't be in the way.

He retreated to the main room and stood gazing out the window, not daring to touch any of the furniture in his present state. The rain had intensified; certainly they did not want to be out in that.

He jumped as something touched his shoulder. "Your turn," Natalie said. She was in her bathrobe, decorously tied. Her hair was still wrung out straight, but looked much better now. So did she.

"I didn't hear you," he said, bemused.

"Water is flowing outside at the same rate as inside. You would have heard me if you had turned it off outside."

"Surely so," he agreed, smiling. He liked her humor, especially because it was occurring in a situation that would have brought out the worst in most women. He went into the bathroom, peeled away his sodden things, laid them on the floor by hers, and stepped into the shower.

The hot water was glorious. It washed away the clammy misery and restored the joy of living to his skin. Natalie had experienced the same restoration, he realized. It was intriguing to think of her as having been so recently naked in this same shower. This was about as close as he was ever likely to get to a naked woman. He would not care to admit it to others, but during his brief marriage he had never seen his wife naked. She had changed in locked-bathroom privacy, and had worn a negligee under the covers even for sex. He had known that wasn't normal, but had lacked the fortitude to protest it. And even if he had protested, what good would it have done? A person couldn't make another person want to have sex, or to be sexy, simply by protesting. But Natalie was not of that type, he was sure. If she gave herself to a man, it would be completely. He envied that man, whoever he might be.

If only he could have the ability to make the kind of impression he wanted to, instead of losing altitude and crashing every time he got near a woman he might like. He had been gratifyingly fortunate in being approached by Natalie, but once she won free of this disaster she would have only a bad memory of the occasion. Fortune always canceled out in the course of time, as with the flips of a coin. How fitting that it happen in a place called Come By Chance!

He turned off the shower, shook himself, reached out, found his towel, and rubbed himself dry. He donned the other bathrobe, drew it closed, then looked for his comb. It was beside the sink along with his wallet and other items of his pockets. He realized that his clothing was gone. Natalie had taken it for cleaning. Now he saw that her rock and other items were sitting on the other side of the sink. She had emptied her pockets similarly. Indeed, there was an accumulation of what must be the contents of the belt-packet she had used in lieu of a purse; she must be cleaning that too. It all seemed so intimate, so homey. His side, her side. Of the sink.

Then he saw the gun. It had to be her police pistol. Where had she carried that? He had never suspected. There it was, clean and dry, lying on the counter beside the other things. He realized that its holster would have gotten soaked too, so she had to fix that before being able to carry the gun on her person again. So she had left it with him for safekeeping, perhaps.

An emotion passed through him that he couldn't define immediately. He focused, and managed to get an approximate registration: it was the peculiar pleasure of being trusted. That gun wasn't for any protection from him; it couldn't be, if she had left it with him. She knew that he was the last person she had to fear.

He went out into the room. She wasn't back yet. She would be taking care of the laundry, his clothes and hers. It seemed best simply to wait for her return.

He turned on the television set. In a moment he found a mixed news/weather station, and verified what the landlady had said: they were caught in a huge mass of rain that would take hours to pass. He realized that he should have had the common sense to check the weather before making an excursion like this. But he had been so intrigued by the prospect of a day alone with Natalie that it had never entered his mind.

Or hers either, evidently. That pleased him, despite the consequence. Actually, now that he was warm and dry, the consequence did not seem bad at all. It was merely extending his date with Natalie, and giving it the semblance of greater intimacy than was warranted, but pleasant for all that. However sterile this night with her might be in reality, he would remember it with fondness for its might-have-been quality.

She returned. "I have them in the dryer," she reported. "It seemed pointless to take the time for a full washing cycle, when it was only water that was the problem. So I just did a quick rinse."

"I should have done my own," he protested.

"Do you know how to operate a dryer?"

"Yes. I'm a bachelor, remember?"

"Then if we ever have to go through this again, you can dry the clothes. But you know, it will be a while before those trousers are dry enough. We might as well see about supper."

"In bathrobes?"

"The landlady knows the situation. They're her robes."

He shrugged. "I'm game if you are. Though I admit I would feel a bit easier if I had something on under the robe."

She made a quick smile. "Yes. The underwear will dry soonest. But let's live dangerously."

"What about your gun?" he asked.

She grimaced. "That's not a gun. It's my service revolver. A Llama .32 automatic. But you're right; I shouldn't leave it behind." She stopped into the bathroom, and returned in a moment.

"But I don't see it," he said.

"Of course you don't; I don't want to advertise it. What would the landlady think?"

What, indeed! He had no idea where or how she was wearing it; nothing showed. That impressed him more than the fact of the gun itself.

She led the way to the front room of the house. He followed, bemused.

It turned out that the landlady had fixed them platters of peas, potatoes, and roast that could be taken back to the room. There was also a bottle of inexpensive wine. Nathan pushed it back on the table, not taking it.

"No, it's paid for," Natalie demurred. "Might as well have it."

"But alcohol—"

"I'm not a teetotaler. I just don't like the strong stuff. Especially in a man. Anyway, I'm trying to discipline my aversion, so as not to be ruled by it. This is as good a time to start as any."

"You're sure?"

"No. But take the wine."

He shrugged and took the bottle. They returned to the room. They pulled out the small table there and sat on opposite sides, their knees almost touching.

The meal was good. The landlady was right: there would be no complaints from this quarter. Nathan hesitated to pour out any wine, but Natalie went ahead and did it. She lifted her glass in a defiant little toast and drank. He followed, reluctantly. He feared that this was treacherous territory.

But they got through the meal without untoward event. Nathan really enjoyed it, despite the awkwardness of having to avert his gaze when her robe started to fall open. Fortunately she realized what was happening and drew it closed before anything showed. Then their knees touched again, and he was off on another flight of guilty fancy.

"Penny for your thoughts," she said.

He shook his head. "I was just wishing this were real."

"Things seem real enough to me. It's hard to forget that rain." Indeed, it was still beating against the windowpane.

"I mean that our relationship would be—I don't know."

"You would like to have an affair with a woman."

"No. Well, yes, I suppose. But not a casual one. I'd like to—to love and be loved."

"Oh. As if we were a married couple, doing this routinely."

"Yes. To have a woman in my life, without stress. A woman like you." Then he feared he had said too much. "I mean no offense. It's just an idle fancy."

"Offense? It's a compliment."

"A dream."

"A good dream. Finish your drink."

He realized that he had hardly touched his wine. "I really haven't much taste for this, tonight."

"Because of what I said this afternoon?"

"Yes. I wouldn't want you to think I would ever be that way."

"Then drink it and show me you aren't that way."

Surprised, he saw her logic. Her husband might have been a nice man, until he drank. So she wanted to be sure that Nathan's character didn't change for the worse when he did drink. It was the kind of calculated risk a woman might take if she were considering getting serious about a man. Better one bad night, than a bad relationship.

He lifted the glass and drank, hoping that he had read the situation correctly.

Natalie stood and collected the platters. "I'll return these to the proprietor."

"I can do that."

"The landlady thinks we're on the verge of married. If we were, I'd be doing this sort of thing. Let's not disabuse her."

"I really don't believe in relegating women to the kitchen," he said. "I don't care what the landlady thinks."

She smiled. "Peace. You can take the breakfast dishes back." She left the room.

Out of sorts, Nathan turned on the TV again. The evening programs were starting. He seldom watched them, normally having better things to do with his time, but didn't care for the awkward silence that might otherwise come.

Natalie returned. She glanced at the TV. "I don't think there's anything worthwhile at this hour."

"I wouldn't know," he said. "I haven't watched much TV in years. I can turn it off."

"No, let it be. It will make us resemble normal idiots. I'll go fetch the clothing; it should be dry by now."

"I can do that."

She shook her head. "Try to act like a normal man, Nathan, painful as that may be." She flashed a smile, making sure he didn't misunderstand.

He returned the smile. "One who would rather watch a rerun of a brain dead comedy than read a new text on invertebrate paleontology."

"Exactly." She disappeared.

Soon she returned with an armful of clothing. "All dry, except for your pants in the crotch."

"That figures." He accepted his pants, finding just a trace of dampness in the pockets as well.

She looked at the bed. "You can have that. I'll make a place on the floor."

"No, the bed is yours. I never meant to deprive you of comfort for the night."

"No, all I'll need is a pillow and a blanket. I've roughed it outside; this will be no problem at all."

"Natalie, I couldn't let you do it. The idea of you being relegated to the floor—"

"Because I'm a delicate violet?" she asked sharply.

"I didn't say that." But something of the kind had been in his mind. He had never questioned her right as a woman to have the softest place to sleep.

"I'm a *police*woman. I've got a service revolver. I'm not going to faint at the sight of a mouse. Give me the extra blanket on the bed." She went to the bed and took hold of the blanket folded at its foot.

He intercepted her, catching the other end of the blanket. "No, I can't allow this!"

"Since when is it your prerogative to allow me anything? Is this sexism in action?" She pulled on her end, making it a small tug-of-war. In the process her robe fell open, and not to any token degree this time.

"No! It's just that—" He paused, bemused by the distraction of her shadowed breasts. "Well, maybe it is. I do see you as a woman, a most appealing one, and it's just not in me to dump you on the floor while I take the best place to sleep. Call it sexist if you will; I confess to it. Please, Natalie—"

She let go of the blanket. "Oh, God, I think we're having a lovers' quarrel."

"And we're not even lovers," he agreed ruefully, trying not to look where he shouldn't.

She paused, cocking her head as if making a decision. "Well . . ."

He stared at her. "I meant that as a joke."

"I know you did. *I* didn't." Now she seemed to become aware of the state of her bathrobe, but didn't touch it.

"What are you saying?" he asked, knowing very well what it was, but afraid to believe it.

"Nathan, I do know what it's all about. I was married, remember. I had a good deal of experience. Bad experience, mostly, but nevertheless enough to dispel a number of illusions.

There's a sexual tension between us, and maybe more. Maybe it's time to tackle it head-on."

He hardly knew how to proceed. This was new territory for him. "I won't deny I'd like to—that I find you attractive—very much so—but that's just the glands. I have no intention of taking advantage—"

"As if I'm an innocent creature to be protected from being dirtied by any man's lustful glance. As if I have no will of my own, no power of decision."

He nodded. "I think you have me dead to rights. All those courtly archaic male attitudes—I've got them. I'm guilty. At least close up your décolletage and stop teasing me." He finally got his eyes clear, for a moment.

"Do you know something, Nathan? I think I like those attitudes. I wasn't exposed to them in marriage."

"You had a bad marriage," he agreed. "As did I, though in a quite different way."

"And you don't want to make love to a woman unless you are prepared to marry her."

"Yes, of course."

"Then with the clear understanding that this kind of thing can happen, let's end this quarrel and share this bed."

Nathan froze. Suddenly a phenomenally new course was opening out before him, almost too good to be true. "If you're sure."

"No, I'm still not sure at all. But I do like you, Nathan, more than is wise at this stage. I think perhaps I won't freeze up with you. It's time to find out."

He remembered her warning: that she could have an adverse reaction to sex, because of the abusive nature of her prior sexual experience. While he had lacked the gumption to force the issue when his wife had denied him closeness. Closeness—what Natalie had said she needed a lot of. "Then perhaps you should lead the way," he suggested.

She glanced at the TV. "Maybe leave that on. We don't know whether the walls have ears."

"Point made." He hadn't thought of that. If they weren't supposed to play it too loud, that suggested that the sound did carry to other rooms. "But the light out?"

"Yes." Then she paused. "Unless you'd like to look at me first?"

"Oh, I would, but not if it embarrasses you. I—"

She opened her robe, flashing him. It was only for about one and a half seconds, but the startling image seemed photographic. She was tall and slender, but definitely female throughout. And—she had just given him more in that respect than he had ever had before. She had not only shown him her body, she had shown him her attitude, and that counted for an incalculable amount.

She turned out the light as he stood, stunned. "Last one to the bed's a rotten egg!" she exclaimed.

Oops. He hadn't thought of the problem of making his way through the darkness. He turned toward the bed and took a step—and banged into it immediately. It was closer than he had judged. Overbalanced, he put his hands down to catch himself—and they encountered her body. He jerked them back, but that left him unbalanced, and he fell half onto her.

"I—I'm sorry," he said awkwardly, trying to get clear. But one hand got tangled in her robe, and brushed what surely was interesting flesh. "I fell." He managed to haul himself somewhat off her.

"I think I beat you, because I'm below," she said, hauling him down again.

"Yes. I didn't mean to—to handle you like that."

She laughed. "Nathan, what do you think we're here for?"

That set him back again. "True. But I mean, shouldn't there be some—some discretion? This is so awkward."

"You are delightfully awkward," she agreed. "You really don't know what to do."

"Yes. I'm not at all good at this."

"In fact you may be worse than I am."

"Oh, no! That is, you're not bad, you're terrific. So much more than I ever deserved."

"Here, let me get us clear for action." She ran her hand across his side and shoulder, to the neckline of his robe. "Um, no, I can't just take it off you. We'll have to stand again. You take yours off and I'll take mine off, and we'll meet again here in a moment. Is it a date?"

It was his turn to laugh. "A wonderful date," he agreed.

They distangled, and got to their feet beside the bed. He drew off his robe and let it drop to the floor, as he wasn't about to try to cross the room to find a chair.

Then she stepped into him, her naked body addressing the length of his. "How do you like me now?" she murmured.

"Oh, Natalie! This is a dream."

"Then kiss me, Nathan."

He wrapped his arms around her and found her lifted face. He kissed her, transported by the sweetness of the act. Yet in a moment he became aware of her tenseness. He drew his head back and dropped his arms. "I think I shouldn't have taken you literally," he said.

"Yes you should have. Kiss me again."

"But you're not ready for—"

"I'll be the judge of that. Kiss me."

He embraced her again, much more gently, and lowered his lips to hers. This time her body slowly relaxed, melting into him. Her arms came around him, tightening. The kiss lasted longer than the first, and was correspondingly sweeter.

Then she broke it, moving her face to the side. "Move your hands," she murmured. He immediately released her. "No," she said, smiling against his cheek. "Like this." She slid her hands down across his back and to his bare buttocks.

"But I couldn't—" He broke off, for she had firmly squeezed one of his nether cheeks. Realizing his foolishness, he slid his own hands down and did the same to her. He felt delightfully naughty, and his desire for her intensified.

"Perhaps you can appreciate the appeal of such interaction," she said, tickling him where it counted.

"I—" He stalled out for a moment. "I think you're teasing me, Natalie. Am I really that stuffy in my language?"

"Not really." She moved her face back into place for another kiss. "I never realized what fun it could be to seduce an innocent man."

"Do what you will with me," he agreed sincerely.

"It's time for the bed."

"Yes. But will you tell me one thing first?"

"Perhaps. What's your question?"

"Where the hell are you wearing that gun?"

She burst out laughing. "And here I thought you were interested in my flesh! You were looking for my service revolver all the time?"

"No. But I thought it should have been evident when you stripped."

"I set it down under the bed a while back."

"Oh." He felt foolish.

"But I suppose I could put it on again, if that's really the way you prefer to—"

"No need," he said quickly.

"I understand that some folk consider firearms to be quite erotic. Masculine symbols, and all that."

"Are you teasing me again?" he demanded.

She pinched his bottom. "Nathan, would I do that to you? Don't you trust me?"

"Can't we just forget about it?" He was both amused and embarrassed. "I'm sorry I asked."

"Maybe sometime I'll show you how I wear it," she said. "But we do have other business at the moment."

"Yes, I think we do." He disengaged. But he remained mightily curious.

They climbed back onto the bed. But this restored his diffidence; he wasn't sure how to get close to her again, because the horizontal dynamics differed from the vertical. He hesitated.

"You haven't gone to sleep?" she inquired mischievously.

He forced a laugh. "Ah, no. I'm a bit nervous."

"You realize that any other man would have done it and been asleep by this time?"

"Yes," he said, ashamed.

"And I would have been tense and hurting," she continued. "Instead I'm loose and laughing. You could not have found a better way to put me at ease."

"I would gladly take credit, if I deserved it. But—"

But she had rolled up against him and caught him with a solid kiss. "Just close your eyes and think of peaceful green fields," she said after a moment.

"What?"

"Advice to virgin brides. They're supposed to just lie there and let the man have his way, they being so innocent they think it is his kiss that makes them pregnant. They aren't even aware of anything happening below the neckline."

"Pregnant!" he exclaimed. "I never thought of—"

"Relax, Mister Naive. I told you I'm experienced. I'm prepared."

"You are? You mean you knew we would—?"

"Hoped, perhaps. Routine precaution."

"You're so far ahead of me, I feel like a babe in the woods."

"Not to me you don't."

He was embarrassed again. "It's impossible for me not to react, when I'm with you like this."

"I know it, and am glad of it. I doubt you'll be ignoring me tonight."

"Ignore you!" he exclaimed. "That is beyond my imagination."

"I like the limits of your imagination."

"You have surpassed them, you seductive creature."

"The funny thing is that that was pretty much the way it was with me, at first. I didn't know about genitalia. I did indeed go numb below the waist."

"I don't think I could ever be unaware of the rest of your body. I'm merely uncertain how to address it."

She rolled him over, climbing on top of him. "Fortunately I do have a notion about that." She paused. "Do you mind my acting or talking like this?"

"Natalie, I don't mind any aspect of you! You're the most lovely, fascinating, exciting creature I've ever encountered. I think I set foot at the verge of heaven when I met you, though I was too dull to realize it right away. Now I'm well into it."

"Into what?" she inquired, wriggling competently.

"Into heaven. Just being with you—" Then he realized what she was doing. "Oh, that was double entendre, wasn't it!"

"Tell me more about heaven," she said.

"Gladly. Being with you like this—I think I could remain this way forever, and never leave paradise. Oh, Natalie—will you mind if I say I love you?"

"Not at all," she said. She found his mouth for a kiss so ardent that he was transported again. There seemed to be nothing in the universe except the two of them and their merged lips and bodies.

"Then I'll say it, and say it, and say it!" he said when the kiss eased. "And not because we're in bed. It's wonderful being with you whether it's in town or on a motorcycle or looking for rocks."

"I wouldn't care to try this on a motorcycle."

"I mean that I'm happy to be with you no matter where we are or what else is happening. Just waiting for the storm to pass is great, if it's with you, or—"

"Or getting soaked?"

"I'd rather get soaked with you than be dry anywhere else," he said fervently. "Look where it has gotten me!"

"All the way through sex," she agreed.

"Through—?" He reconsidered. "Oh, my! I didn't realize!" He felt himself flushing. "That is, I wasn't thinking of it in exactly that way."

She began to laugh, her breasts shaking against his chest. "First we had a lovers' quarrel without being lovers," she gasped. "Then we were lovers without knowing it."

"There's just so much going on, it's hard to keep track," he said, bemused.

"I love it." She lifted her head. "And I love you, Nathan. I'm right here in heaven with you."

"You certainly are," he agreed, kissing her yet again.

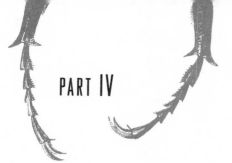

PART IV

Phantom Killing

Let the phantoms go. We will worship them no more. Let them cover their eyeless sockets with their fleshless hands and fade forever from the imaginations of man.

—Robert G. Ingersoll,
The Ghosts and Other Lectures

Life is a narrow vale between the cold and barren peaks of two eternities. We strive in vain to look beyond the heights. We cry aloud, and the only answer is the echo of our wailing cry. From the voiceless lips of the unreplying dead there comes no word; but in the night of death hope sees a star and listening love can hear the rustle of a wing.

—Robert G. Ingersoll,
The Ghosts and Other Lectures

CHAPTER 23

Mission

LISA WAS NERVOUS as she approached the car. Then she saw the policewoman Natalie Sheppard at the wheel, as promised, and relaxed. She quickly opened the back door and got into the back seat. There was a man up front beside Natalie. Both were in civilian clothing, and looked more like a dating couple than professional people.

"Have you two met?" Natalie inquired as she put the car in motion. "Nathan, this is Lisa James, who works at Martha's Fish Store. Lisa, this is Nathan Smallwood, a zoologist who is investigating the monster sightings."

"Hello," Lisa said awkwardly, smiling as the man turned his head back to see her. She was not socially adept, but her smile normally made up for it.

"Hello, Lisa," he said. "Martha's Fish Store? I understand that Martha can be a bit difficult to work with."

"I need the money. And I do like the fish; they're interesting."

"Uh-oh," Natalie murmured.

"Did I say something wrong?" Lisa asked, alarmed.

Nathan smiled. "By no means, Lisa. It's just that fish are my specialty; I'm the Curator of Fishes at the Harvard Museum of Comparative Zoology. Natalie's afraid I'm going to talk for four hours about obscure fish."

"Oh, that's all right; Martha does that all the time. And invertebrates."

"And invertebrates," he agreed. "But I'll try to stifle it, for now." He paused. "Forgive me if this is unkind, but I understand that you are related to the victims of the sea spider?"

"Yes. My brother. His wife was killed, and I don't know what he's going to do now. He really loved her."

"I know," Natalie murmured. "They were the loveliest couple I've encountered."

"Well, we hope to catch the monster that did it," Nathan said. "Though this may be complicated because—"

"Because you need to catch it and study it, in case there are others like it," Lisa said, remembering what Elmo had told her.

"Exactly. Normally creatures like this do not exist in isolation, unless this is a remarkable fluke. So while we certainly need to protect ourselves from it, it is also a potentially remarkable bonanza to science."

"I just wish it hadn't gotten Kalinda," Lisa said, the hurt returning.

"Let's change the subject," Natalie said. "We have a four hour drive to Twillingate, and we don't want to get depressed."

"Of course," Nathan agreed. "I couldn't get depressed, because we'll be passing through Come By Chance."

Lisa was happy to latch on to a new subject. "What's there?"

There was another silence, worrying Lisa. Then Natalie spoke. "Might as well tell her. It's not as if there's any secret to keep."

"As you wish," Nathan said. He turned back to Lisa. "Natalie and I visited Come By Chance recently, and found love. We are now a couple."

"That's nice," Lisa said. "I wish I could find that there."

Natalie laughed. "All you have to do is get caught out in a storm on a motorcycle with the man of your choice."

"Oh—you mean like wet T-shirts?" Lisa asked dubiously.

Nathan laughed. "That would surely do it, for you. No offense."

"No offense to whom?" Natalie asked.

They all laughed. It was obvious that nice as Natalie might be, her strength was not in her T-shirt.

"Seriously," Natalie said after a moment. "If you have a man in mind, the key is getting with him and doing things."

"Every boy I date wants to do things," Lisa said, frowning. "Because I'm—" She hesitated to continue.

"Because you're one strikingly lovely girl," Natalie said. "I see the problem."

"But I don't have a man, anyway," Lisa said. "Though—" again she hesitated.

"Oh, you do have a prospect?" Natalie inquired. "We have a long drive, and romance is always interesting. Will you tell us about it?"

Lisa mulled the matter over, uncertain whether to let others know her concern. But she did need some advice. "No, not a prospect. Trouble, maybe."

"That's even more interesting," Nathan said. "Someone's stalking you?"

"No, I don't think so. Just—I don't know."

"There's no need to talk about it if you prefer not to," Natalie said. "We don't mean to pry."

"It's not that. It—he's—maybe I'm imagining things."

"I doubt it," Nathan said. "A man who looks at you is bound to have notions."

"Really?" Natalie inquired. "Maybe you had better stop looking at her, then."

Nathan winked at Lisa. "She's a jealous creature," he confided.

"Oh, I don't want to make any trouble!" Lisa protested.

"Lisa, we're joking," Natalie said. "We're newly in love, and just overflowing with it. I think it's the kind of love your brother and Kalinda had. They showed me how it was, and then I found it for myself. Don't take our games seriously; you'll be sick of them by the time this trip is done."

Oh. They were indeed acting much the way Garth and Kalinda had. "It must be nice."

"Very nice," Nathan agreed.

"Well, maybe you can help me. There's this older man, and I—I think he likes me, maybe. I don't know what to do."

"If he bothers you, call me in my official capacity," Natalie said. "We don't have to tolerate any stalkers here in Newfoundland."

"No, he's very polite. And he's never actually said anything, or acted fresh. So maybe it's nothing. He's a responsible person. I'm sure he wouldn't—do anything bad."

"That depends," Natalie said. "If he's staring at you, making you uncomfortable, it could lead to worse. A man's position means nothing; a judge can harass women. We've had cases—"

"No, no, nothing like that. I think if I just told him to go away, he would. But—" She lost her way again.

"But you're intrigued," Natalie said wisely.

"I guess—maybe. I mean, he's an important person, I think, and strong, very strong. So I can't think why he would even notice me."

"I would tell you why, but this jealous female would put me out of the car," Nathan said. "So just take my word, Lisa, that there's no particular mystery there. The questions are the extent of his interest, and your reaction to it. Do you like him?"

"I'm not sure. I would have said no, never, because there are things about him that are pretty weird. But then he helped me in the store, and I appreciated that, and then he left, and when I got to thinking about it, I started wondering. It's just a feeling that sort of grew on me. Can a man be interested in a girl, and not give any sign?"

"Yes," Nathan and Natalie said together.

"But why? Why not either say something, or go away?"

"I can readily answer that," Nathan said. "Because he may like her, but be afraid she will reject him if he gives any sign."

"And sometimes she feels the same way," Natalie added.

"But I'm nothing at all, and he's a fishery officer—"

"Oh my God," Nathan said. "You're not speaking of Elmo Samules, Martha's brother?"

"Yes," she said, abashed. "How did you know?"

"I was with him when we discovered your brother's boat. I remember his hands. That's what bothers you, isn't it?"

"Yes. Of course I'm used to it, with Martha, and the teeth. I know they're just the way they are. I mean, they're not monsters or anything. But still, the idea of those hands touching me, or kissing—"

Nathan and Natalie exchanged a glance. "We see the problem," Natalie said.

"But you know, Elmo *is* a good man," Nathan said. "He's not the way his sister is; she's maybe a bit twisted."

"A *bit* twisted?" Natalie asked. "You should have seen the scene she made in the restaurant!"

"She does get sort of mean, sometimes," Lisa agreed. "But she's never actually done anything to me, just made me feel real uncomfortable. I think she doesn't much like people. *Any* people. But she treats them fair, and she does love the fish. She spends a whole lot of time in her lab, making new fish or something. She can do some really weird things with sea creatures. But Elmo doesn't seem to be like that."

"He isn't," Nathan agreed.

"What would Martha do, if her brother took an interest in you?" Natalie asked.

"Oh, she'd fire me, for sure. I think he's the only person she likes, though she fights with him too."

"So if he likes you, he wouldn't want to get you fired," Nathan said.

"I suppose. But I don't know that he likes me. It's just a feeling."

"You're in doubt because he is perhaps twice your age, and well established," Nathan said. "And because he is careful not to show anything."

"Yes."

"What kind of reaction do you suppose he gets from other women?" Natalie asked.

"Oh, they wouldn't like him. Because—you know."

"So it's not surprising he figures you wouldn't like him either," Natalie continued. "His course is entirely understandable. The question is, what about yours?"

"My course?" Lisa asked, baffled.

"When I got interested in a man, I asked him out," Natalie said. "I think in retrospect that was a good decision."

"But I couldn't—I mean I don't think I even like him. I just don't know what to think."

"Let's look at this logically," Nathan said. "Forget about his age; men often are interested in younger women, and it often works out if other factors align. Let's assume that he likes you, and if you smiled at him he'd float away on a cloud of bliss. That he'd marry you, if you were willing. In that case you hardly need to worry about your job; he's got a good one. You would never need to see Martha again, so her ire wouldn't mean much."

"Though Martha might simply be wary because she doesn't want to see her brother hurt," Natalie said. "She might change her mind if you married him. Did you resent Kalinda?"

"No! Never!"

"So the consequences aren't necessarily bad," Nathan continued relentlessly. "The question is whether you can see any of that happening. Could you learn to live with his hands and teeth, for the sake of love and security?"

Lisa hadn't thought of it that way. If such a man were actually within reach, and he really did love her, and marriage was possible, would she be able to ignore the hands? She pondered the matter carefully, and from her depths the answer welled up: "No. Those hands—they freak me out."

Nathan nodded. "Then I think you have your answer. Avoid him, or tell him to go away, and it will be over. Just as long as you know your own will."

"Yes, I guess." She saw that it did make sense. She didn't need to worry about how Elmo might feel, if there was no chance for a relationship anyway. She was a little sorry about it, because she realized that it wasn't his fault, but that was just the way it was. "Thanks."

"We aim to provide your money's worth," Nathan said, smiling. "We specialize in only the best quality romantic advice."

"We being sudden experts in the subject," Natalie said. "Having both failed in marriage before, we figure we know exactly what to avoid."

"We have an avoidance relationship," Nathan agreed. He leaned over and kissed her right ear. Lisa thought again of Garth and Kalinda. How nice it must be!

They rode in silence for a time. Then Natalie spoke. "Come By Chance."

Nathan peered out the window. "It looks less romantic in sunlight."

"We could close up the window and turn on the shower to sound like rain," Natalie said.

"Yes! Let's do that."

"Not now," she said, laughing. "We're on business. And what would Lisa do, meanwhile?"

"We could put her in the shower."

Lisa kept her mouth shut, not entirely comfortable with this banter.

Natalie reached out to punch his shoulder. "You'd like that, wouldn't you! One woman in bed, and a backup in the shower."

"One is all I could handle, I fear."

"So you'd go to the shower?"

He glanced back. "We'd better stop. I think someone's blushing."

Natalie glanced back herself. "Make a note, Lisa: when you're that sure of your man, you'll know its love."

"OK," Lisa said, wishing she could stifle her flush.

They passed through Come By Chance and Sunnyside and moved on north toward Clarenville and Shoal Harbor. "These are like the places of dreams," Nathan remarked.

"Just because you found your dream doesn't mean it's all dreams," Natalie said.

"I found only one dream here. The other I'm still working on."

"You *are* looking for another woman?"

"No, the other is a literary dream. I've always wanted to write decent-selling science fiction. I've written hundreds of strange short stories in my spare time, but most of them are too strange for the market."

Lisa perked up. "You write science fiction? I read that, sometimes."

"You haven't read mine, because only about one in a hundred ever sees print."

"What are they about?"

"Oh, everything. One's about a big black bug that mates with an old computer."

"A computer with a bug in it?" Natalie asked. "Are you punning?"

"Not in this case. This was a BIG bug. It tried to mate with an old broken computer, but that didn't work very well. Then it found a functioning portable computer, and mated, and died. Then hundreds of smaller bugs flew out from it, looking for more computers."

"So what happened?" Lisa asked, interested.

"That's where the story ends. You can figure that there's going to be a whole lot of mischief coming up."

"*I* can't. I want to see it happen."

Nathan shrugged. "Maybe that's why that story didn't make it."

Lisa wasn't satisfied. "Maybe another one will make more sense to me."

"OK. I wrote an absurd and mysterious story about a man who woke up in the center of a big field of cows. Some were real and some were robots. The robot cows protected the living ones from being killed, but didn't worry about little things, such as if the man just cut a bit of meat to eat from a living cow. So he survived, but he couldn't find his way out of the field. The funny thing was that a number of the cows were rather odd, having extra feet or tentacles or whatever. And the man seemed to be gradually turning into a cow himself. He tried to pile the cows into a mountain he could climb to see if there was any way out, but all he could see was more cows. Then he slipped and fell down the mountain and hit his head, losing consciousness."

"So what happened?" Lisa asked, as before.

"That's it. The reader's supposed to work it out for himself."

"Not *this* reader," she said, annoyed. "I like to read how it ends."

"I think we're zeroing on your problem," Natalie said. "You're not properly addressing the needs of your reader. This isn't like love, where the other party eagerly makes up the difference."

Nathan shook his head, frustrated. "I thought I was."

"But you never say how it ends," Lisa repeated. "You just sort of start it, and let it fade."

"Hear the voice of your literary critic," Natalie said without malice. "You know, if you find a way to score on her, maybe you'll have your key to success."

Nathan considered. "Very well, let's see if I can score on you, Lisa," he said with half a smile.

She was getting used to their banter. "OK, do it to me," she agreed.

"What kind of story do you like?"

"Do you have any with princesses, magic, adventure, and romance?"

"But that's not science fiction—it's fantasy."

"You asked what I like."

He pondered. "How about one with a princess, science, adventure, and romance?"

"OK."

"It's the year 2030, and I'm on beautiful Ganymede."

"Where?"

"Ganymede. Jupiter's major moon, about three and a quarter thousand miles in diameter."

"How big is that?"

"You should have told her how big it is," Natalie said reprovingly.

"But—"

"In her terms, dummy."

He paused, assessing the situation. "About twice as big as Earth's moon, measured across its disk."

"Oh, now I understand! It's big."

"Yes. I'm with lovely Princess Tau. We walk toward a green ocean with glittering fairylike nodes of life dancing on its translucent surface."

"Yes," Lisa breathed.

"We are looking for advanced creatures who might share their food with us. Then five green-skinned creatures come, riding massive black horselike things. We fight."

"Yes. Unicorns."

"Finally I kill the last one. Princess Tau tends to my wounds. Then we walk on to a Royal Palace. A creature comes out and leads us into a swamp. In time I realize that he is not our friend, and I make ready to fight him. But he attacks first, using a weapon of chaos, and the princess and I are killed."

There was a silence.

"That's it?" Lisa finally asked.

"Yes."

"But he never even made it with the princess!"

"Well, he might have, offstage."

"And they both got killed."

"Yes. They miscalculated. Life is rough on Ganymede."

"Too rough. That's not a romance, that's a tragedy."

"I fear you aren't scoring," Natalie said.

Frustrated, Nathan faced Lisa squarely. "How would *you* write it?"

She concentrated. "Gee, I don't know. I'm not a writer."

"Suppose he arrives on Ganymede, determined to explore it and claim it for his country," Natalie suggested. "And there's Princess Tau, who looks—well, like Lisa. But she's really an enemy, so he better watch out."

"Yes," Lisa agreed. "So she's out to seduce him, to get his guard down, so he can be killed, like Samson and Delilah."

"Only every time she starts to really tempt this innocent slob," Natalie continued, "something happens to interfere."

"Like those five green-skinned ogres he has to fight," Lisa said.

"And at the end she finally succeeds in seducing him, and absorbs his body into hers," Natalie said. "He realizes as he expires that this is how she mates."

"So it was true love after all," Lisa finished triumphantly.

"But he dies!" Nathan protested. "I thought you didn't like that."

"But he dies romantically," Lisa said. "If you wrote a story like that, I would like it."

"See—you can score with Lisa," Natalie said. "All you have to do is die for love."

Nathan sighed. "I'll think about it."

They laughed. "Maybe we have just shown him the way to ultimate literary success," Natalie said. "He will be world famous, and no one will ever hear of us women, his true reason for greatness."

"Maybe," Lisa agreed, enjoying it.

They drove on, and it really didn't seem like four hours before they reached the town of Twillingate, where the ferry to St. Anthony and points north was.

Elmo met them there, with Joseph Falow, the police chief. They had come by boat. Elmo seemed hardly to notice Lisa. Had she been wrong about him? She hoped Nathan and Natalie would not embarrass her by saying anything about the matter.

They walked to the ferry. Lisa was always surprised by the size of such crafts. In childhood she had somehow confused a ferry with a tugboat, and had a mental picture of a brave little boat trying to haul monster ships into the harbor. In reality the ferry was massive and powerful, capable of forging through the sea waves at amazing speed.

But the monster that had attacked her brother's boat had been huge and horrible indeed. Suppose it attacked the ferry? Lisa shivered, fearing the very thought.

She saw that a number of other people were boarding, including a party of teenagers. But they were not from St. John's, and she didn't know any of them. So she preferred to stay fairly close to Natalie Sheppard, if she could.

It was early evening, and the cold sea air was closing in. Lisa was glad she had had the sense to put on blue jeans and a waterproof jacket. Some of those other teens were bound to get cold before the ferry trip was done.

Soon they were all aboard, and the boat cast off its line and moved out of the harbor. They were on their way.

But on their way to what? she wondered. Now she hoped that they would not after all find the monster.

CHAPTER 24

Hunt

THE PYCNOGONID QUIETLY waited beneath the ferry lane between Twillingate and St. Anthony on the Island of Newfoundland. The creature was hungry: its multiple eyes trembled as they surveyed the environment for signs of food. Fish were becoming scarcer.

Above the sea spider was ice—red ice. Internal pigments in tiny plants called phytoplankton on the bottom surfaces of the ice gave it a reddish hue and the appearance of a raspberry ice pop. Beneath the ice was a brilliant three-dimensional cosmos overflowing with a zoo of translucent organisms. Some looked like jellyfish which glittered like jade. Others called tintinnids looked like glass paraboloids. The tintinnids propelled themselves with hundreds of thin evanescent tentacles. Tiny krill also swam about and fed on the red phytoplankton. The krill could live without food for a year and survive, a much needed defense against seasons in which phytoplankton were not plentiful. Unfortunately for the pycno, these organisms were too small to satisfy its hunger.

All around the pycnogonid were silica-spiked sponges, bright amber spiny crabs, and ultra-thin invertebrate animals that looked like yards of intestines. In the last few years waves of immigrant organisms had begun to colonize the local waters, threatening the harmony and existence of local species. Strange species of zebra mussels, daphnia, and ruffe fish were among the intruders. Most stowed away in the ballast water used to balance and stabilize large ships. As the big freighters loaded their cargos in faraway waters, they filled their ballast tanks with water from the local seas. Later, in Newfoundland, the crew released the ballast and any freeloading aquatic life the ship was carrying into the local waters. The new creatures, initially coming from places like the Caspian Sea and New Zealand, became firmly established along the Newfoundland coasts, competing with and displacing native species.

The sea spider had changed over the past three years. As the pycno matured, optic nerves were induced to grow out along its long flexible proboscis, 20 feet in length, by various processes of which the pycnogonid was unaware. Just in the last few days, increased cellular activity was occurring at the ends of the nerves. Today the spider felt a tingling along its proboscis and suddenly it had additional sensory input. Each optic nerve now bore a huge eye at its end. The spider could see with less light. It was with these new eyes that it viewed the colorful world in its nearby environment.

Recently, beautiful red and azure sponges were beginning to dot the ocean floor. They never moved, never visibly responded, even as the sea spider trampled them to death in the mud on the sea bottom. Although the sponges could not flee from the pycno's crushing limbs, they were complex animals with a repertoire of behaviors. Fifty years ago, marine biologists considered the sponge to be a plant. More recent studies showed that the sponges were active animals, their bodies dotted with small holes through which whiplike appendages beat and pumped water. The holes filtered food morsels from the surrounding ocean. For their sizes, sponges were in many ways as voracious as the pycno. Before a sponge could gain even an ounce in body weight, it had to filter a ton of water.

The sea spider treaded water and began to rise from the deep.

As it ascended, it fed on drifting jellyfish, white-tipped sharks, a few blue marlins and a rare *Chaenocephalus aceratus* which wore a crocodile-like nose. It particularly enjoyed the slim male pipefish which carried the fertilized eggs of the female in its stomach pouch.

As it continued to rise to the surface in search of more food, a fish known as *Pseudochaenichthys georgianus* swam by. It oozed slime and bared saberlike teeth. The pycnogonid did not stop to ingest the fish. It ignored the fish, not because it feared the fish or found it unwholesome, but because it grew bored with small animals, which could not come close to satisfying its insatiable needs.

The sea spider finally reached the surface where larger specimens might be more plentiful. Its head and proboscis rose out of the water like a sub with a periscope. It saw a large moving object. Its proboscis began to undulate and twitch, as if it had a life of its own. As if it were a separate, sentient organism.

The prey was larger than the pycnogonid. Faster than most fish. It was a ferry boat.

About a mile away from the ferry the spider patrolled a few feet beneath the surface of the sea. Clinging to one of its right legs was a creature that looked like a spiral soda bottle, except that its reproductive system flared away from its body like tendrils of flame. Its eyes were translucent globes filled with a luminescent milky substance. Although the pycno hunted using all of its eyes and keen sense of smell, it was not aware of the spiral creature's presence. Its multiple eyes could not see objects directly beneath its belly.

The sea spider was not here by accident. It had come up from deep water as dark as blood, attracted by the ferry's lights and engine vibrations. For a minute it became disoriented because it had lost visual contact with the ferry's lights. There was just darkness. Its proboscis began to dance up and down like a child on a pogo stick. Then the creature ascended to the surface so that its eyes poked out of the water. Its whole body began to revolve slowly until its eyes locked onto the ferry, and then the creature began to swim toward the source of the sounds and lights. It followed the ferry for a few minutes.

Its long legs were built so that it could swim as fast as the fastest fish in the sea. Now it was using its swimming prowess to track the ferry. To the pycno, the ferry was a big fish or sea mammal, and the creature followed the boat with one emotion: hunger. Its claws contracted spasmodically. It was not intimidated by the ferry boat's size. The sea spider was built to feed on all the fishes of the sea, even the largest sharks and killer whales.

CHAPTER 25

Ferry

IN THE COFFEE shop on the ferry's deck, Nathan sat with Elmo and the two police officers Falow and Natalie around a felt-covered table. Natalie's hair caught the light from the overhead bulbs and was illuminated with wild drama. She appeared tense. In this light, she seemed tall and formidable, with a shiny smile that was the softest thing about her. She looked out the windows at the fading panoramic view of turquoise waters and snow-capped mountains, at the wondrously intricate lacework of bays, islands, and coves. A whiff of pungent sea air drifted through the windows. Her dark eyes moved to Elmo's.

"Do you think all of us going to the scene of the last attack will help?" Elmo said. "What can we learn?" They all felt some of the rough sea winds that swept like lost souls through the open windows of the coffee shop. Nathan rose and closed a few windows.

"If we can learn how fast the sea spider moves by interviewing some witnesses, it might help us to prepare some kind of defense—or attack," Nathan said. Their destination was somewhere out in the darkness of the barnacled pilings and rotting timbers of the forgotten Grey Islands 50 miles south of St. Anthony, near the northern tip of Newfoundland.

As the ferry pulled away from the island, all four of them

looked out the window and watched a party of cross-country skiers gather in the town of Twillingate. The skiers were celebrating the completion of a 40-day, 500 mile journey across Newfoundland, from Cut Throat point in the northern tundra region to Twillingate on the Notre Dame Bay. By sheer luck, they had arrived only two days after the anniversary of that bitter day when British explorer Robert Schmid discovered that Norwegian explorer Gary Login had beaten him to Twillingate by 10 days. Login survived and won fame. Schmid and his five fellow explorers perished and won glory.

On the other bank were a number of teenagers in snow vehicles. Each vehicle had a large snow ski attached to the front. Half dirt bike, half snowmobile, the vehicles made it possible for the kids to whiz around the hills like hockey pucks on smooth ice. Fog, with a clammy feel of something dying, rolled in from the sea. Pine trees and railroad tracks disappeared as if dissolved by turpentine poured on an oil painting. Faraway street lamps became tiny eyes which blinked on and off in the gathering gloom.

Natalie got up and went to the food counter paneled in knotty pine. Behind it was a teenager wearing a red and white uniform. He was brewing some coffee. "Can I get you something?" he asked. The teenager reminded her of some of the perfect faces on a TV show. The boy's name, Bill, was written on his uniform in bright red letters. On the shelf behind Bill were row upon row of fruit drink bottles. The lime green, lemon yellow, and bright orange colors created a miniature rainbow of glass jars which sparkled in the fluorescent counter lights.

"What's left? Any flame-broiled salmon?" Natalie asked.

"No, just junk food," Bill said. "And a few frozen dinners."

"I'll take the cookies."

"That's a dollar."

Natalie withdrew a dollar bill from her pocket, dropped it, and almost banged her hand on the edge of the counter. She then looked back over her shoulder at the three men.

"There are still some Devil Dogs at the counter, if anyone is hungry," she yelled to them as she paid the boy for the chocolate snack. "Also some chocolate and honey-glazed doughnuts, Yodels, Ring-Dings, Pez, and other healthy snacks."

"No thanks," the others said in unison.

Natalie looked up, and Nathan's gaze followed hers. High above the counter was a small color TV. Geraldo was on. Nathan's gaze shifted to the wall on the right where a small plaster crucifix hung. He wondered what that was doing there.

A poster taped to another wall of the coffee shop caught Nathan's eye. "Look at this," he called to Natalie. The poster showed Martha Samules, the fish store lady, wearing a floaty peignoir shimmering with large pearls. Around her waist was an African mud-cloth belt. Pinned to her peignoir was her famous red button with the words FISH ARE FUN.

Natalie walked over, took Nathan's hand, and smiled. "She sure is everywhere," she said. "I guess this is an advertisement for her tropical fish store."

Chief Falow looked out a window and breathed deeply, perhaps hoping it would ease his apprehension. It didn't seem to. They could smell decomposed wood along with the odors of creosote and lime which frequently drifted from the paper mills in Twillingate. Falow began to pace.

In contrast to Falow's agitated actions, Elmo sat quietly at the table leafing through the local newspaper. Nathan and Natalie looked out another window, Nathan noticing the remarkable ice-sculpted valleys, numerous lake basins, and rounded rock knobs—the classic signs of glaciation. In the distance he saw a few men wearing goggles against the icy wind as they tracked caribou, using snowmobiles.

"What are those men doing over there?" Nathan asked. From the deep chilly waters of Newfoundland, the men were pulling an unusual treasure: huge, century-old logs of virgin timber.

"The bottom is covered with pine," Elmo said. "Thousands of logs sank in the harbor during turn-of-the-century lumber operations. The timber is knotless and fine-grained from slow growth. Worth a lot in today's market. The lumber is well preserved by low oxygen levels and the cold temperatures."

"Look over there," Falow pointed to their left. "It's a MOG canal boat."

"Are those solar panels on the top?" Nathan asked.

"Yep, it has twenty 60-watt solar-cell modules, enough to charge 16 lead-acid batteries."

"How long will the power last?" Elmo asked.

"The batteries should power the boat for 10 hours," Falow replied. "The boat's not too fast. The 30-foot-long craft is designed for intercoastal waterways and goes only five miles per hour."

The ferry ride started to get bumpy. The ship rocked back and forth as if it had Parkinson's disease. Nathan glanced nervously at Elmo.

"Why's the ride so bumpy?" Nathan asked.

"Could be the wind," Natalie said.

"Shouldn't cause a ship this big to rock," Falow said. A few of the diners pushed away their food, no longer interested in their hamburgers, french fries, and fish sandwiches. A glass of orange juice fell to the floor and shattered. "I don't like this," Falow said as he stood up and began to pace again.

"Look, some of the passengers are going to the rail of the ship," Elmo said. "Maybe they're seasick or just curious about the rocking motion."

"That's the worst place to be if the pycnogonid is in the vicinity," Nathan said. "What if the sea spider is attracted to the hum of the engines? Should we slow down or speed up?"

"How can we get those kids away from the rail without causing a panic?" Elmo asked.

"Get a hold of yourselves," Falow said. "Set a good example."

Before anyone could comment further, the captain's voice came over the ferry's loudspeakers: "We're experiencing some turbulence in the waters and think it best to continue at half our usual speed. No need to worry. The crew will keep you advised when we know more."

"Sounds more like an airline pilot than a ship's captain," said Elmo. "What's he mean by *experiencing turbulence?*"

The MOG canal boat, now about a half-mile away, seemed to be unaffected by the water "turbulence." Whatever the problem was, it seemed localized to the vicinity of the ferry.

"Sheppard, go to the car and get your gun," Falow said. "I'll go find the captain and see if he can announce to the passengers that it's best to stay away from the rails."

Nathan hoped that would be sufficient. He did not like the feel of this at all. They had come to spy on the sea spider; was it possible that it was spying on them?

CHAPTER 26

Captain

LISA, NOT FEELING easy about joining the others in the coffee shop, because Elmo was there, elected to stay outside and see the sights. She had not been on this route before, and was interested. The sea was fairly calm but had an occasional swirl and swell.

The large ferry sloshed toward St. Anthony through gathering veils of darkness and mist. She understood that this was actually one of the warmer areas of Newfoundland. For four months of the year, more northern regions were virtually inaccessible. Further south were the lakes and bogs, and then the big cities like L'Anse au Meadows and Parsons Harbor.

She spied the ferry captain, and approached him. Concerned that he would order her out of his way, she protected herself with her most useful armament: her smile. "Hello," she said, catching him with it as he turned at the sound of her voice.

Captain Calamari was a big man, surely rarely fearful. He stood six feet two inches tall on the bridge and was dressed in a seafarer sweater patterned with clipper ships. Emblazoned on the shirt was the proud insignia of the Newfoundland Merchant Marines. With one hand he sipped on a steaming cup of good Jamaican coffee to jump-start his heart. He was clearly satisfied with his job. The roar of the ocean waves invigorated him. Lisa had heard that he was the only captain the new ferry had ever known.

Now, spying Lisa's smile, he softened somewhat. "What can I do for you, Miss?"

"Lisa. I'm Lisa James. I'm here with the—the monster-hunting party. But I'm really just a spectator. I was just admiring the ferry. It's such a nice boat."

If her remark lacked something in precision, it nevertheless evoked a warm response.

"She's on her last ride of the evening," the captain said affably. "She's a Norwegian-built UT-904 ferry combining the speed of a catamaran with the smooth ride of a hovercraft when traveling at faster speeds. Two fans beneath the craft create a five-foot air cushion that is trapped by the rubber skirts at the bow and stern section. She's a slim 128-foot-long craft that slices through the water with little drag. She could theoretically hold 360 passengers, and her top speed is fifty knots, about fifty-seven miles per hour."

"Really?" Lisa asked with her eyes evincing rapt wonder. It wasn't entirely an act; she was impressed despite her inability to follow all of the description.

Calamari shrugged. "Such high speeds, however, are rarely attempted in the icy waters."

Lisa forced a laugh. "Maybe if the monster chases us."

The captain pulled a cord which activated a horn to produce one long whistle followed by three shorts. The whistle echoed weakly against nearby cliff walls. For almost half a minute the reverberations could be heard from the tall pine trees. The echoes rolled off the fragile houses cradled between the wind-scoured land and the wind-tossed waters of the Labrador Sea.

"That's something," Lisa breathed. "It just goes on and on."

"I don't like all the fog around my ferry," Calamari confided. "Thick fog, created when the warm Gulf Stream and the cold Labrador Current come together, occurs between March and June. Today's fog in autumn, however, is unexpected and unusually murky. Fog used to be the quiet killer of the sea, robbing sea captains of their most important sense: vision. Although I prefer to use my own two eyes, the ferry is equipped with two radar scopes to help me at times like this. Today nature seems alive, like a phantom or an angry predator."

"You know so much," Lisa said. "No offense, but I thought someone who ran a ferry wouldn't be, well, smart."

The ensuing discussion evoked the captain's life history. Calamari was the son of a Somerset Quaker and lived at Westson-super-Mare in England during his childhood before coming to Newfoundland. His schooling was fortunate, having several exceptionally gifted teachers who imparted to him a keen interest in the sea and a love of good literature. Quiet and studious by nature, Calamari was also athletic, playing cricket and enjoying long bike rides through the Mendip Hills. When he was 15 his family had moved to Newfoundland, where they remained ever since.

Meanwhile, he was busy running the ferry. He let Lisa tag along as he did, and she appreciated that. She was learning a lot, and much of it was interesting in ways she hadn't expected.

A bank of fog now stretched ahead of the bow of Calamari's ferry. He strode back to the wheelhouse, issuing orders to the engine room to reduce speed to 20 knots. Although a ferry's captain was evaluated on his ability to meet the ferry schedules, he explained, the tent of dense fog and waves demanded caution. The danger of actually running into an object and sinking was remote, since the ship contained eight watertight steel doors below the A deck. This compartmentalization made the ship virtually unsinkable should they hit something. The ferry theoretically could remain afloat if three adjacent chambers were flooded. The steel doors would keep the remaining compartments dry. That was comforting to know, because Lisa knew that the monster was truly awful and powerful.

As Calamari looked out to sea a light drizzle began to mist down. He reached for his binoculars, which he said combined an infrared range finder and an electronic compass. Even with his high-tech instrument, he could see very little into the night. His spirits, like the *Titanic,* were sinking rapidly. Lisa's worries were increasing accordingly.

Up on the bridge, Calamari stared at the sonar screen but did not see any signs of the sea spider. If it was periodically flattening itself out near the ocean bottom with its legs spread wide, it might avoid the sonar. So he wasn't at all sure that this monster chase would work. But he didn't like that inexplicable bumping they had felt; that had never happened before.

Rudolph, the engineer, joined Calamari. They stared at the screen for a few more minutes and looked warily at each other like condemned criminals. No, Lisa did not like this at all.

CHAPTER 27

Teens

THE COLD GUSTS of wind made the ship's Newfoundland flags flap like ghosts in a graveyard. Keeping her hands in her pockets to protect them from the chilly air, Natalie Sheppard walked over to the several people near the ferry's cold gray metallic rail. Some were peering out into the mist. Others were actually hanging over the rail and dangling their legs into the fog. "I'm a police officer," Natalie said. She adopted an aggressive machine-gun-like tone to insure compliance. "Please move away from the rails. The seas are choppy and it's dangerous to stay by the edge of the ferry."

They looked at her, and several began to move. Their apparent eagerness to stay near the rail surprised her. Although she made no mention of the pycnogonid, certainly some of the travelers must have read about it in the newspapers or seen the stories on the local TV news. Apparently the stories provoked curiosity rather than fear.

Natalie gazed at the motley group remaining before her. There was a big man who looked like a lumberjack with a beer belly. His hair glistened with grease, and he drank from a bottle of soda pop. Most others were teenagers. One girl rocked to the acid beat of her radio. She wore a very short skirt, and Natalie could see the blur of her panties as she moved to the music. Another kid was trying to read a book by the dim light provided by the ship's incandescent fixtures.

One teenager, wearing aviator glasses with dark gray lenses, played a Viotar, a six-stringed instrument that looked like a cross between a violin and a guitar. He played it with a bow, as he swayed back and forth. The *Star Trek* T-shirt he wore was stained with perspiration. As he played, his glasses fell from his head and onto the deck as a result of his gyrations. The boy was evidently not too skilled. Natalie usually loved Viotar music, but the boy produced sounds like a parakeet being vacuumed out of its cage.

When the boy finally finished his song a few of the girls clapped. A braless woman, about eighteen years old, bobbed along the ferry's rails toward the boy and then gave him a kiss. He stooped down to pick up his glasses and tucked them into the V of his shirt. He looked around with an expression of amusement. He then popped a few peanut butter candies into the girl's mouth and smiled.

Natalie was losing patience. With the exception of a few punk teenage girls wearing body fatigues and fluorescent makeup, most of the other travelers had complied with her request to move back from the rail. One of the teenage girls' pants was so heavily encrusted with rhinestones, it might have stood alone. The girl looked at Natalie and raised her hands in a don't-shoot pose. Then she brushed back some hair that the wind had blown out of place.

"Are you hard of hearing?" Natalie said. "Move away from the rails." The girl looked up and said, "Are you going to shoot me if I don't move?" She spoke with a thick, clotty voice with an uneducated accent. If Falow were here, he probably would have picked her up bodily and moved her. Instead Natalie decided to let her do what she wanted.

"OK, it's your life," Natalie told the girl, using a tone of voice one might use to intimidate a dog.

Natalie walked away and then gazed out to sea. The boat started to rock. Then it made sounds like those of a boar being slaughtered. Something was scratching the hull. Natalie backed up a hasty half-step while she looked out to sea. It was so dark out there, so forever. Well, she had done what she had come to do, as far as feasible. She made a hasty retreat back toward the coffee shop.

Then she spied Lisa, standing near the bridge. Was the girl bothering the captain? She detoured to check on that. But as she got there, she paused, seeing the men distracted by something. She had a sick suspicion what that something might be. She came to stand silently beside Lisa, eavesdropping.

Inside, she saw Calamari check his sonar screens, and saw a strange green blip on the luminescent sonar display. "What is that?" he said out loud in an expression of bewilderment to Rudolph, a blond, stocky engineer.

"It's big," Rudolph said. "And it's moving." He seemed frustrated by his inability to do anything about the lurking unknown object. Natalie knew that sonar could tell them only so much. She knew that the term "sonar" was derived from the initial letters of the words *so*und, *na*vigation, and *ra*nging—and it worked by transmitting spurts, or pings, of high-frequency sound waves through the water. By examining the echoes from objects in the water, Calamari could determine their distance and size. Sonar was used in World War II as an antisubmarine device, but the peacetime value of sonar was safe navigation in the presence of shipwrecks, icebergs, and other submerged obstacles.

"Too big for a school of fish or a large mat of submerged seaweed."

"Perhaps a whale, but it's so close." Rudolph's pale Teutonic features were slowly taking on the coloration of pimento cheese. Natalie couldn't tell whether his new complexion was due to anger or fear.

"It's right under us!" the captain exclaimed.

Natalie had seen enough. "Come on, Lisa," she said, and started off. But the girl didn't follow. Well, maybe she would be as safe near the captain as in the coffee shop. And now it occurred to her that there were other places she should check before seeking her own comfort.

Natalie stumbled down the steps to the ferry's parking deck, which contained about twenty cars. Even though the area was enclosed on two sides, she was still constantly assaulted by acid air and brine. The ferry was new, but some of the walls of the parking area looked old: rust bloomed like a skin rash in great brown blotches.

Natalie moved in and out of the rows of cars with a quiet economy of effort that would have been unusual in a woman not trained for efficiency. Suddenly there was a heavy shaking of the deck that made her lose her footing. She fell across the hood of a canary yellow passenger car and finally steadied herself with one hand against the window of a pickup truck. The truck had a rack holding four bicycles and six pairs of skis. Natalie almost knocked the skis off as she regained her footing.

"You OK?" a woman asked as she leaned over in the passenger seat of her car. Another family was huddled together in a silver station wagon. They looked at Natalie with nervous eyes.

"Yes, OK. Thanks," Natalie said even though she had more than a premonition of danger. The parking lot was taking on a new, manic quality with the approach of darkness.

Natalie turned to look out to sea—and she saw what had to be the pycnogonid coming toward them. The spider did not seem to hesitate as it treaded water and accelerated. Somehow Natalie realized that the spider had no fear at all and would do as it wished. That would not be what any human beings wished.

She withdrew her service revolver and ran upstairs to the upper deck. Most of the passengers were looking in the opposite direction so did not see the spider's dreadful approach. She shouted only two words in a voice that could cause a hearing impairment: "It's here!"

The pycno closed fast astern. As Natalie assumed a defensive position with her legs apart, with her gun pointed at the sea spider, she saw its triangular mouth open and close spasmodically, and she saw its myriad polyhedral eyes. There was another sound: the clicking chop of its chelicera. The spider's head was out of water. The all-swallowing sucker waved in Natalie's direction. It was a hateful organism, bad smelling, a scavenger as well as a killer.

"Brace yourself," Natalie screamed to the passengers in the parking lot.

The pycno reached out of the water and cast a leg onto the ferry's deck. Then it cast more legs, embracing the ship. It hauled its impossibly huge body up close, like a phoenix rising from the burning ashes. But this was the opposite: freezing water. The gross head came up to the level of the deck. It moved its proboscis from right to left as if scanning the deck for signs of life. When it ascertained that the ferry was a virtual banquet of warm-blooded mammals, it seemed to feel something akin to pleasure. Its legs trembled in anticipation.

Nathan and Falow appeared and ran next to Natalie. No one fired a shot; they waited for the perfect time to aim at the primary brain. They all knew that careless shooting would be worse than none, because it would only aggravate the monster.

"*Colossendeis*," Nathan whispered in a mixture of fear, surprise, and awe. "I know that species. It's a huge *Colossendeis*."

Natalie looked at the creature, as if mesmerized. She couldn't shake the feeling that the huge beast was evil Fate clutching the ship in embodied form. This was Death, Satan, Lucifer, the Grim Reaper, the Beast. She realized her thoughts bordered on madness, and she quickly tried to channel her emotions to something more productive.

Natalie edged closer to the beast. It seemed to be carefully studying them with the cold black orbs of its multiple eyes. One eye swiveled to Natalie and then the creature reached for her, its multiple legs moving in such fluid harmony that it sometimes seemed more like a perfectly functioning robot than a living, breathing creature.

Falow raised his service revolver and fired three quick shots in succession at the creature's body. A series of dry, sluggish reports echoed from across the hills. Natalie drew her own revolver, aimed, and shot. The gun barked four times, and bullets ricocheted off the deck peppering the spider with splinters of wood and metal. The bullets hit the creature with a cracking sound. Black ichor looking like tar began to ooze out of an opening in one of its legs. The pycno proboscis shot upward to the sky and let out a low mewing sound, and then the creature slid off the deck and into the sea.

A split second later the elephantine pycnogonid's wake hit the ferry, causing it to roll and toss its passengers to the deck. Natalie grabbed for the railing, missed, and fell down on her wet butt. The sea rose up and snarled.

Then silence. There was a faint moaning of new ice on the edge of the sea. A miasmic mist. The oily fumes of diesel fuel and the faint ozonic smell of rain.

Some of the passengers broke down and screamed. Others wept. Some applauded Natalie.

"Is it dead?" Falow yelled.

"Don't know," Natalie said. "Probably wounded to the point where it can't scramble on deck again. I wish we had a .44-Magnum with us. These smaller caliber guns are close to useless against a thing like that."

"Hope it can't come back," said Elmo. She hadn't seen him arrive. He was already going back up to the deck.

They waited. The silence was eerie. Everyone was afraid to go to the rail and peek over the edge into the water. Captain Calamari gazed down from his position high on the bridge.

"I don't see it," Calamari shouted. He was looking through binoculars.

"You better radio for help," Natalie said.

"I will in a minute."

"Did you see those large eyes at the end of its proboscis?" Nathan asked. "Normal *Colossendeis* don't have them. But we know so little about the deep-sea pycnogonids. Maybe this is a mutation. It must be able to see better than I expected."

Before Nathan could finish his thoughts, the sea spider's legs shot out of the water and onto the deck like a cannon ball fired from a cannon. They scattered the passengers away like pigeons. One boy, as he ran away, shoved an older man who then bounced off the deck as his upper dentures shot out of his mouth. The dentures flew through the air and into Natalie's long hair.

CHAPTER 28

Prey

BACK ON THE deck, Elmo Samules glanced at Lisa James. He should have had more pressing concerns, considering the horror of the situation, but in this instant he seemed able to focus only on her. He wanted to shout warning to her as the monster's snout loomed at the side of the ship, but was afraid he would merely cause her to jump backward—into it. So for the moment it was as if he saw a snapshot, a still picture, with a little bit of animation superimposed.

Lisa stood just a few feet away from where the creature loomed. She was silent, with a radiant smile, somehow unaware of the mayhem about to take place. Apparently she had been watching the increasingly frenzied activity by the captain and his engineer, and never thought to look out to sea. Oddly, a bright blue butterfly seemed to follow her every step, fluttering happily near her hair and eyes. She grinned as she let the arctic butterfly land on the top of her hair. She did not see the pycnogonid behind her, but now she felt the ship tilt in its direction. The blue butterfly fluttered away.

The monster's snout loomed above Lisa's head. Still Elmo couldn't find the words he needed. The universe remained almost frozen.

Something liquid dripped on her. Drip. Drip.

Lisa suddenly revealed her incredulous fear as greenish goo oozed from the sea spider's proboscis and splattered onto her cheeks, hair, lips, and white coat.

And Elmo dared not move or shout, lest she react by fleeing him and blundering right into the monster.

Drip. Drip. Drip.

The pycno's two front black eyes peered at Lisa with an alien intent. As the proboscis got closer, its unwinking eyes fixed on hers. Someone on deck had slapped on a flood light and pointed it at the creature. Elmo saw that its body was a bristly beige. Its legs made a horrible clattering sound.

"Aaah," Lisa screamed as the digestive fluid burned into her skin, putting her into extreme agony.

So close were the spider's front legs that they dripped salt water onto her white windbreaker and blue jeans. The punk girl with the rhinestones immediately took action and threw a chair at the spider, which had no immediate effect. She threw another chair. After a few seconds' pause the spider reacted, as if it were surprised at resistance, at a defense. One of its leg spikes caught the girl in the shoulder, slicing above her ribs and puncturing some major blood vessels. Then the entire leg came down on the rhinestone girl's head with a terrible raking that seemed to take much of the hair and skin off.

Lisa collapsed to the floor in near shock, and lay motionless. She was pale, like an angel sculpted in white marble in a giant cathedral. Her white coat spread open like wings. Her beautiful shiny hair trailed along the deck like golden seaweed floating in a still sea. Elmo couldn't draw his attention from her.

Another woman watched only a few feet away but did nothing. Her hair, a lifeless shade of black, was mostly covered by a chador. She surveyed the scene for a moment, her granite eyes locked on the pycno. She screamed something in Arabic, but did not run. She found a bucket with some water and dashed it onto Lisa, diluting and washing away the burning digestive juices. But that brought her into range of the spider. One of the legs came down on her arm, severing major nerves and rendering her arm useless. She took one look at the arm flopping at her side and continued to scream.

Finally Elmo broke out of his weird stasis. He took a fire ax and ran toward the sea spider. "Haa," he bellowed as the ax came down on one of its legs. The pycno quickly moved its leg, carrying with it the ax, which had sunk a few inches into its flesh.

The spider's proboscis started to shake as the creature now went for Elmo. Elmo backed up, slipped, and was struck on his ribs by one of the thing's legs. The ax cut might have taken some of the power out of the spider's strike, which would ordinarily have killed him. A leg spike bounced off his rib cage, and he felt something snap inside. He rolled away, got up, and was struck again in the ribs. The throbbing hurt exploded into a lightning bolt of seemingly scorched nerves. He bit his lip and started to scream.

"Damnnnnn!" Elmo bellowed. He tasted blood and was getting dizzy.

Lisa came out of her stupor and started to crawl away. Her pert nose wrinkled as the odor of the creature hit her.

Now Elmo saw Nathan looking for a weapon. Elmo himself was weaponless and hurt, but he edged closer to Lisa, needing to try to help her. He was already so close he thought he could see the girl's pulse pounding rapidly in an artery in her forehead. Or was he imagining it, in the stupor of his pain?

Meanwhile Nathan was there and charging in. The man certainly didn't lack courage! But in his distraction he tripped over a gull that had frozen solid to the deck. Its mouth was opened in a horrible rictus as if caught in a scream. Its eyes bulged as if in protest against a Newfoundland chill too cold for even arctic gulls to survive. As he tripped, Nathan hit his knee on the gull's beak.

"Damn," he cursed.

Elmo knew how he felt. Everything was going wrong. They were trying to help each other, and only getting themselves hurt. The trained police had been better, on the parking deck below;

they had taken time to aim and fire their guns, driving the monster off for a moment.

Elmo looked back to Lisa. Another of the pycno's legs moved toward the girl, and then its terminal claw scissored forward and pinched her outstretched hand. Her thumb seemed to unhinge in a horrible spray of blood. A scream bubbled in her throat, frothing on her tongue like specks of sea foam. Elmo thought he felt the amputation in his own hand. He tried to get up, so as to lurch forward and reach her, but could not. All he could do was watch her.

Another leg scratched her forehead, and blood began to trickle down into her eye. For a second Elmo saw the spider as if through her eye, through a crimson lens.

"Help me," Lisa screamed as she wiped the blood away. She dodged as a leg crashed to the deck near her. Another leg crashed down behind her, and she dodged again. It was as if the creature were toying with her as it tried to smash her face, break her teeth, shatter her legs, making it impossible for her ever to walk again. Actually, Elmo realized, it simply couldn't locate her readily, because of the awkwardness of having to reach up across the deck and haul its snout up there. The monster was working hard to hold on to the ferry, so was clumsy about grabbing morsels from its deck. But they could not depend on that for very long, he feared.

The creature simply ignored Elmo, who could not move to help Lisa. He needed not only more strength, but some effective weapon. So for the moment he successfully wedged himself behind a table. He cast frantically about for something, anything that might do. Anything to throw, to prod with, or merely to heave into the maw and perhaps block it.

The pycno turned its full attention to Lisa. "Please!" the girl implored. Elmo realized with horror that it was her sounds it was orienting on, as much as anything; every time she screamed or cried for help, it closed on her more accurately.

The spider then grabbed Lisa around the waist. Her left arm was twisted at an odd angle. Her lipstick-red lips peeled back from her teeth and a long howl burst from somewhere deep within her throat: "Aaaaah." The pycno's listless black eyes stared into her own. Blood was running from her forehead and her windbreaker was mostly torn off.

"Please," Lisa screamed. Elmo tried to lurch to his feet, but collapsed before getting anywhere. He had to watch the confrontation, helplessly. A claw like a pair of wire cutters reached out and grabbed her arm and turned her toward the creature's proboscis. The proboscis opened wide and Elmo could smell the stink of ammonia and rotting meat. He knew it would be much worse for Lisa. She held her arms in front of her in an automatic defensive maneuver which had little effect. Seconds seemed to turn to hours.

Next he saw the proboscis touch her arms, at first gently like a moist warm rag, but then more forcefully.

Suddenly, up, up, up the proboscis carried her into the air. She screamed again, despairingly. Then the pycno threw her into the ice-cold sea. It happened in just an instant. The girl had no time to react. The pycno looked at the passengers on the deck, seemed to hesitate, but then let go of the boat and sank back into the water, in search of the girl.

Elmo's whole body seemed to go numb, as if the water were chilling him to insensitivity, instead of her. Lisa—dying! He staggered to his feet, determined to do something, anything, if only to throw himself into the sea after her. If all else failed, at least he would die with her.

"Get the passengers inside the parking area or the coffee shop," Falow shouted to Natalie and Calamari. Even though Falow wore a wool cap, the sweat on his scalp looked icy. Shivers wracked his body visibly as he ran to the rail and looked over.

Elmo followed him, clutching at his side. He might not feel the pain, but his body did. He reached the rail and stared out at the roiling water. Lisa, Lisa—where was she?

The boat bumped. Jellyfish creatures with purple bladders floated to the surface of the black sea, swirling in an eddy current. They looked a little bit like Portuguese men-o'-war. Seconds later a vast white mass, perhaps their mother, joined the jellyfish. Its myriad long arms curled and twisted like a nest of boa constrictors.

"What are those weird things?" Elmo shouted as he scanned the ocean for the girl. He had spent a great deal of time at sea, but never seen anything like this before.

"The seas around here seem to have a lot of strange organisms lately," Natalie said through clenched teeth.

Then his desperate gaze caught a glimpse of white. Her tattered windbreaker! It had to be!

"There she is!" Elmo screamed. He saw Lisa about fifteen feet from the ferry. The gloom was tenebrous, making it difficult to see her against the dark waves, despite her bright jacket. She was still quite conscious and trying to swim to the boat. Cold drops of sea water stung her face as the freezing wind drove them against her cheeks and forehead. She screamed in surprise, this time because the arctic bath chilled her bones. Her long red hair glimmered under a lacework shawl of ice crystals. Each stroke of her arm and each kick of her legs seemed to be slower than the last. The intense cold of the water was rapidly draining her strength. She was losing her energy amidst the jewels of ice which drifted by like a slow swarm of bees. Again the shock of the frigid sea against her face made her wince with pain and sapped her strength. It was if her limbs were run by hidden clock springs which needed to be rewound.

Without thinking further, Elmo climbed down a rope ladder at the side of the ferry. The crippling effect of his injuries was fading; he knew he had to act right now if it was humanly possible.

"Quick, swim to me," he cried to the girl. He held out his hand, the oddly shaped fingers stark against the heaving background of the sea.

The sheer physical smoothness of the jellyfish near the girl was alien, intimidating. The pycno was nowhere in sight. Soon something resembling a green and red möbius ribbon with blue eyes and a twist of greasy hair came out of the depths and wriggled closer to the girl. The girl swam as fast as she could to the edge of the ladder where Elmo knelt. She came closer to him.

Closer. But still out of reach—and he couldn't go to her, because he depended on his hold on the ladder. If he lost that hold with his other hand, they would both be helpless in the water.

Her arms were out, reaching for Elmo; her eyes pleaded for help, and she was moaning. Several spiral soda-bottle creatures also emerged and drifted toward her. The translucent globes of their eyes grew slightly in size as they approached.

Then the pycno emerged and treaded water. Now its eyes looked like dark plumbs. Its proboscis pointed in the girl's direction, as the orifice at the end dripped a pale fluid.

The harbor seemed even colder, and Elmo knew that Lisa felt the last vestiges of heat leaving her body. Her fear became panic as her screams escalated in volume. Her eyes were sunken. But she was still moving forward, finally coming into the range of his long fingers.

Just as Elmo got hold of the girl's hand, their grips locking, the pycno grabbed her left leg. She kicked, weakly. The vein in her leg started to leak more blood into the ocean. The shoe on her other foot came off and floated in the waves like a gull on the water.

Elmo pulled. The pycno pulled. The girl moaned.

"Elmo, take this," Nathan shouted. Elmo's breath caught in his throat as he saw a crowbar. The girl was now holding onto him with both her frozen hands. Below her, the sea appeared bottomless, like a black hole in a vast space.

"I can't! I can't let go of the ladder or Lisa!"

"But the legs!" Nathan cried, as if this were new information. "They're pulling on her!"

"I can't hold her much longer!" Elmo yelled. Sea water poured out of the girl's mouth along with vomit that was now rising from her stomach like lava from a volcano.

The pycno started to grab her thigh.

Nathan bashed ineffectively at it with the crowbar. He couldn't reach it from above.

"I'll shoot it," Natalie said and took a few shots at the creature from her position on deck.

This wasn't getting them anywhere. They couldn't win a tug-of-war with the monstrous spider. Elmo realized that he would have to gamble. Suddenly he let go of Lisa for a second, grabbed the crowbar from Nathan with his right hand, and swung it down onto the pycno's retreating leg. But nothing seemed to stop the sea predator.

A slimy brown thing flapped out of the dark sea and pulled at the long hair of the woman. It was the pycno's bumpy tongue. Lisa moaned, then started making little sounds of horror, like the bleats of a sheep being led to slaughter, as the pycno yanked on her, forcing her to gaze into black eyes on the end of its long pulsating proboscis.

Elmo looked where she looked, sharing her horror. The proboscis was smooth and fleshy. As he gazed into the enlarging opening before her he thought he saw something scurrying frantically within the opening of the sucking appendage. Was it a parasite, or the living remains of some non-digested prey? He saw how Lisa's revulsion increased, her mind shattered. The ocean level was just below her chin as he saw cakes of ice floating away on the currents and waves. He saw her became drowsy as hypothermia took effect.

Water gurgled and foamed around the girl's mouth, and she stopped struggling against the deadly undertow. Elmo almost felt linked to her mind, sharing her dying thoughts. Keeping her head above water seemed a pointless task. Above her the dark sky looked like an ocean, as cold and dangerous as the one below. The beats of her heart bounced round like a marble in a roulette wheel: this was cardiovascular destabilization. Both her body and mind were shutting down. In her hypothermic stupor, the murmuring waves seemed to beckon to her like the voices of angels.

Finally the pycno pulled Lisa into the cold ebony sea. As she plummeted down into the darkness, bubbles rose to the surface. The last thing he saw through his cold disoriented eyes was the blue glow of bioluminescent jellyfish. They swarmed around her face, eerie and supernatural, like a mysterious radiance of a divine presence.

"No!" Elmo hurled the crowbar away, let go of the rope ladder, and dived after her. He didn't even feel the shock of the water; he had been half immersed in it anyway. But his dive wasn't effective; he realized belatedly that he should have done it from the deck, so as to gain some momentum to carry him below the surface. In a moment he was gasping for air amidst the waves.

"Elmo! Here!"

Dazed, he turned his head. There was Joseph Falow, in a lifeboat. The man had a coil of rope. Good idea!

The boat nudged up to him as he faced it. "Tie rope around me!" Elmo gasped. "Get me dead weight!"

"Got it." Falow quickly looped the rope around Elmo's trunk, then handed him the anchor. Elmo took a breath, clutched the anchor to him, and sank down into the freezing brine.

In a moment he saw Lisa. She was relaxed in her unconsciousness, her hair floating around her head in a reddish cloud. Beautiful even in death. Except that he wasn't going to let her be dead.

He kicked with his feet, still clinging to the anchor. He was falling through the water, but able to move laterally this way. He had to get over the pycno. He saw the monster's action, in slow motion. One huge spider leg was drawing the girl in to the snout. The monster didn't seem hurried, being certain of its prey.

Elmo reached the leg. He hooked the anchor over it and let go. Of course the anchor could pull on the elephant-sized leg just slightly, but it was enough for the pycnogonid to take notice. As the creature grew curious about the anchor, Elmo caught hold of the girl by her nearest extended arm and hauled her in to him as hard as he could.

The leg felt the jerk and moved. It caught at the anchor, perhaps taking it for the girl. Lisa came free. Elmo kicked his feet and stroked with his free arm, heading upward, hauling the girl along with him. He was aware that the spider could readily intercept them and eat them both. But it was an animal, and tended to focus on one thing at a time. Right now it was the anchor. He used his fading energy to get them as far as he could, saving nothing for the future.

He reached the surface. He lifted Lisa as high as he could—and his last strength gave out. He found himself fading, his sight dimming. He would drown—but he had saved Lisa. That was what counted.

Then she was roughly hauled from his flaccid grasp. He realized that he had failed after all, and now he had no reserves to summon. The agony of his rib cage, suppressed for the duration of his effort, was now surging back to overwhelm him. No choice but to let it happen.

"Get him up!" And hands were on him, hauling him out of the water. Falow, on the lifeboat—but where was Lisa?

"Lisa," he gasped as he flopped into the boat.

"We've got her," Falow said. "We stopped the bleeding. Giving her artificial respiration. She'll make it."

That was all he needed to hear. Elmo let go of the last vestige of his consciousness.

CHAPTER 29

Shop

"THAT WAS A brave thing he did," Natalie said. They all looked over the rail as the lifeboat was hauled up to the deck. There was no sign of the sea spider. Occasionally they felt jerking bumps coming from the underside of the ferry, but they did not want to think about what it probably signified—meat being torn away from the body, and limbs torn asunder. Lisa and Elmo had been saved, but they were not the only ones who had gone overboard. The captain was trying to make a survey, but all they knew was that there were several people gone. Their body parts now made a trail through the cold sea as wide as the ferry lane, for all sharks.

"Get this boat out of here fast!" Falow shouted to Captain Calamari as he clambered out of the lifeboat.

"Top speed is 50 knots. It will take a minute," Calamari shouted back.

"Do you have any explosives or flare guns?"

"Just a few flare guns."

"OK, get them out; we may need them."

Many hands took hold of the unconscious man and girl and carried them across the deck. "Take them to the coffee shop," Falow directed. "It's the best place to attend to them."

"It's *warm,*" Natalie said. That was the most important thing, for people who had been almost fatally chilled.

The ferry's engines made a humming noise, growing louder and louder, passing through a cry and into a scream. Natalie saw Captain Calamari looking at Rudolph the engineer.

"Something's slowing the ferry's forward motion," Rudolph said.

"I can guess what it is," Calamari said with an exasperated sigh.

Natalie followed the bodies into the coffee shop. Both were breathing, but neither looked good. Lisa was missing her left thumb and had scrapes all over her raggedly clothed body. There was blood on her leg from the cut vein. Elmo had a great bruise on his chest, and his breathing was labored; he probably had several broken ribs. "I'll tend to Lisa," she said, kneeling by the girl as the others cleared back. "You check Elmo, Nathan." She tuned out the others.

She checked Lisa's hand. There was little bleeding; that was one benefit of the freezing water. But the girl would never have a thumb again. Then she felt around Lisa's body, heedless of any proprieties; she needed to know whether any bones were broken or skin torn. There didn't seem to be any such damage, apart from scrapes across her abdomen where the spider had picked her up. Then she bandaged the rip on the leg, stanching the bleeding there. It would have been worse, but for the numbing cold.

As Natalie was about to do the same for the shorn hand, Lisa groaned and opened her eyes. Natalie shook her head in appreciation; the young had marvelous powers of recovery. "You're safe," she said soothingly. "Elmo rescued you."

"Elmo," the girl repeated. "I saw—his hand. Coming to save me."

Now Elmo stirred, hearing his name. "Lisa?"

"I gotta get up," Lisa gasped, trying to sit.

"Relax," Natalie said, pushing her back down onto the mat. "It's over. You're in the ferry, in the coffee shop."

"I know. Gotta. Get to. Elmo." She struggled up again.

Natalie sighed, and helped her, providing support. Lisa made it to her hands and knees and crawled over to where Elmo lay. She winced as her thumbless hand ground into the deck, but didn't stop. She halted with her head over his. "You saved me," she said.

Elmo managed a smile. "I had to," he replied.

Lisa put her head down to his. She kissed him on the mouth. Then she collapsed, exhausted.

"I think Lisa has changed her mind," Natalie murmured.

"I agree," Nathan said, handing her a bandage.

Elmo's eyes moved to her, questioningly.

"She was aware of your interest, but she didn't like your hands," Natalie said, sure that she was not now betraying a confidence. She lifted Lisa's mutilated hand and got to work on it. "Now she has lost her thumb, and I think it's safe to say that she believes you will not hold that against her."

"That, too," Lisa breathed.

"But—" Elmo protested weakly.

"I think the two of you need to talk. Can we get you to a chair? I think you'll be more comfortable, if you can manage it."

Nathan helped Elmo sit up, and then to stagger a few steps across the room. Natalie helped Lisa similarly.

Natalie checked the bandages on the abrasions which covered Elmo's right side, where the pycnogonid scratched him. The man was sitting in a metal chair as he planted his feet flat on the floor and gripped the edges of his seat.

"Ouch," Elmo said. As Natalie adjusted the last bandage on his skin, the flesh around his cheeks went white. His head was a dull red, gorged with blood. That was one reason she had thought it best to get him vertical.

"Just sit there for a while and rest," Natalie said. "I'm sorry we don't have a medic here, but in my first-aid opinion you will survive if you take it easy until we can get you to the hospital."

"I don't think I could move if I wanted to," Elmo replied. His long teeth were clenched tightly together and his voice was shaky.

Lisa, now sitting beside him, reached for his hand with her bandaged hand. "When I was drowning, I had a vision," she said, her voice getting stronger. "I saw myself, six years of age, at play in the pine forest by my white and brick colonial house. The pine needles on the forest floor rustled as I walked through them with my sneakers. My parents held my hands. My frisky German shepherd dog, Princess, wagged her tail and followed us. It was sort of nice. Then I woke on the boat, feeling *awful,* and I knew you had saved me."

Elmo smiled wanly. "Sorry about that."

Falow, Nathan, and Natalie retreated to a table far enough distant to give the couple some privacy, though near enough so that they could offer help swiftly if necessary. At their table was a huge ashtray. Natalie looked with distaste at the smoking cigar sitting in the ashtray but did not get up to remove it. She became aware of the tension in the coffee shop. The ferry passengers were now well aware that they faced a threat as horrible as any they could have imagined.

Bill, the teenage boy behind the counter, produced a giant-sized pink bottle of anti-diarrheal medication. He stared at the label for a few seconds, shook his head, and put the bottle back on the stand full of medicines. One of the men on a stool at the counter pealed nervous laughter so loud that other people at the counter—fishermen and tourists for the most part—craned around. The laughing man looked as if he were going to have a nervous breakdown.

"Look, we may only have a few minutes before it attacks again," Nathan said. "Even with the ferry moving at full speed, it may be able to catch us." He sketched a diagram on a piece of paper showing the anatomy of the sea spider. "Here's what I think the insides of this monster look like, according to what I know from smaller species."

The others listened intently as he pointed to the diagram with his pencil. "I've circled areas which you should aim for," Nathan continued. "The small palp legs are located just behind the chelicerae and have sensory hairs. If you hit these, the animal will probably be in extreme pain and unable to attack. The small leg just behind this is the ovigerous leg. It's used by the male to carry the female's eggs. If you knock this out, it will prevent the monster from breeding. The nervous system is made up of a dorsal brain, circumesophageal ring, paired ventral gangila, and ventral nerve cords. If you hit the cord, it will probably paralyze some of the legs. But try to hit the main brain."

"How about the legs?" Natalie asked. "Can we cripple it by taking out the legs?"

"Each of the huge walking legs contains eight independent segments. They're quite tough, and the pycnogonid can survive and walk even if a few of the legs are completely destroyed. Don't bother aiming for the big legs."

"What about the eyes?"

"Its five eyes are located far apart, helping it to triangulate on prey. Very efficient. But it's doubtful you'll be able to knock out all five of them. Go for the brain or those strange eyes on its proboscis. It evidently uses them to zero in on people on the deck."

When she was sure she understood their best strategy of attack, Natalie walked over to the counter, away from Nathan and Elmo, curious to hear what the passengers were talking about. Bill motioned her to join them.

"Coffee?" he said.

"Please," said Natalie. The boy placed a cup on the chipped Formica counter and poured hot coffee into it. A few of the other men at the counter had sodas. The lumberjack with the beer belly was eating from an aluminum frozen dinner tray.

"How about some pumpkin pie to go with that?" The boy spoke quickly, obviously nervous. "Homemade. Pumpkins from Tiffany's orchard over on Main Street. Picked today."

"No, thanks," Natalie said. "How can anyone think about eating?" The boy did not answer her, and just nodded his head.

"Why don't we all just stay in the coffee shop until morning?" another passenger asked. "It can't get us in here."

"That's just what we're doing," said Bryan, the lumberjack, in a pensive tone. Bryan was a big, almost handsome man with the ruddy complexion and strong presence of a man who often worked in the woods. "Just stay in here until someone rescues us."

"Good idea," Natalie said. "You should stay in here with the others. But we're going to try to destroy it if it attacks again—before it has a chance to destroy parts of the ship or break through some of the wooden doors and glass windows. Assuming that we don't get moving fast again soon, and leave it behind."

"Think you'll kill it?" the boy asked.

"Yes," Natalie said. But she was afraid the boy detected a hesitancy in her voice that was not at all reassuring.

CHAPTER 30

Hunger

UNDER THE SEA, delicate, evanescent sea anemones flowered beneath the pycnogonid's legs. Polyps were in bloom, undulating to some unheard rhythm, combing the sea water with long, slender tentacles. Nearby were strange corals. Some had convoluted surfaces, like the sulci of a human brain. From within the convolutions rose thin worms resembling red strands of rubber. The sea floor looked like a living carpet. A few small fish patrolled, searching for food, but shied away from the spider whenever it moved its legs. Some were large—barracudas and the like.

The sea spider looked up and saw a golden cone of light cut through the water. It was the light from a high-powered flashlight held by a passenger on the ferry. As the light penetrated the clear waters it reflected off a school of small fish, which sparkled like stars.

Suddenly the billowing skirts of a lion's mane jellyfish glimmered beneath a small vault of ice. The jellyfish was a mobile restaurant for small crustaceans, which snatched scraps of food from the jellyfish's open maw. This area of the sea seemed to be a zoo of life, because of the abundant nutrients and rich oxygen concentration.

As the jellyfish drifted, its skein of stinging tentacles touched the pycno's back leg, but the sea spider did not feel any pain. More important were the distressing signals from other parts of its body. For the first time, the spider felt pain from some of the gunshot wounds. A new experience. No critical nerve paths had been destroyed, so it retained full mobility.

But the pycno was still hungry. The moving cone of light from the ferry acted as a magnet, a beacon, for the creature. It rose again from the frigid blackness to intercept the ferry.

The sea spider rose through a cloud of four-inch ctenophores, which looked like a herd of half-inflated footballs gliding in the icy sea. It rose through cigar-shaped shell-less snails known as sea butterflies.

It ascended through a world of teeming life, but its only purpose now was to cause death.

CHAPTER 31

Snack

A LEG CAME over the rail. Then another, followed by the great snout. Another siege was starting.

Natalie saw it. She had her Llama .32 automatic, but only one more bullet. Her mouth opened wide, making a short guttural sound. The muzzle of her gun wandered back and forth. She trained the gun at the head as it appeared, knelt, and fired.

She missed. The head had made an unpredictable jerk, dropping back down into the water. The pycnogonid couldn't have timed it better if it had tried. It was as if fate was with it.

The boy with the viotar had just removed his hexagonal rimless glasses, cleaned them, and put them back in place, hiding two pink spots high up on his nose. Suddenly he saw the sea spider and his glasses dropped as he screamed. One lens cracked. He should have run immediately, but instead he got down to scramble for his glasses.

The creature's sinewy organs of manipulation groped for the boy and grabbed him around the thigh. The pycno's leg tapered from a thickness of a human hand at the point where it held the boy to more than two feet in diameter where it disappeared over the rail and descended into the sea. It was brown on top and pearl white on its underside, where various sharp spines protruded.

The boy looked to his right, seeing what had grabbed him. His eyes opened wide. "Get it off me! Take this friggin' thing away!"

"Oh God," Nathan whispered.

The leg began to pull the boy toward the rail. From the boy's pocket fell a small aerosol bottle of breath freshener. The deck began to leave splinters on his arms. As he was just about to be pulled into the sea, he grabbed onto the rail and yanked himself back onto the deck.

"Help," he yelled as he looked at his hand. A sharp crescent of metal on the rail had torn the nail on his thumb right off; all that remained was a bleeding half-circle of ragged flesh. The leg pulled some more.

"Hey, help me. Do something," he cried in shock and pain. As he opened his mouth, some of the smooth bristles from the creature's leg entered it, caressing his tongue and gums. A quick gagging noise came from his throat. "Damn it, do something." One of the bristles abraded his lips, surely igniting sparks of pain all the way to his skull.

"Christ," Nathan said as he came out of the coffee shop to see what was happening.

Natalie was the closest, and she grabbed the boy around under his armpits and pulled as hard as she could. For a second she made some progress, but than the leg began to exert even more force. The spider might be somewhat haphazard when it cast about, but once it had something, it had enormous power. Both Natalie and the boy were drawn across the deck. A half empty pack of chewing gum fell from another of the boy's pockets.

Nathan joined them and pounded on the pycno's leg with a ballpoint pen. It was all he had at the moment. For a second it seemed to have an effect, surprisingly, but he realized it was probably because the spider was trying to take stock of this minor distraction.

Then another giant leg rose out of the water toward them. It grabbed a chunk of Natalie's hair and pulled it out by the roots. Just as suddenly as it appeared, this second leg disappeared back into the water, with the black hair still in its grip. Natalie thought of all those shampoo commercials about split ends, and started to laugh, and then to scream.

The leg appeared again and began to make scratching sounds on the ferry's deck. The tip of the leg slapped Nathan in his side. It felt as if he had been hit by a cold hammer. Then it slammed Natalie and grabbed her arm.

"Someone give us a hand," Nathan shouted, not having time to consider how strange those five words sounded in this context.

But no one came. Those who hadn't sensibly fled remained too terrified to respond effectively. They just stared, backing away. *Where was Falow?* Nathan thought.

Natalie looked down and saw the first leg around the boy's hips. It was working its way into his skin. The boy grimaced in pain as some of the spikes tore like razors through the fabric of his *Star Trek* T-shirt. The spikes dripped some clear liquid. Where the liquid touched the boy's shirt, tiny holes appeared. One spike dug deep into his shoulder and blood began to ooze from the deep hole the leg spikes left.

Natalie tried to wedge her hands beneath the creature's leg to dislodge it. Nathan saw her grit her teeth; she should have had heavy gloves for this, because the surface was rough and spiked throughout.

Meanwhile the motion across the deck continued. Now the boy's legs dangled over the ferry's side. One of his sneakers fell into the sea. Natalie and Nathan continued to pull at the boy while trying to avoid the creature's legs. Nathan wished he had the crowbar that had been lost in the sea.

From out of the ocean appeared the pycno's proboscis. It was black and muscular like an elephant's trunk, except it was much bigger. It slowly made its way to the boy like a snake crawling toward its prey. Halfway from the end of the proboscis were two large death-bright eyes, which began to swivel in the direction of the boy. The beast hung there, half on the deck, much bigger than an African elephant—still, fierce, colossal.

The pycno waited a moment in all its majesty, and then it slowly moved. When the proboscis was a foot from the boy's face, his screams became continuous. Then he just gave up, stopped screaming, as if he could scream no longer. His eyes bulged. He collapsed on the deck, as far as the leg's grip on him allowed. Other legs were closing in, forcing both Nathan and Natalie to let go of the boy and retreat, lest they suffer the same fate. The power of the monster seemed overwhelming.

The proboscis stroked the boy's belly—then seemed to reach *into* it and started sucking on him. The boy let out a single shallow gasp. His fingers twitched, an involuntary nerve reaction. Green goo oozed from the sucking appendage, perhaps digestive enzymes, and poured out onto the boy and the deck of the ferry. The lidless, clear-glass eyes seemed to radiate hatred and hunger.

More legs were rising from the deep. Some were small, others thicker than the trunk of an oak tree. The bigger ones had little claws on their ends. Natalie and Nathan charged in again and pounded on the proboscis, which started to withdraw from the boy's belly. But then it re-established its position and they saw it was sucking his organs and blood, eating him alive. The legs closed on them again, and again they had to retreat.

"God almighty," Natalie murmured, horrified. The pycno seemed totally unconcerned with all but the boy. It ignored the man and woman and continued to feed as if they were not there. The boy began to cough, and an ugly blue color began to spread to his cheeks.

"Take this," said Bill from the coffee shop as he handed Nathan a broken cola bottle. Nathan grabbed the bottle and tried to shove it into the pycnogonid's body, but the hard exoskeleton resisted all his efforts to puncture it.

"Falow, where are you?" Natalie screamed. The tension was building to a crescendo. She touched the boy's face, but he did not move.

"I have another idea," Bill said as he ran back to the coffee shop. A minute later he came running back with a hot dog in his hand. He shoved it into one of the leg's pincers, and jumped quickly back. Maybe the hot dog would distract the sea spider from the boy, Bill evidently thought.

The pincer squeezed the hot dog and brought it into the sea. For a moment the proboscis withdrew from the boy's belly and quested for the hot dog. The spider wasn't well coordinated, with the snout seeming not quite to know what the pincer was doing.

As the proboscis left the boy, a loose slew of the boy's intestines spilled from the hole in his belly. The boy's face was ghastly with its colorless lips and waxen skin.

Unfortunately, the creature soon figured things out, swallowed the hot dog in an instant—and immediately went back to feeding on the boy. Natalie approached again and touched the boy's neck, attempting to find a pulse. The boy seemed sunk in a deep level of unconsciousness and did not react to either Natalie or the pycno. He was limp, every muscle unresponsive.

"There is a pulse," Natalie said as the legs drove her back again. "I think his heart is oscillating strangely and occasionally exhibiting severe tachycardia."

"What?" Nathan asked.

She almost smiled. "Sorry. I mean it's beating excessively rapidly. It's a bad sign."

"Because his guts are being consumed," Nathan said. "And we can't do a thing about it. I hate this!"

"Here, tie this to his body so he can't be pulled off the deck into the ocean," yelled Bill. He handed Natalie a half-inch, hawser-laid nylon rope with a breaking strength of one thousand pounds.

Falow came out of the coffee shop and when he saw what was happening he started to run. He grabbed a nearby chair and flung it across the deck at the pycno. The shattered pieces of the chair fell to the floor: instant junk.

Other legs began to rise from the sea and to grab at Natalie and Nathan, so they retreated farther from the boy and dropped to their hands and knees.

Falow pondered a moment, watching one of the spider legs spasm, then ran to within six feet of the creature. He had his gun. The spider did not have an instinctive fear of the man or the gun, but it was evidently capable of cold caution in these unusual circumstances. Perhaps it remembered the sound the gun made and the pain it had caused. Maybe, Nathan thought, its bowels undulated nervously within its body and legs as it prepared to finish imbibing the boy.

Meanwhile the boy seemed in a coma as deep as the ocean. Nathan saw his body shuddering with the force of its own heartbeat. His heart rate might have risen to over two hundred beats per minute.

"Get away," Falow shouted to Nathan and Natalie who still crawled along the deck. Falow then fired at the pycno and probably hit a ventral ganglion. As a result, nervous information to and from the spider's fourth walking leg was halted. The creature's leg hung limply at its side.

"Got you," Falow cried, his voice rising with the increased pounding of his heart.

"Score one for the home team," Natalie muttered.

The boy's body remained on the deck. The boy was not yet dead. His arms moved and his blood dripped like raindrops onto the wet floor. Sometimes his eyes rolled back into his head, as if he were having convulsions, but these episodes were now interspersed with near lucidity. A low moan escaped from his barely moving mouth. His gaze met Nathan's and had a pleading look. Then his deep-set eyes dilated in sudden pain as more of his intestines were yanked from his body by a spike in the creature's leg.

Bill then grabbed a fire extinguisher and sprayed it at the proboscis eyes, and the creature immediately responded. Its leg shot out at the rail, tearing it off as the proboscis lifted the boy into the air, broke the nylon rope, and tossed him into the sea. There was a dull snapping sound as the boy hit the water. He was probably still conscious as his broken body floated on the cold ocean waves.

Nathan saw the boy's eyes look at him, cold blue eyes barely alive, bleak with the pain of dying. A few snowflakes frosted his eyelashes. This was no longer a carefree musical teenager; this was a person who had aged a lifetime in a few awful minutes. Suddenly he fell forward into the swelling waves, swallowing a mouthful of salt water so cold that it might have made his tongue ache. His face was shriveled, the skin of his fingers blanched of all color. Deep water, impenetrable as ink, stretched all around him, with no possible escape. He seemed to struggle for a second and Nathan noticed three pale gray slugs as big as men undulating toward him. Their mouths were full of needle-like teeth that quivered like quills on a porcupine. A moment later he was dragged beneath the water.

Nathan turned away, his own eyes wild and searching. He felt a lump in his throat that presaged considerable emotional turmoil to come. Then his eyes met Natalie's, and he realized that she was near tears as surely as lightning bugs were a sign of approaching dusk.

But Natalie could not afford to go into emotional retreat now, any more than he could. She was looking for Falow. When her eyes finally met Falow's, Nathan could see that they were radiating both anger and despair. "Where where you?" she screamed at him, as if she were the chief and he a deputy. Nathan hadn't seen this side of her before, but he understood her anger. If Falow had been there when the pycno first grabbed for the boy, they might have saved him.

Indeed, Falow recognized his error. "I was in the bathroom, didn't hear what was happening—" He was cut off by a splashing sound in the sea. It was the pycno.

From high above on the bridge, Captain Calamari shone a bright spotlight into the pycno's eyes, trying to further blind it. The deck below smelled of death.

"Look at its eyes," Calamari whispered. Anyone who cared to look over the deck saw the furious reddened orbs of the pycno peering out from inflamed, irritated sockets. Falow shot a few more times. They were good shots, considering the fact that

Falow had a bad angle leaning against a table and was firing at shadows which moved against a bright background. Brains number two and four were soon destroyed by the gunfire.

For a moment, the beast seemed as if it were paralyzed and unable to move its great mass. However, within a minute ganglion seven evidently took over, and the spider began treading water again. Its motions were more jerky. It began to submerge like a submarine.

A deep cry came from Falow's mouth. "If we ever survive this, I'm going to kill that son of a bitch, no matter where it tries to hide." The anger and despair seemed out of place on Falow's face, like a splattering of ink on a Mondrian painting.

Captain Calamari was on the radio to the Coast Guard. "Get out here now!" he screamed into the microphone. Rain started to fall from the sky, streaking through the floodlit section like sugar threads from a cotton candy machine.

"What is your position now?" said a voice on the radio. Before Calamari could respond, Nathan looked to his left and saw the pycno rear up on its posterior legs, catch hold of the boat, and begin to climb up to the bridge. As he watched, he caught a whiff of the fragrant melange of blood and ammonia. When the creature came to the smooth metal surfaces of a tower, it hauled itself up with the agility of a spider. Its legs were near the ferry's antennas as it pawed obscenely at the metallic projections.

Nathan saw a black bird take off from a small nest on the antenna. He saw Falow shoot the creature again. It backed up, mashed the antennas, taking with it a guidance computer for the ferry's engine, and fell into the sea again. The black bird's nest floated on the waves, but there was no sign of the pycno.

"Newfoundland Coast Guard!" Calamari shouted into the microphone. "Do you read me?" There was just static. All communications with the mainland were cut off as a result of the absent antenna. He paused for a second, as if hesitant about speaking his next thought. He replaced the microphone in its holder, surely dismayed at the prospect of guiding a ship with no communication. He tried to start the engine, but could not get it to respond. He looked to his left and saw a pipe from the engine belching blue smoke and roaring like an old lawnmower. He probably couldn't get over the obsessive sense of everything going wrong. Nathan understood perfectly.

Nathan slumped with Natalie against a chair on the deck and noticed a piece of paper by the rail. At first he simply rolled his hands into fists and placed them on his hips, ignoring the paper. But he kept thinking that something was peculiar about it. It was wet with sea water and didn't seem to have been there before the pycno arrived.

Then Falow walked over to the paper, picked it up, and read the words to them all:

THE AVERAGE HUMAN ESOPHAGUS IS 10 INCHES IN LENGTH.

CHAPTER 32

Siege

THE SEA HAD become a black meringue of foam and froth. Occasional waves vaulted over the ferry's sides and crashed down on the deck with a shattering force. *Whoosh.* A swirl of gray fog curled up along the outsides of the ferry's coffee shop windows like an old cat. The mood inside was tense. A five-year-old boy and his mother joined Natalie, Bryan, and Bill. She introduced herself as Brenda.

Bryan stood up, stretched his big body, and put his hands together making a tent of strong, hairy fingers. Bill looked out the windows, his large eyes filled with fear. In order to distract the little boy from the scary atmosphere around them, Brenda, his mother, brought out beautifully crafted wooden jigsaw puzzles and placed them on the Formica counter.

"Want to put together the Mickey Mouse puzzle or the Star Wars puzzle?" Brenda asked him with forced cheer. She was in her late twenties, a quiet woman, with smoke-blue eyes that tilted catlike. She had surely been quite striking a few years back, but now her ample bosom was becoming matched by a solidifying body.

"Star Wars," the boy replied as he clutched a tiny, ragged blanket. His eyes were enormous as he watched his mother dig through an assortment of toys in her large pocketbook. Their small white poodle snuggled up to the boy with affection.

The lumberjack had finished his greasy meal and tossed the aluminum dish into the garbage. "How about a beer?" he said to Bill. Bill smiled and pointed to an old sign on the wall. It read:

ABSOLUTELY NO ALCOHOLIC BEVERAGES SERVED!

"No exceptions, even now?" Bryan leaned his big arms on the oatmeal-colored chair. He looked around, perhaps belatedly noticing how the recent deaths weighed heavily upon the passengers.

"I'd be happy to make an exception now," Bill said. "But we don't have anything except soda and orange juice. Try this." He handed Bryan a cola. Bryan popped it open, tilted his head back, and took a swig. Then Bryan walked over to the window and gazed outside. There was no sign of the spider. Outside the moon was like a lacing of quartz on the black-velvet sea. He began to pace back and forth.

"I'll take an orange juice," Natalie said, as she handed the boy a dollar bill. He went to the refrigerator and poured a drink.

"It's on me," he told Natalie. "No charge today."

"We can't just sit here and do nothing," Bryan suddenly yelled. He pushed a coffee cup blindly to the side. It fell off the counter and shattered on the hard vinyl floor.

"We're waiting for the Coast Guard to come," Natalie said. "It should be here soon. Try to stay calm."

"If I were any calmer, I'd be in a body bag," Bryan said. Natalie winced; all they needed now was a hysterical lumberjack!

"Our engine's dead," Bill said. Natalie cast the boy a look that said, *Why did you have to say that?* Bill began to fill a water cooler with a plastic jug labelled FRESH WATER.

"I know that," Bryan said, facing the boy but not looking directly at him. "The engine's dead. But Captain Calamari mentioned that the ship had something called a radio direction finder. Maybe that helps." Natalie did not tell him that the radio direction finder was used to help the ferry determine its own position at sea rather than for the Coast Guard to find the ferry.

A shy looking Inuit woman came into the coffee shop and sat by herself, away from the others, in the corner of the room. She never said a word as she looked outside the coffee shop windows.

"Actually, I think we could all use a little coffee," Bill said.

"Good idea," Natalie agreed quickly. Anything to break up the mood of apprehension and gloom.

Bill brewed a pot of coffee, and soon the delicious aroma filled the air. It had a tranquilizing effect on the passengers, taking away some of the horror of the night.

Suddenly from the bathroom at the side of the coffee shop came a muffled cry. Natalie's heart skipped a beat. But then she reluctantly walked to the bathroom door. At first she knocked on the dried-up wallpaper which covered the door. As she knocked, the wallpaper curled itself away from the door's metallic surface.

"Anyone in there?" Natalie said, as her hand rose to her quivering neck. The door slowly opened. From inside came a gust of hot, oily-smelling air.

"Smells like a pack of skunks," Bill whispered.

The bathroom began to exude a smell of disinfectant that could not mask a melange of putrid biological odors. For a moment, Natalie didn't see anything in the shadows. The place was eerie and damp. It reminded her of the pendulum pit of Edgar Allan Poe. Brenda's poodle started to growl.

As her eyes adjusted to the dim light Natalie saw movement. A shadow, perhaps a leg or arm. She found it easy to imagine that the shadows on the walls moved like tarantulas which dripped poison from their fangs. Then from within the dark interior emerged a long hand with fingers all the same length, except for the ring finger, which was a good seven inches in length. They all had large bile-green nails at their tips. "Elmo!" she exclaimed. "What happened to you? You gave me a scare."

"Sorry, I got stuck in there," Elmo said. "I'm still pretty weak. The stench didn't help."

Indeed it didn't. The skunk smell followed him like a cloud of pestilence. Bryan cried out in disgust. Brenda looked bewildered. The little boy looked as if he were about to say something naughty, but caught his mother's warning look and didn't.

But Elmo merely smiled and went to rejoin Lisa. Natalie was surprised at how good-natured he was, considering the discomfort he was in. Was it an act? Did Elmo and his sister Martha suppress an anger which would one day explode in a fit of sudden fury or in a warped act of revenge? Martha, perhaps, but she had seen too much of Elmo's courage in adversity to believe that he had any such problem.

Natalie returned to the counter, along with Bryan, Brenda, and her five-year-old. The child had finished the Star Wars puzzle and started the Mickey Mouse one. Brenda brought out *The Cat in the Hat* by Dr. Seuss and an old-fashioned kaleidoscope to keep her son occupied after the puzzle was finished.

"Could I have a cookie, Mom?"

"Sure." Brenda handed her son a bag of Oreo cookies, from which he withdrew two. The boy carefully separated the chocolate wafers and licked at the white icing. "Good," he said as the sweet icing dissolved on his tongue.

Without a warning, Bryan withdrew a steak-knife from his pocket and threw it across the coffee shop at the wall. It landed precisely on a large stag beetle that was crawling along the white woodwork of one of the windows. The knife protruded from the black beetle's back like a skewer in shish kebab.

"Why did you do that?" Natalie asked, rolling her eyes in total incredulity.

"I hate bugs," the lumberjack replied.

Natalie let it go. This was going to be a long night.

"Wow," the boy exclaimed, forgetting about the kaleidoscope. "Can I touch the knife, Mom?" He looked at the steak-knife in the wall and then back at his mother.

Nathan exchanged glances with Bill, indicating they thought Bryan was off his rocker. "What a nut case!" Bill whispered.

"Brenda?" Nathan said. "You look a bit pale." His face was furrowed with genuine concern. "Let me get you a drink of water."

"I'm OK," Brenda said as a single tear dripped from her nervous eyes. Nathan handed her a glass of water. She continued to run her finger around and around on a water spot on the glass.

Bryan persisted in playing with his large knife. "Put it *away,*" Natalie said to him. Her fist slammed down on the Formica surface of a table. A bottle of ketchup in the center of the table teetered, rolled, and fell to the floor.

"You mind if I stack a few chairs behind the windows?" Bill asked Natalie. "Might help if the spider shows up again."

She shrugged. "Go ahead." She seriously doubted that chairs would stop the pycno, but if this made for greater confidence among the passengers, it was worthwhile. In fact, if it just got the freaky lumberjack settled, it would be enough. The sea monster was bad enough; panic would double or triple its effect.

Bill began methodically placing chairs against the many windows in the coffee shop. Brenda watched him and then whispered to Natalie.

"Think he's dangerous?"

Natalie smiled, preferring to interpret the question as humorous. If it referred to Bill, it was; if to Bryan, it wasn't. "Probably harmless, but I'll have to watch him."

A beeping sound came from behind Bill. It was the microwave. "I made some popcorn," he said as he gave a small dish to the little boy. The boy looked up from his puzzle and smiled. "Thanks," he said, as his mother nudged him.

Natalie looked at Brenda and the child and was surprised to find herself suddenly on the verge of tears. She turned away and walked to one of the windows that Bill had not yet barricaded, trying to get herself under control. If she broke under the strain, who else would keep the situation under control? She loved Nathan, but he wasn't the type, and Falow couldn't do it alone.

She looked out into the darkness and a queer, all-consuming feeling of being watched stole over her. She pressed her face against the glass window and cupped her hands in order to see better, but nothing was visible out there. Nothing but heavy banks of clouds, which were coming in their direction. For a moment she thought she caught sight of some nearby movement, and she took a step back before realizing the movement was just the reflected blinking of her own eyes. She almost smiled a little at her own nervousness.

"Everything OK?" Nathan asked her as he followed her to the window.

"OK, considering what we've been through, and the fact that we don't know if it will attack again." She was relieved to find that her voice sounded normal. The passengers would lose confidence if a police officer even *sounded* strained.

She held Nathan's hand but rather than receiving comfort she felt as if she were doped with Novocain. Fear did that, sometimes. Fear was the drug which numbed touch. Still she required closeness, so she took his hands in hers and pressed the side of her face against his. There was, after all, no need for secrecy; they had become a couple, and if the whole world didn't yet know it, that was because the world was a bit slow on the uptake. Nathan was being careful not to interfere when she was performing her police duties, but right now was an interstice. Others would assume that it was merely affection she was showing for him; her own awful fear and need of comfort was being masked.

"No," she murmured. "This can't be happening. Real life is not like a science-fiction novel." The words came out with a trembling moan. Tears filled her eyes. Nathan understood; just so long as no one else caught on to her weakness.

With all the chairs blocking the windows of the coffee shop, Natalie was beginning to feel like a caged animal with claustrophobia. "I'm going to go out on the deck and grab a few minutes' breath of fresh air," she told Nathan, disengaging. "You should stay here, and let me know the moment anything starts coming unglued." Her eyes flicked toward the lumberjack meaningfully.

Nathan nodded. "Please stay away from the rails," he said. He placed his hand on her arm comfortingly, a small kindness that seemed huge to Natalie. Her feelings for Nathan were still deepening. He stirred her heart with his little ways as much as his large ways. She felt her tears coming again, but then stopped herself.

"You don't have to tell me that." But of course he had been joking, in his sometimes ineffective way. "I'll stay right next to the coffee shop door. I just need a little fresh air to snap me out of this."

But at the door she hesitated. Thunderheads were stacking up on the northern horizon. Loud boomings muttered over the ocean waves from that direction. More trouble brewing. Unless the storm caused the monster to go away.

She turned, glancing back at Nathan, changing her mind about going alone. She saw him nod, catching on immediately. Bless the man!

"I think I'll go up to the bridge and see how Captain Calamari and Rudolph are doing," Nathan said.

"Don't go out there!" Bryan screamed. The five-year-old boy dropped his kaleidoscope and its glass shattered. Brenda and Bill turned around to see what the lumberjack would do next. Natalie thoughtfully evaluated the man's mental state. Could she afford to leave the coffee shop even briefly? She decided to risk it, because not only did she need to get out of here for a while, she needed to know exactly what the situation was outside.

"Something's—out there," Bryan repeated.

As if that were news! "We'll be out just for a minute," Natalie said reassuringly.

"Don't go out there! I feel its presence. Walking death," the lumberjack said, slurring his words as if he had been drinking something stronger than pop. An artery on the left side of his neck visibly throbbed. Brenda and Bill looked at him with impatience and irritation.

"Why not keep your mouth shut," Bill said. Bryan looked at Bill and kept quiet. The lumberjack might have weighed twice what the waiter did, but now had none of the youngster's poise. Natalie realized that the business with the chairs had helped Bill recover confidence in the safety of his bastion.

The other teenager laughed, but then decided it was best to be quiet. The little boy began to cry. Yes, she had to leave now—and return soon. Before things came apart.

Natalie opened the door to the coffee shop, letting in a gust of cold wind that spat drops of rain on the linoleum floor. Various gray mists rose off from the sea in big steamy columns, enclosing the occupants of the coffee shop in their own private world. The rumbles of the approaching storm cooled the air a few degrees.

The sea grew choppy and seemed to be in the hands of demons.

CHAPTER 33

Snout

NATHAN STOOD ON the bridge with Captain Calamari, Falow, and Rudolph while Natalie checked the decks. Outside thunder boomed as an occasional streak of blue-white lightning stabbed the ocean near the horizon. Mists flowed onto the bridge, making the ferry's steering wheel the only solid reality in a shifting world. To their left were several cigarette butts which had been crushed in the congealing gravy on mashed potatoes. Some of the men from the engine room had been smoking more than usual.

"Uggh," Calamari said. "My stomach's grumbling with acid indigestion and I'll be lucky if I don't get diarrhea. I don't need this."

"You do look tired, Captain," Falow said. "Dark circles under your eyes."

The captain's face was white, his eyes listless. "You don't look so great yourself, Chief," he retorted.

"The weather is not helping matters." The ferry seemed to be swallowed up in a murky olive-brown fog, shot here and there with shimmering streaks of an ochre tint. Falow quickly grabbed hold of a life preserver that the wind had torn free and was about to toss into the sea.

"How does a man as big as you move so quickly?" Calamari

asked. He winced as a cramp evidently wracked his bowels but luckily passed. Outside there were little lines of lightning that reminded Nathan of a sparkler. The flickers continued.

"Years of practice."

They talked about inconsequentials, perhaps trying to distract themselves from the horror of their reality. Like most Newfoundlanders, the captain said, he usually enjoyed all the local wildlife—both the animals and the plants. He particularly liked the flowering plants. In Newfoundland, beautiful wild flowers bloomed, seeded, and died all in a rush; plants flourished and perished quickly in areas of short summers and longer winters.

In northern areas of Newfoundland, he remarked, where flowers were less plentiful, the sea ice buckled into canyons of blue and turquoise pastel, and Eskimo women searched for crabs. A herd of reindeer would sweep across the tundra by the Labrador sea, food for the Eskimos and wolves. Bowhead whales were still caught and butchered. Their skin was cut into strips called muktuk, considered a delicacy. When a local entrepeneur had approached Calamari and the ferry line management to open a muktuk bar on the ferry, they declined, pointing out that muktuk would not appeal to the tourists or ecologically-minded tourists. Nathan understood how that could be the case.

Suddenly Rudolph cried out, "Big object on the sonar screen, closing fast."

"Any chance we could be running into an iceberg?" Nathan asked.

"Ice is a poor reflector of radar waves," Calamari said. "Even with a strong signal, which we don't have, we can't definitely identify icebergs. I wish we had one of those microwave radiometers. That would have told us more."

"So it could be an iceberg," Falow said. "Let's hope we don't run into it."

"On a clear day," the captain said, "I can see a berg from this ferry more than ten miles away. Tonight of course, we couldn't see it until we had hit it."

Calamari picked up the intercom microphone and spoke just

two words to the passengers, "Brace yourself." He then turned toward Rudolph. "Tell the men to get the life-rafts ready."

The captain's orders rang through the ferry. Aft and forward, the small crew snapped into action. The ferry's clock chimed out 10 P.M. in nautical couplets. Calamari studied the incredible maze of gauges and dials before him—manometers, shaft revolution indicators, vent opening indicator boards and various levers glistening with elbow-grease. He looked so helpless. Nathan knew that there was little he could do without working engines.

A small electrician crawled down into the battery pits under the compartment decks and was able to get some of the backup power restored to the ferry. As the dwarf Dutchman rose from the pits he sneezed from the acid fumes but gave Calamari the thumb's-up signal. The lights on the ferry's control panel lit up like a Christmas tree and then began to dim slightly.

The captain turned on a nearby sodium-vapor light and aimed it at the murky ocean waves. A urine-yellow glare reflected from the waves, but there was no sign of the leviathan. Calamari's light penetrated into a gray fog that hid the ocean and made it seem to Nathan as if he could invent any shape in the water that he wished.

The reports came to Calamari's control room over intercoms. Unfortunately all but one of the life-rafts had been destroyed. Simultaneously, the intercom poured out an incredible message: the engine rooms were flooding.

Nathan saw Rudolph go into action automatically. He knew what a flood of water in the engine room meant. Time was of the essence. Rudolph opened the high pressure air pipes to the main ballast tanks. The air roared into the tanks with the force of a tornado, expelling the ocean water in a bubbling spray. The entire ferry shook from the inrush of air.

The intercom signal was fading. Instinctively, Calamari pushed his ear near the speaker with a violence that must have made his ear ring, straining to catch any further information from forward and aft. "Ready the one remaining raft," he barked. Nathan knew that the order was a formality. The men were already lowering the raft. The captain then turned to an Eskimo junior lieutenant. "Please gather some of the passengers towards the raft."

Rudolph had connected a radio transmitter to the batteries in the pits, and he tapped out word to the Newfoundland Coast Guard that the ferry was in trouble. He hoped that some of his S.O.S. message would go through despite the broken antenna. Forward and aft, the passengers and crew settled down and waited.

The dwarf Dutch electrician drank a little brandy from a metal flask he carried in his hip pocket. He pulled a photo from his wallet. Nathan conjectured that perhaps now that the man thought death was knocking at his doorstep, he was beginning to wish that he had treated his beautiful wife a little better over the last year, that he had paid more attention to her, and had been a little more loving. Of course Nathan didn't even know whether the man was married, but it seemed reasonable.

It was time for him to return to the coffee shop; Natalie was probably already there. Once they had gotten out into the open air she had felt better, and gone about her business efficiently, checking for lost or injured people, and for signs of the sea spider. Apparently having a definite task to do restored her; it had been the tense inactivity inside that had gotten to her. He hadn't wanted to hamper her; he wasn't a policeman.

The first tiny drops of rain began to patter down on the glass windows of the coffee shop, whose occupants nervously waited for the approach of the pycnogonid. Inside there was little place to hide. Nathan was with them now, but Natalie was still outside on deck somewhere. He tried not to let it bother him too much. And he decided that the direct truth was best, for the people here. "The shaking of the boat was the pressuring of the ballast tanks," he reported. "But there is something coming." He looked around, trying to judge how they were taking it. Apparently they were OK; confirmation was better than doubt.

He went to Elmo and Lisa, but they seemed to be all right,

though both were pale. Someone had found them a blanket, and they were huddled together under it.

Bryan was the first to hear a noise beyond the coffee shop door—a slurping wet noise accompanied by scratching. "It reminds me of the noise my mother's garbage disposal made after putting soft garbage inside," he said. He seemed to have steadied down in the interim, which was a relief, and his analogy seemed apt: that was what it sounded like.

"Can it get through the doors or windows?" Brenda asked. Nathan saw the front of her full blouse quivering rhythmically, and realized that it was echoing her pulse; her heart must be beating like a jackhammer. She reached inside her pocketbook for a tranquilizer to calm her escalating anxiety. After a minute of searching, she gave up. "I took the last pill weeks ago," she muttered. Instead she began to pace back and forth but stayed very close to her son. That didn't do it, and soon she was back in her chair.

"I checked a window," Nathan said. "It's inch-thick plate glass. Maybe if we are quiet and don't move, the pycno won't know we're in here."

Now Nathan had the feeling that he was being watched. He quickly looked toward the windows but saw nothing. His heart skipped a beat because the dark windows reminded him of a row of black dead eyes. The door and windows were filling up with shadows, making his nervousness increase. But until Natalie returned, he had to put on the confident front, so as to keep the others calm.

Suddenly the ferry began to tilt rapidly to stern. Brenda lost her footing as the angle of the ferry reached 30 degrees, and she was propelled from her seat, like a pellet fired from a shotgun. Salt and pepper shakers crashed to the vinyl floor. A quiet Inuit woman held onto a table, but then tumbled to the floor when the table began to slide. Elmo and Lisa were holding onto each other, seeming stable, physically and otherwise.

The steady white noise of the air conditioner suddenly stopped. Water began to pour from the air conditioning vent in the side of the room, dousing Bill with bitterly cold salt water. Nathan knew what was happening: sea water was coming down the ship's air conditioning system, and the pipes that normally carried air out of the coffee shop to the outer deck were now alive with frothing ocean water.

But understanding it didn't solve the problem. Several hundred gallons of sea water roared into the coffee shop, hitting Brenda full in the face, sweeping her across the floor and bringing her hard against the glass door. Even as the icy water cascaded into the coffee shop they heard some sounds coming from outside.

"It'll stop in a moment!" Nathan cried. "Get out of the flow!"

Brenda's white poodle, dripping with water, laid back her ears and whined. The rush of water slowed to a trickle in a few minutes.

"Mommy, what's out there?" the little boy said. He started to tug nervously on his cartoon T-shirt. Brenda hugged him closer as she shivered in her wet clothes. Water continued to gush, churning up foam that refracted the light from the ceiling bulbs like garlands of silver tinsel.

"Nothing we should worry about," Brenda said bravely. "Let's read one of your books. How about Dr. Seuss's *Green Eggs and Ham?* You love that Sam-I-Am."

"How about *The Cat and the Hat?*" said her son.

Nathan continued to gaze at the windows of the coffee shop, trying to shake the feeling that reality was on the verge of slipping out of control. Bill and Bryan followed Nathan's gaze around the periphery of the room.

"OK," Brenda said as she rummaged nervously in her bag of toys and books. The poodle wedged herself between Brenda and her son.

Bryan carefully stirred the cup of tea in front of him. The sound of the fork bounced off the sides of his cup and grated on Nathan's nerves. But the last thing he wanted to do was set the lumberjack off again, so he ignored it.

Seconds later the sea spider's large proboscis stuck its opening to a window as if it were searching for food. Right at the pinkish end of the proboscis were little shriveled black lips that pressed and flattened on the glass like two balloons. Green goo poured from the opening and dripped down the plate glass like a river of mucus. Several feet away from the window, Nathan saw the glittering black eyes of the proboscis. One eye swiveled toward Brenda as the incandescent bulbs of the coffee shop threw white rhomboids of light on the dark, shiny orb.

"Ahhh," Brenda screamed. The boy whimpered like a homesick puppy.

"Shut up," Bryan said. "It might not know we are in here."

"Look at that thing," Bill whispered in a sickened voice.

As if it had overheard them, the pycno stopped moving, then turned slowly toward the plate-glass window and raised its huge sucking appendage in what looked like a slow, sarcastic wave. A whitish-brown vapor poured from the snout; it was the methane by-product of digestion—flatulence—hitting the ice-cold Newfoundland air. Outside thunder boomed and lightning sparked, as if sounding an entry fanfare for the monster.

The large proboscis withdrew from the window, stopped for a few seconds, and then thudded into the glass hard enough to make the whole frame shake. In a moment it repeated the strike.

Thud. Thud.

Bill looked at the window with mounting fear.

The door burst open, startling them all, but it was only Natalie. "The spider's—" she started, then paused as she saw the thing at the window. She tried to smile. "But I see it's already here."

Nathan went to her and took her hand. "We're OK here, so far. Brenda got soaked by water from the air conditioning vent, but the monster can't get in that way."

Thud! Thud!

Natalie's hand tightened in Nathan's.

"The window won't stand up to much more of that," Bill said. Lightning flashed and gave the window the look of a shiny yet gloomy black eye.

The banging on the window became louder. Brenda started to scream. She had been doing well, but now was losing it.

"Shut up," Bryan shouted at Brenda again. The poodle started to bark.

Things were coming unglued, but Nathan didn't know how to stop the process, and it seemed Natalie didn't either. His testicles contracted in fear. Bill slid behind the counter as he looked for some defensive weapon but found only a ketchup bottle. Brenda's mouth opened and closed. For a second, she reminded Nathan of a kissing gourami in an aquarium.

As the banging became louder, Nathan's mind was filled with all the images of the science-fiction films he had watched with his father in his boyhood. Several small shivers ran up his spine.

For a moment, the coffee shop door opened a few inches. Nathan looked at Natalie, then at wide-eyed Brenda, and back at the half-open door, wondering what would happen next. Natalie's grip on his arm became extremely tight. He looked at her, and saw sweat beading her forehead. What was out there?

The thudding on the window had stopped. All was quiet for the moment. Then slowly the coffee shop door opened to its maximum extent. Now they saw the massive, horrible snout, questing, trying to get in. The dooway, however, was too small to permit the proboscis to enter the coffee shop. After a moment it withdrew from the door in a seeming fit of rage.

"It can't get at us," Nathan said, relieved. "The angle is wrong, the snout's too thick, and the thing's not smart." He went to the door and pushed it shut, hoping the latch would hold if the monster tried again.

Thud! This time the sound of the proboscis banging on the glass windows was louder than a shotgun blast. The smooth curves of the giant snout gleamed under the overhead fluorescent lights.

The next moment a glass window shattered, the thick plate glass pulverized to diamond-like pieces and projections which scattered colored light in all directions. A few pieces hit Brenda in the face and she screamed, perhaps blinded by the exploding glass. Natalie immediately went to her.

The big black sucking appendage started to squirm its way through the jagged hole in the plate glass. Long triangles of glass which pointed inward from the window frame did not seem to slow the creature.

"What do we do now?" whispered Bill. A few tiny shards of glass were sticking to the proboscis and forming a dark obsidian sparkle. No one had an answer.

It was heading toward Bill. Bill retreated as they continued to hear the scratching of the sharp glass against the strong proboscis. The thin lines that the glass made in the appendage were apparently so shallow as not to be even noticed by the creature.

The long sinewy organ of destruction suddenly hurled itself through the hole in the glass like a striking cobra. Remaining pieces of glass in the window flew apart in a million shards. The glass fragments showered up, rained down, and tinkled against the floor like little Christmas bells.

"Oh God," Brenda whispered. Her face was scratched and bleeding, but she seemed to still see well enough. "Oh God, oh God."

The coffee shop was filled with the heavy aroma of ammonia with the underlying scent of decaying meat. At first, the passengers were still, each one afraid to move. Their worst nightmare had come.

Suddenly Bryan grabbed *The Cat in the Hat* book from the little boy, ran to the snout, and began to slam it with all his might. The proboscis simply vomited some green digestive goo onto the Dr. Seuss book, and then it grabbed the mucilaginous Seuss from Bryan's hands and threw it across the room. Bryan wiped some of the green gel onto his pants and then ran from the undulating proboscis of death.

Nathan stared at the stuff on the floor. Within the goo were tiny skeletons, no doubt the remains of some partially digested fish. The small bones of the fish began to curl as if magically still alive. Their small, bony mouths seemed to open in a silent cry.

The proboscis began to make its way to the little boy, who was now crying wildly. Nathan couldn't blame him; he felt like doing the same.

Bill grabbed a garbage can and threw it at the sucking appendage. As the can hit the floor, a big chunk of watermelon rind fell out. This was eagerly gobbled up by the pycno.

"Don't go so close to it," Nathan yelled, distracting the pycno. The creature started to overturn a small refrigerator, reducing a multitude of soda bottles to dull green shards. It seized some of the food in the refrigerator and started heaving it against the ceilings and walls as if frustrated by the minuscule samples of food. These could never satisfy its appetite. Everything was broken and crushed.

Bill searched for something else to throw at the creature, found a chair, and then broke it across the proboscis with little effect. The proboscis banged Bill on his arm, and he cried out in pain. He rose to his feet with great effort. His legs surely felt like spaghetti. Slowly the proboscis made its way to the food counter shelves which were stocked with health drink bottles. With one mighty swing, it knocked the shelves to the ground. Puddles of orange and lime liquids mixed on the floor like a fading Miró painting.

It then made a strange hungry humming sound as it propelled itself through the counter and exited on the other side. Bill ducked, but not quite in time. It hit his face, and his gashed and battered forehead started bleeding copiously.

Brenda screamed again. A bag of Cheez Doodles was knocked off the counter, and some of the orange contents scattered across the vinyl floor. As the proboscis pulled itself out of the crumbling remains of the counter, electrical wires were ripped out of the wood and began to pop and sputter, sending up clouds of black smoke from the burning insulation. The live wires began to dance back and forth like whirling dervishes.

"Get away from the salt water on the floor," Bryan said to the Inuit woman, who stood sallow-skinned against the rear wall of the shop. She stood still as if paralyzed with fear and confusion.

Her hands opened and closed around a crucifix she wore around her neck.

The poodle started to bark and growl and snap at the proboscis. Brenda screamed for the poodle to get back. Then, in one single, fluid motion, the pycno flung the poodle through the glass of a window. Brenda and the boy screamed in unison.

The wires on the floor continued to sputter and spark. It looked like a swarm of fireflies.

"Get away from the water," Bryan shouted again to the Inuit, but could not seem to make her understand that the danger of electrical shock was equal to or greater than the danger from the pycno who had trouble reaching her.

Bryan tried to walk along some dry spots on the floor to reach the girl. Suddenly she understood the problem but it was too late. The wires entered the water, and her scream was burned out of her vocal cords by a few thousand volts of electricity. Her body continued to twitch for a few seconds but gradually stopped as the electrical current locked her joints, muscles, and tendons. There was the smell in the air of fried meat.

"Get some salt," Bill said to Bryan as he pressed a pack of napkins against the wounds in his forehead.

"Where? Why?"

"We can throw it at the creature's mouth or eyes."

"Where?"

"In the storeroom. On the left." The proboscis had left a dark maroon weal on Bill which ran from his wrist to his elbow. An exposed region of flesh on his wrist was sweating small beads of blood, and a sick throbbing in his arm seemed to distract him from the pandemonium around him.

Bryan ran to the storeroom and opened the door. Styrofoam cups, burger packages, packets of ketchup, and paper napkins lined the shelves. "Where's the damned salt?"

"On the left," Bill called. "Behind the napkins." Bryan immediately saw a few shakers filled with salt, and removed them from the shelves and threw them to Bill. The proboscis was only a few feet from the crying child.

"We're all going to die!" a woman screamed.

"Shut your trap," Bryan said. Now that there was an immediate problem, he was doing well.

"We're all going to die!" she screamed again.

Brenda was at first paralyzed with fear but then tried to pull the boy away. As she pulled him she slipped on ochre jellylike muck which oozed from the proboscis. She tried to scream and pull away from the creature, but she continued to slip and slide. The snout swung around, seeking.

"What in hell is that?" Nathan muttered as he gazed into the interior of the proboscis and saw something inside, something scurrying frantically in the large cavity.

"Something's inside it!" Natalie cried.

Then they heard a sound Nathan could not quite identify, coming from within the beast. A soft hungry licking. Even as he was seeing it, he couldn't believe it. This was not like any pycno he had studied.

A frigid breeze blew through the broken window, drying rivulets of perspiration on Brenda's face.

"What did you see?" Nathan cried to her.

"I don't know."

"Probably an internal organ, or a parasite, or something it ate. Could it have been a fish or crab?" He was hoping that she had a better answer than he did.

Brenda stopped talking. She and her son were backed into a corner of the shop with little room to move. Both were staring at the snout as if mesmerized.

Bill took off the top of the salt shaker, ran to the proboscis, and dumped it into its opening. The snout responded by beating the floor of the coffee shop, as it attempted to scrape off the salt in its sucking appendage. The covering membrane of the proboscis glistened with a shifting phosphorescence, and dark brown chromatophores on its exoskeleton exploded into bright crimson. It began to yo-yo up and down like a broken marionette. In doing so the snout banged into Bill's crotch.

"Oooh," he screamed, as he backed up, bent over, and covered his aching testicles. The probocis gave Bill a shove into the counter, fracturing his collar bone.

"Oh God, oh God," Brenda whispered. Her hands clenched and unclenched like the pincers of a lobster.

Nathan was not much better off. He could see the big black eyes of the pycno as they rolled in their sockets and fixed their attention on the woman. A piece of goo flew at her from the creature's drooling sucking appendage and hit her on the arm.

"Jesus," she screamed. It reminded Nathan of warm petroleum jelly, although it had the exact color of lime gelatin. Brenda quickly wiped her arm briskly on the leg of her jeans, trying to dislodge the gruesome material, which stuck to her skin like flypaper. "Get off of me," Brenda spoke to no one in particular. She continued to wipe even after the last traces of goop were gone from her skin.

Nathan glanced at Natalie, but she seemed to be as revolted and helpless as he was. The monster was just so big and so awful that it was almost impossible to organize any coherent plan of opposition.

Brenda looked at the thick liquid shimmering on the linoleum floor as if it were luminous paint. Her heart seemed to be thumping rapidly again behind her ample bosom. The proboscis slowly came toward her, and she raced away with her son, her low heels tip-tapping on the linoleum floor. The creature's eyes were as shiny as diamonds as they pursued.

Then the sucking appendage was upon her. Nathan saw a conga-line of squirming bristles ascend her thigh under her dress. The large eyes fixed on hers again.

"We're all going to die!" the woman screamed again.

"We've got to do something!" Natalie said. "Maybe I can get something from the deck." She went out the door.

Nathan cast about for anything that might make an effective weapon. He found a fragment of broken chair. He hefted it like a spear, trying to locate a vulnerable spot on the immense snout. But the situation seemed hopeless.

The opening of the proboscis widened in what seemed like a yawning snarl. In a few seconds, Brenda was standing on her toes, the proboscis wrapped around her neck. The whites of her eyes were marbled with crimson, while the dilated pupils opened up and stared at the others in the coffee shop. Her pupils were like dark circles painted on paper by an avant-garde artist. A few wisps of her hair were damp with sweat.

Nathan struck at the proboscis, but could make no impression. He used the spear to shove against the monstrous living column, but he might as well have been pushing at a mountain. It ignored him.

The digestive walls of the esophagus turned inside out, making it appear as if a tongue were being formed from the inner folds of flesh. It happened ever-so-slowly, in much the way of a ketchup commercial where the ketchup seemed to take minutes to ooze from the bottle.

From about ten feet away, Bryan pointed at the creature. Then he got the steak-knife, aimed it, and threw it into the interior of the proboscis. A fist-sized chunk of the wet walls of the proboscis's interior fell from the muscular organ and onto the cold tile vinyl floor of the coffee shop. The flesh began to wiggle. Then it started to croak like a frog. The wounded proboscis unwrapped and withdrew from the window, and for a few minutes there was silence in the coffee shop.

Brenda dropped to the floor and curled her body into a tight ball. Her elbow popped with a metallic sound of tearing tendons. She ignored the pain, covered her face with her hands, and peeked out through the cracks between her fingers.

Bryan came closer to the chunk of pink tissue on the floor, which convulsed as paroxysm after paroxysm ran through the dying flesh. Then it began to flap around on the floor, like a bird taking a dust bath, and then to wiggle like a caterpillar. The lumberjack raised his huge boot and crushed the living flesh beneath his heel. It lay there limp, like a dead worm.

"Thanks," Brenda croaked to him over the boy's screams. She

sounded as if she were speaking with a mouthful of marshmallows. Her bruised voice box must have felt as if it had been pushed back into her esophagus.

Then her eyes took on a wild look as if the enormity of what happened had just hit her. She ran to the chunk of tissue and pounced upon it, spat on it, kicked it. A piece of its flesh flew off from her shoe and struck Nathan on his chest. Another piece catapulted to the chipped Formica counter of pastries and assorted candies and stuck there for a moment, a few of its blood vessels still pulsing feebly, before it loosened and fell with a splash into an open jar of lime drink. Another piece struck Bill on his face and splattered open in a clot of viscous glop. Bill began to gag.

Nathan dropped his useless stick and went to the woman. "That's enough, Brenda." She collapsed into his arms.

Bryan retrieved his steak-knife from the shiny vinyl floor, cleaned it on a paper napkin, and placed it back in his pocket. An ammonia smell continued to fill the air.

"Let me get rid of that stuff on the floor," Nathan said. He found a mop and bucket in the bathroom and pushed the dead piece of flesh into the bucket. The stench of the pink flesh was maddening. As he scraped some of the remains, he broke a few pustules of flesh, which began to emit a vague banana-lemon smell. Nathan walked quickly to the broken window and tossed the bucket out onto the deck. Brenda broke into tears, and Bill handed her some napkins.

"Thanks," she said, her red eyes still streaming tears. Bill stayed next to her. After a few seconds of silence, she caught another whiff of the banana-lemon odor.

"I'm going to throw up," she said, unable to hold her churning gut back any longer. She ran to a corner of the room, opened her mouth, and vomited.

"Mommy, Mommy," her son cried.

"It's OK," she said from the corner of the coffee shop, to comfort the boy. Billy went over and handed her some more tissues.

"Mommy, what was that thing?" the little boy said. "I want to go home. I'm scared."

"It's over. All over. We don't have to worry."

"Where's Natalie?" Bryan asked, remembering that the policewoman was no longer with them.

"She went outside for some fresh air," Bill said.

Nathan knew better. He went to the broken window and shouted, "Natalie?" There was no answer; in fact there was little sound coming from the deck area. "Natalie? Are you there?" Suddenly he sensed that Natalie was in grave danger.

Still no answer, but he thought he heard a cough. What if the cough were not really a cough but the sound of the spider dragging its legs along the deck? What if the spider was silently stalking Natalie or other passengers? Worry escalated to fear. Nathan walked to the door.

"Don't go outside," Brenda said. Her voice trembled. Her eyes twinkled with madness.

Brenda was concerned about him? As if she hadn't just had the world's most horrible experience! "I'll be careful."

As Nathan reached for the door's handle, he stopped. His heart hammered in his chest. From outside came the screams of women which rose like prayers to the night sky. One scream stood out above all others in intensity and volume. It was Natalie.

CHAPTER 34

Attack

NATALIE HEARD A flapping noise from behind her, a liquid sound, like something from an X-rated movie, but several octaves too low. She knew what it was.

"Ahh," she said as she felt liquid on her shoulder. She wiped at it with her hand and saw it had turned dark sepia and crimson with syrup of some unknown composition. The sepia syrup smelled like ammonia. It was beginning to sting like burning lava. With praying-mantis speed, the pycnogonid had somehow hauled itself onto the deck with little sound. Of course, despite its silent entry, its massive bulk could not be hidden and the boat now rocked with the additional weight.

Water cascaded from its monstrous body. Its huge eyes were afire, its colossal pincers working and gnashing back and forth. In a moment it oriented on her.

"Nathan," she screamed as the huge creature rose in twitching terror against a starless, black sky. She had become relatively ineffective since her gun had run out of ammunition. She had simply stood and watched as others reacted to the predations of the monster. She had hoped to clear her head out here, and return ready to act like the policewoman she was supposed to be. But the sheer size and ferocity of the thing, and her lack of firepower, unnerved her, leaving her emotionally feeble. She was disgusted with herself—but also terrified.

The ghostly mass of legs began to reach for her. She retreated a few steps and slipped on a burger wrapper. Her knee crashed into a discarded beer can, causing a sharp pain to climb her leg.

"Damn," she said as her empty automatic skidded away from her and clattered on the wet deck. She reached for it, hoping she could use it as a kind of club, but could not get to it in time. She was not normally a woman who cried readily, but she sobbed now. Her hair was plastered against her head like a wet, straggly wig, surely making her look exactly as messed up as she felt.

"Falow," she screamed, trying to quell her rising panic as she breathed harshly from her open mouth. The spider was only a few feet from her. She felt as if her eyes were taking on a dull sheen as of plastic pottery.

Something thick and soggy pressed against her legs. It felt like a cold, sticky tongue caressing her. *What is that?* she thought as beads of perspiration formed on her temples. But her thought was rhetorical; she knew what it was, having seen it with Brenda in the coffee shop.

It was a segment of the sea spider's digestive tract, which had evaginated through its proboscis like an inside-out balloon. As its digestive walls made contact with her, the creature trembled with anticipation. It made a slurping sound.

"It's trying to eat her," a passenger screamed. "Help!"

Natalie felt a burning on her skin, like a high fever. It had to be from the digestive fluid. She tried to twist away from the fleshy thing looming in front of her.

Like a scene out of an adventure movie, Falow leaped from an upper rail near the bridge and landed on his feet on the deck about thirty feet from Natalie. Without a moment's hesitation, he emptied his gun into one of the spider's eyes and legs closest to her, and the pycno backed away.

But it paused for only a second. Natalie got up, her right ankle striking a deck chair. It was only with the greatest effort that she continued to rise to her feet and steady herself by holding onto the back of a table. She was only vaguely aware that her leg was bleeding as she cast a horrified glance back over her shoulder in the direction of the creature.

Before she could think of what to do next its long proboscis shot out of the main mass of its body with the speed of a chameleon's tongue and enveloped her. Dark stars of light skated across her field of vision. One of the spider's leg spikes ripped through the remains of her shirt like a razor and punctured her left lung. A growing numbness spread through her chest.

"Gah," she choked as she gasped for air. She fought with all her waning strength, knowing that she had to tear herself from the beast's embrace because soon she would be unconscious. Dull drum sounds, harbingers of approaching asphyxiation, began to bang in her ears. Her weakening screams rose and fell with the thumping of her own heart.

Fear drove her to try a final attempt to dislodge herself from the creature. First she bit at it, tearing away a mouthful of horrible urine-stinging flesh. She bit down again and something crunched like the cartilage and gristle from a chicken bone. The warm, sour taste of aging bacon filled her mouth.

She tasted vomit in the back of her throat. Then she poked the nails of her right hand into the fleshy interior of the proboscis as hard as she could.

This had a momentary effect. The pycno's grip relaxed, as brown juice oozed from its injured flesh. It was evidently not well equipped to deal with a creature who fought back from the inside. But this was probably more like a mosquito trying to sting the inside of a frog's mouth; it was hardly a fatal strike.

Natalie continued to chew and gnaw at the interior of the creature's sucking appendage. She would not give up. Not give up, no matter how little it ultimately counted.

"Ummph," she grunted through a mouthful of blood. Her lips felt as dead as bone.

"Keep shooting at it," she heard Nathan scream to Falow as

he gazed at the tattered rags of Natalie's shirt. She caught a glimpse of his face. He looked as if his stomach was twisted with nausea. But at least he was here!

"I don't have any more bullets," Falow yelled back. Him, too! Why hadn't they thought to prepare for the worst? They had come to this fray like rank amateurs. Had they thought that a few little bullets would scare away the monster? What utter folly! Falow was evidently on the edge of exhaustion, astonished as he saw Natalie continue to fight, and her angry refusal to relinquish hope. He didn't know how weak-kneed she had been, until she had to fight for her life.

Natalie's eyes caught Nathan's for a moment. *I will not let you die,* his gaze promised her as he searched for a weapon with which to attack the beast. But he had to be wondering whether it was a promise he could keep.

Then the pycno must have suffered a lapse of attention. For a moment Natalie broke free. She stood unsteadily, not quite believing it, trying to get sufficiently organized to run to safety. She looked back at the passengers on the ferry boat. The burnt bacon taste lingered horribly in her mouth. Stroboscopic flashes of lightning made the scene seem like something out of a horror movie. She knew she had little time to get away. But her body just wasn't responding well.

As she tripped again, she saw some of the passengers staring back at her with the red bloodshot eyes of little rabbits. All around her was the stink of sulphur, rotting meat, and the smell of her own half swallowed vomit.

But she tried. She was on hands and knees now. She crawled about six feet. Then she heard the horrid scraping of its legs against the deck. Close, way too close. Then, to her right, she saw a leg inches from her face, a bristly tan limb with multiple spikes. She looked up, looked into the charred hole where one of its eyes should have been.

For some reason, Natalie had a vision of her friend and the apartment they had shared over the barbershop on Main Street. Then of the house she had lived in before her parents died. She wanted her mother. She missed her mother. For a moment she heard a piano playing. Again it was her mother, this time playing the old baby grand piano in their house; the song was *Moonlight Sonata.*

The vision was suddenly cut off. With a muted screech, the sea spider grabbed her torso and lifted her high up into the air. It was wrapped around her, smothering her. It waved her body round and round like a rodeo rider twirling a lasso. She would have screamed if she could, or fainted, if she could. Why hadn't she fled the monster faster, when she had the chance? Or had it freed her deliberately, playing cat and mouse with her?

Her mouth broke free from its muscular surroundings for a moment. She gasped for breath and continued to scream. The pycno applied pressure to her head, and then her body began to convulse and jerk like a puppet guided by an amateur puppeteer. She saw the skin on her hands changing colors, and thought that her face must also be changing colors like a traffic light, from red, to orange, to a sickly green. She stopped screaming—and the monster dropped her limp body onto the deck like discarded rubbish. She never felt the landing.

CHAPTER 35

Battle

A FEW PASSENGERS far away from the pycnogonid ran forward to help Natalie, but the monster twitched and frightened them away. Some peered over the rail as if expecting to find her in the water. There was only a faint glimmer of light from some exotic bright-eyed fish which swam near the murky surface.

Nathan ran toward the body, but the legs and snout oriented alertly on him. He knew that they would grab the moving target first—but that there was no guarantee he could distract it permanently from Natalie. It might simply hurl him into the water for later consumption, as it had Lisa. So he had to find a way to distract it that would keep its attention indefinitely, or at least until others could get to Natalie and drag her to safety.

Assuming that it was not already too late. She had been wrapped in that awful proboscis, and then had taken a bad fall to the deck. Was she all right? He thought he saw some motion, but the lights from the boat were too dim to reveal her clearly. She was only a shadowy shape against the dark deck. She had to be alive—but wouldn't remain so unless he got her clear very soon.

What could he do? He gazed wildly around, seeking something, anything that might offer itself. His frantic eye crossed the dark water. For a moment he thought he saw her body out there, with albino mutant crabs crawling on her outstretched arms. A few grasped her hair with large wicked claws, and then she was pulled under.

No! That was horrible imagination. Or maybe it was the body of a passenger he didn't know who had fallen into the water. But Natalie, still alive, was clearly on the deck, about to be gobbled by the spider, and he had to get focused and save her, no matter what it took.

"Natalie," Nathan screamed in frustration as he grabbed Bryan's knife. She couldn't be dead. Not the woman he had just spent a beautiful evening with in town, in the forest, and on the beach at night. In Come By Chance, discovering glorious love. Not Natalie who never had a mean word to say, who seemed so kind. Who had evoked his love, full-blown, when he had never expected to find anything like it here.

He looked across the deck, running wildly, brandishing the knife. He could not lose her. His throat was tight, his eyes watery. Maybe he could attract the attention of the monster to himself, then cut quickly into the joints between its limbs, its proboscis, crippling it. Anything, to save Natalie!

The pycno seemed to be watching him. Good! He would lead its attention as far away as possible. He charged up onto the bridge.

The monster moved, its legs reaching for Natalie's body.

"No!" Without warning, Nathan suddenly leaped from the bridge onto the pycnogonid's bony back and drove Bryan's steak-knife into a line on its exoskelton where the primary brain joined the spinal cord. He buried it to the hilt, splitting the shell with a sharp crunch. He knew exactly where to strike a creature like this. Nathan realized that he looked like a cowboy riding a bucking bronco, although he was more like a matador thrusting the barb into the shoulder of the bull.

But he doubted that the knife was long enough to do enough damage to a creature this size. He had to find a more vulnerable target. He withdrew the knife and drove it again into one of the five black eyes. "Take that, you filth!" he screamed. "Take your own medicine!"

But the sea spider jerked backward and the knife blade snapped. He had lost his weapon!

Yet Nathan did not stop. He took the remnant of the large knife handle and slammed it down with all his might. This time he felt the spider's exoskeleton near the base of the brain crack, and he hit it in the same place again and again. A loose slew of mucus-like substance spilled from the crack. He was getting somewhere!

The pycno jumped, dropping something like a disembodied arm from its mouth, and regurgitated the half-dissolved contents of its many stomachs. The jellylike substance from its stomach churned itself on the deck for a few seconds as if alive. Had he managed to stop the monster?

The pycno continued to eject various marine and human pieces in mangled lumps with little form. Then its legs quivered as if about to descend on Natalie's body. In any other circumstance Nathan might have admired its single-mindedness. But not now. What did it take to stop this horrible thing?

A brief gagging noise came from Nathan's throat. The knife handle, his main defense, fell out of his hand. He began beating at the creature's five black eyes with his bare hands. The rage within him was a living thing. It was as if the spider had awakened a sleeping giant within the man. A giant to rival the sea creature itself.

"Die!" Nathan cried. He rode the pycno, screaming and yelling as it whipped him around and around and even tried to turn itself upside down in an attempt to dislodge him from its back. It had finally recognized that he was dangerous to it; he had its full attention. But he was riding a tiger. Would he ever be able to get off it? It hardly mattered, for he had no intention of getting off. He had come not to ride it, but to kill it.

Lightning shattered the gray heavens and lit up the mayhem on the ferry. One bolt struck the ship's deck, severing some of the remaining railing from the boat. The electrical crackle continued for a few seconds but did not slow the fury of Nathan's attack.

The pycno rose up on its posterior legs, pawing obscenely at the air. Its huge body cast shadows even in the darkness of night. Nathan realized that deadly as the monster was when attacking other creatures around it, it was at a serious disadvantage dealing with a creature *on* it. Its legs weren't made for this.

"Yeeeee!" The creature was doing something with its proboscis that caused it to emit a high-pitched whine. Its multiple eyes bulged like balloons being filled with air as it slashed at the steel hull of the ferry. The wind stung Nathan's ears, made his eyes tear, and pasted frost on his mustache. He knew that the creature was trying to get at the source of its pain, and didn't quite know how. He understood that feeling, for it had been his own until very recently.

Natalie still lay on the deck. The pycno was distracted, but had not moved far enough away from her to allow anyone else to approach. The sight of her motionless body set Nathan off again.

"Not enough?" Nathan demanded as he drove his hand into the open wound near the nerve cords. The anger exploded in him so intensely that his fingers trembled and his teeth were clenched. He screamed with fury and a hunger for violence. He reached deeper into the creature and felt some of the tissue tearing in his hand as he pulled out gobs of white muscle and membrane. "Then have some more!" He jammed his hand in again.

The pycno tried again to dislodge him but could not reach him. Then its wild eyes met Nathan's. Its strange, alien face seemed contorted with rage. Nathan hesitated for a second as he gazed at those gleaming empty eyes that looked more dead than alive. Did his own eyes mirror that rage, that deadness?

A lightning streak reflected off the colored orb and drove Nathan to increase his attack. He crushed one eye as he struck with the flat of his hand: short, vicious, hard. He smashed his fist into another eye and felt the black globe crush and ooze dark liquid. It trickled down his legs like steaming soup. Step by step, he was blinding it.

The pycno went wild, with all of its legs attempting to reach Nathan, but as he had discovered, the thing could not reach him if he huddled close to its body. Now all he had to do was hang on and let it lose strength. Just so long as it didn't go for Natalie again.

Its movements slowed, became imprecise. A pool of green blood, not yet congealed, bloomed from the pycno's eye sockets in a small puddle. After a minute, he realized that all of the eyes on the body had been destroyed. The spider was blind, except for the two eyes at the end of its proboscis.

It swung that proboscis around to gaze at Nathan, and then vomited on him. As Nathan wiped the ooze away from his eyes, a heavy wet thing, its digestive wall, started slobbering its way up his belly and chest. It then expelled green corrosive substance from its mouth, but the bulk of the goo missed him.

Now the rest of the world returned to his awareness. "Here, take this," the captain shouted as he threw a flare gun to Nathan. Nathan reached for it but dropped it. The gun clattered to the deck. "Try again!" Calamari shouted. He threw a second gun, and this time Nathan caught it.

Nathan cried out and shoved his left hand into the digestive walls, which opened and closed spasmodically. Then he took away his hand and pulled the end off the flare gun. Orange flame shot out of the gun, which he jammed with all his might into the beige mucus walls of the sea spider's digestive tract.

Suddenly the digestive walls withdrew. Nathan smelled an unpleasant aroma, a cross between burnt bacon and ammonia. The pycno's legs thrashed madly, but they weren't taking the creature anywhere. A minute later the creature was motionless, as if hypnotized with pain and failure.

Nathan reached into the open wound, reached deep, and pulled out a majority of its primary brain. The creature was now anencephalic, left with merely a brain stem, a tiny stump of a brain, and a few minor brains—the ganglia. If it were to survive it could now exist only in a persistent vegetative state—the remaining stalk of its brain allowed the body to perform basic, reflexive functions like breathing. Its primitive heart, the hemocoel cavity, would continue to pump blood, and its flesh would be maintained, assuming someone fed it. But the spider would never again be conscious of its environment, never see, never feel.

As if aware of its state, it began to keen so loudly that it masked the approaching sirens from the Coast Guard boats. Rescue was coming at last.

Nathan could have let the pycno "live" in a tenuous vegetative existence, but instead he reached deep into its body and tore out its last vestige of life, the brain stem. The mass in his hand was gray, slightly wrinkled, the size of a plum. It throbbed, trailing torn nerves and arteries. It pulsed, not because it was still alive, but because the torn nerves continued to provide an ever-weakening electrical impulse. He held the beating organ in his left hand until its metronomic pumping stopped. Then he threw it to the ferry's deck. It flattened like a piece of dough as it hit the wet surface.

The spider collapsed. Its muscles trembled, went rigid, and ceased to move.

Off in the distance the sounds of sirens continued, the lamenting wails of Coast Guard boats hopping though the waves like a small school of fish. They grew louder, winding up like an invisible clock spring in the dark autumn air. Reflections from the revolving lights atop the Coast Guard boats cast a red stroboscopic pattern on the deck. The fog looked like a red wounded mist, like blood on a de Kooning painting.

The passengers did not bother to turn in the direction of the sirens, but merely continued to stare at the man with wild, bloodshot eyes on top of the spider's corpse. The storm clouds, which had covered the sky so densely that no moon or starlight could penetrate, were starting to move southward.

At first Nathan stood defiantly, gazing up at the dark sky where several beams of moonlight were beginning to shine like rays of hope from a beneficent god. But seconds later he collapsed, fell to the deck, moaned, and was quiet. He had had the strength of madness, and now it had deserted him. He felt lost.

Behind him was the dark and broken wreckage of the great pycnogonid. It look ominous in the misty night, like a ghost, a skeleton, a grim reaper, a phantom which never moved but only gazed at the little man who should be bones. No one moved on deck. They just stared. Nathan realized that he now looked like a thin old man, never moving, never caring, lying near the creature's still brain on the deck, frozen on the edge of fallow fields forever.

Then there was a groan. "Natalie!" Nathan cried, bursting out of his trance. He hauled himself past the brain and lurched toward her.

Then everyone was converging. "She's alive!" Falow cried.

"Alive," Nathan echoed, prayerfully.

CHAPTER 36

Decision

AFTER THE COAST Guard arrived and helped all of the passengers off of the ferry, they secured a rope to the battered craft and started pulling it back to shore with a tugboat. The pycnogonid's body was left to sit alone on the ferry's deck, its long legs trailing back into the sea. Overhead the gulls cried, hoping to get an opportunity to probe at the rotting flesh of the sea spider. Around the ferry, the ocean waves seemed to lift to the stars.

The ocean water was beginning to take on a rainbow sheen of oil that glimmered like mercury on the twilight sea. Above in the sky was a trailing veil of gold. Dawn was approaching. It had been quite a night.

From beneath the spider's body there was movement. A hinged door beneath the chitonous exoskeleton opened downward. A hand appeared. The hand's fingers were all the same length, except for the super-long ring finger. Dr. Martha Samules, owner of the largest aquarium store in Newfoundland, crawled from the hollowed-out region in the dark interior of the creature's body. She had on a diving mask and oxygen tank. The skin on her hands looked blistered, as if some of the corrosive substance from the pycnogonid's digestive tract had seared her with some mystical and unknown heat. Her arms were splattered with blood and brains and tiny broken fish bones.

"Ahh," she said as she gently pulled herself from some of the creature's muscles and veins, and let the fresh sea air rush into her lungs. Her neck was dotted with large beads of sweat despite the chill of the air.

The dawn grew colder as quick-moving shadows of clouds skimmed over the water. The drizzle continued. But the woman seemed to notice neither.

Martha gazed up at the spider's long thin legs, so much like her own fingers, and trembled. She looked left, then right, and saw no one. Her wild, exotic sapphire eyes sparkled in the moonlight. Her inch-long teeth were clenched in a large sharky smile.

"So one male wasn't enough," she said. "The big female won't be able to do it alone, either. But what about a hundred—or ten thousand? Suppose three had tackled this boat, coordinated? I think we are almost there."

Then she reconsidered, gazing at the hole that had been carved to remove the creature's main brain. "But stronger protection is needed in some sections. May have to implant some steel plates. And the eyes—how can those be shielded? It's a challenge."

She walked quietly over to one of the creature's shorter legs and reached into a small crevice in its underside. As she thrust her hand in, she felt hundreds of juvenile pycnogonids in their larval stage of development. She withdrew a handful, and held the writhing tiny bodies in her left hand. She reached into another body cavity and pulled out the creature's cold, dead heart.

"But we'll have to do something about your taste in prey, too," she said, as if addressing the dead sea spider. "Can't have you eating all the fish and squid and other creatures in the sea. Maybe we can give you a special taste for human flesh alone. Then you'll *have* to seek the right prey, even when not guided." She nodded as she pondered the matter. "Oh yes, there's work to be done yet." She smiled, looking forward to it.

Above she heard the cry of a mournful gull. Her hand still held the larvae. Then, as quick and quiet as a ferret, she crawled to the edge of the ferry, gazed over the rusted railing as the noisy surf flung crystal splinters onto her wrinkled face, and then dropped into the dark blue sea filled with golden froth of autumn's russet.

Epilogue

The human race has been guilty of almost countless crimes; but I have some excuse for mankind. This world, after all, is not very well adapted to raising good people. In the first place, nearly all of it is water. It is much better adapted to fish culture than to the production of folks.

—ROBERT G. INGERSOLL,
The Ghosts and Other Lectures

"HOW DID YOU know about this place?" Lisa asked, her wide-eyed wonder coming naturally.

"Well, I *am* the local fishery officer," Elmo replied as he guided the car along the diminishing road to Cape St. Mary's, at the southern tip of the southwestern projection of the Avalon Peninsula of Newfoundland. "This is a sea bird sanctuary, and fish are essential to sea birds."

"Oh, of course." She smiled at him, as she did so often now. He had told her how her first smile had captivated him, and now that was important to her. He did not return the smile, and that was by mutual agreement. Her smiles were performed for both of them.

He brought the car to a halt. "We'll have to wait here until they catch up," he said. "They don't know where the sea stack is. I hope you don't mind the delay."

"Whatever will we do with the time?" she inquired rhetorically as she unsnapped her seat belt and slid across to hug him. She planted a wet kiss on his cheek. "Am I boring you?"

"Not unduly," he admitted. "But you know you really don't owe me anything. I would have tried my best to save you even if you'd been old and ugly."

"Well, I do expect to be supported in excellent style for the rest of my life," she said. "Once you get up the nerve to marry me."

"It's not nerve, it's caution. You need time to realize that the loss of one thumb does not make you unattractive to the great majority of men."

"But it does make me realize how unimportant hands are," she said. "Except when they are reaching out to pull a person from freezing, monster-ridden hell. So I can focus on things like decency, security, and commitment." She kissed him again, this time on the ear. "Love was there waiting for me, only I couldn't see past the—"

She broke off, for she had spied an oncoming car. The other couple had arrived.

The car pulled up behind theirs. In a moment Nathan and Natalie Smallwood got out. They hadn't wasted any time about getting married, Lisa thought. That was because he had to return to Harvard, and they hadn't wanted to separate. Police Chief Falow would have to hire another policewoman for St. John's, because this one would be working in another state, at least for a while. Natalie had actually gotten married in a wheelchair two weeks after surviving the monster spider. Her first week of marriage must have been good for her, because she was on her feet now. This was technically their honeymoon. They liked going to obscure places together. In fact, they seemed to like anything at all, together. It certainly looked like fun, from Lisa's vantage.

Lisa and Elmo got out to join the others. "It's a good thing you arrived when you did," Elmo said. "This teen was getting fresh."

Natalie smiled. "Oh? Did she do this to you?" She planted a kiss on Nathan's cheek.

"Yes, twice," Elmo said indignantly.

"He's lying," Lisa protested. "The second one was on the ear."

Natalie frowned at Lisa. "For shame!" she said severely. "Are you trying to corrupt this innocent man?"

"I'm trying to get him to marry me," Lisa said. "But he ignores me."

"Keep working on him," Natalie advised. "It's just a matter of trial and error until you find his weak point."

"What was Nathan's weak point?" Lisa asked mischievously.

"His imagination. It was limited."

Lisa was perplexed. "But how could that—?"

"Never mind," Nathan said. "Some things must not be revealed."

They laughed. Then Elmo led the way to the sea stack. This turned out to be a small steep-sided rocky mountain by the coast. They had to navigate a trail down the cliff-like shore and cross shallow water to reach it, but didn't get their feet wet because there were stepping stones leading to it. There was also a crude path slanting up it, so that they could climb without having to scramble four-footed. That was just as well, because neither Natalie nor Elmo had yet recovered strength for anything beyond routine exertion, and Lisa was not yet fully recovered either. They wouldn't have come out here, if the matter weren't so important.

"What a place for a mountain!" Lisa remarked. "How did it ever get here?"

"It was here first," Elmo explained. "The waves of the sea cut through behind it, washing out the dirt and gravel, causing the cliff to collapse. So it remains as an island, protected by rock that was too solid for the waves to defeat. It's a perfect breeding place for northern gannets, because neither land nor sea predators can conveniently reach it. It's past the birds' nesting season, but there may be some remaining."

Sure enough, as they reached the top several goose-sized birds squawked and took off. The group paused in place, waiting for the birds to settle. Lisa saw one of them swoop down into the sea, going for a fish. "I wish I could do that," she said.

"Wouldn't work," Elmo said. "Your mouth's too small."

They found comfortable rocks and sat on them. "Do you think she'll come?" Lisa asked, concerned.

"She'll come," Elmo said. "She knows I don't bluff. We disagree philosophically, but we trust each other. My note was clear enough."

"Just what did you say to her?" Lisa asked. "I never saw the note."

"Because you had to remain anonymous, until this time," he said. "She would have fired you, if she knew that you and I were comparing notes and fathoming her secret."

"And what a secret it is!" Natalie exclaimed. "We never suspected. If it hadn't been for that pycnogonid attack on the ferry—"

"And for our coincidental acquaintance," Nathan agreed. "We had a personal as well as professional reason to figure it out."

"And when I looked deep into its snout and saw that thing moving," Elmo said, "I didn't realize its significance right them. But later it registered: there was something *inside* that giant pycnogonid. Something that wasn't its natural innards. Something that seemed almost independent. That started me thinking, during my recovery. And when Lisa mentioned how my sister was able to train small sea spiders in her lab, I started making connections. It all started coming together, in an amazing way. That's why I mentioned it to you, Nathan, when you visited."

"And that got me going," Nathan agreed. "I would not have believed anything like that was possible, if I hadn't actually seen and fought that monster. Then it was not *if* but *how*—and who. Who could have generated what we encountered?"

"And there was only one person," Natalie said.

"So I simply wrote MARTHA—YOUR PET ALMOST ATE ME. MEET ME IN PRIVATE—OR IN PUBLIC." Elmo smiled. “So she called me, and we said nothing, only agreed to meet on the stack.”

“You threatened her?” Lisa asked. “She gets mean when threatened.”

Elmo smiled. “So do I. We know each other. She knows I won’t bluff. She knows she has to settle with me, or I’ll blow the whistle on her project and she’ll be arrested for murder. Because of the people that pycno killed.” He glanced at her. “Like your sister-in-law.”

Lisa shuddered. How well she understood how savage the monster was! “But won’t she come with a gun or something, to—so that you won’t tell?”

“No. She knows I’ll have the information documented and primed to be released on my death. But she wouldn’t kill me anyway. I’m the one person she would never knowingly harm. Nor would I harm her. We’re two of a kind.” He held up one hand, showing the odd fingers. “So we’re here to negotiate. In complete, guaranteed privacy.”

“I don’t know,” Lisa said. “I’ve never seen her give way on something she’s set on.”

“I’m the same way,” Elmo said. “That’s why we have to negotiate. She knows that.”

“You will both have to compromise, you know,” Natalie said. “There has to be some middle ground.”

“And you and Nathan will be the judge of it,” Elmo agreed. “And Lisa. We’ll probably accept what you agree on.”

“I hope so,” Lisa said, not completely reassured.

After a while they heard a scraping from the seaward side of the stack. “She comes,” Natalie said. None of them moved.

A head appeared, and then the shoulders and torso. It was Martha, in her wetsuit. She saw them, and came to sit on a rock facing them all. She looked at Lisa. “So you’re part of this,” she muttered. “I should have known.”

“Her brother’s wife was killed by the spider the first week,” Natalie said.

"I didn't think she had the wit to do anything about it," Martha said.

"Lisa's with me, now," Elmo said.

"If I had known you were on that ferry—" Martha shrugged.

"You had to know I'd be looking for the giant pycnogonid," Elmo told her. "And that I'd find it, sooner or later."

Martha sighed. "I had hoped later." She looked around at the rest of them. "So you all know. What's your deal?"

"Lisa will explain it," Elmo said.

"Lisa can barely explain a sign that says NO REFUNDS. Leave her out of this."

"No, she'll do it," he said, his jaw set.

"Why her?"

"Because she will use the simplest, most straightforward language," Nathan said. "There will be no confusion."

Lisa knew that he also regarded it as a good exercise for her to boost her self-confidence. Fortunately he didn't say that.

Martha nodded. "And no subtlety." She faced Lisa, grimacing. "So?"

Lisa tried to quell her nervousness. Never before had she faced Martha on any basis approaching anything other than servility. But this time it had to be done. "You're breeding monsters. You have to stop."

"Those monsters will stop a worse monster," Martha said grimly. "The one that's destroying the world. You know that humankind will never cease its overbreeding and consequent pillage of the animate and inanimate resources of the world until all other life and all usable features of the globe have been extirpated. Then it will be too late. Better to cull that rampant species now, and save the world as we know it."

Lisa knew the answer to that; they had discussed it carefully. "That may be true, but this isn't the way," she said carefully. "If too many monsters attack too many ships, the—the government of some country will strike back. Like maybe by poisoning the water, or setting off bombs. They wouldn't care that it hurt ten times as much as was necessary."

"That's not true," Martha said defiantly. "The governments wouldn't poison their own waters or use bombs. Countries bordering on the oceans know that they need the shipping lanes, the fish, and the beaches for their own economic well being. They'd never drop bombs."

"You mean some governments actually care about the well-being of their ecosystems?" Lisa countered. "Why, Martha, how could you say such a thing?"

Martha snarled, evidently stung by the sarcasm. Lisa was privately thrilled; she had never before dared to speak this way to her employer.

"Even if you are right that most governments would hesitate before poisoning their waters, not all governments would be careful," Lisa continued. "And if you actually managed to exterminate thousands of people, there's no telling what the government and local people will do to protect themselves."

Martha's lips pursed appreciatively. "I *have* been too distracted by my work," she said. "I should have thought of that. The stupid government is capable of doing a hundred times the damage it has to, in pursuit of some shortsighted objective." She squinted at Lisa. "You didn't work that out yourself, did you, girl?" The tone was insulting.

Lisa smiled, briefly. She had been primed for this tactic. "Of course not. Elmo did. But it's true, isn't it? Even if no one knows about you, they'll do terrible harm to the environment, trying to kill the monsters. So your program will be—"

"Counterproductive," Martha finished. "I'm trying to save the world, not harm it myself." She glanced at Elmo. "But since when does my brother care about the environment? He's always been a human-first idiot."

Lisa stifled a laugh. She had come to know how extensive Elmo's knowledge of the sea and its creatures was. He was just as smart as Martha was, only maybe in a different way. It was one reason she loved him, as she had come to know him. He had saved her life, but he was a considerable man regardless. "He cares about humankind. And the other creatures of the world.

He wants to help them. He just thinks you're going about it wrong."

Martha looked at Elmo again, assessing him anew. "If she turned you around on that, she's a hell of a lot more girl than I took her for."

Elmo remained silent, refusing to be provoked into a retort, because they had agreed to let Lisa speak alone, unprompted. They believed that would be more persuasive. So Lisa had to speak for him. "It wasn't me. He had time to think, while he was recovering. He realized that humankind *is* like a monster, maybe, and maybe has to be stopped. But peacefully, without bloodshed. And he talked with Nathan and Natalie, and they worked out a way, maybe." She wasn't saying it well; Martha's remark about her competence, or lack of it, had put her off her rehearsed words. Exactly as Martha had intended.

"What way?" Martha demanded.

"You—you have a knowledge about marine life that they—they say is genius," Lisa said, cursing herself for her halting delivery. But this was the crux, and if Martha didn't buy it, there would be trouble. "You can make monsters no one else could. So maybe you could make—something else. Like a way to feed humankind, instead of—"

"Feed humankind!" Martha screeched, startling several gannets into flight. "I don't want to make the situation even worse! Humankind should be starved, not fed—especially not at the expense of the marine environment."

"A special food," Lisa continued with determination. "Algae, maybe, a new variety that grows the way the sea spiders do, that feeds on wastes and oil spills and stuff, to fill whole bays with high quality green food that man can harvest instead of hunting fish. Like—like manna from heaven. So people could farm it, and there'll always be more than enough. The fish could eat it too. You could develop this, and—"

"Of course I could!" Martha snapped. "But why should I? It would only be helping my enemy to quadruple his population even faster."

"Because—because it would have—have another property. A secret one. It would reduce fertility. For man, not for fish or other creatures. The poorest countries, which unfortunately have the highest birth rates, would be your first consumers. If you were to manufacture the food in bulk and sell it cheaply, you'd still make a profit. So the more of it people eat—"

Martha was staring at her. "Good God, girl—this is insidious! The more people eat it, the fewer babies they'd have. Only they wouldn't catch on right away, because it would be like red squill, the rat poison that thins their blood a little at a time, so by the time they notice it they've OD'd and are dying. A slow, cumulative effect, difficult to prove because there would be so many variables. especially if they weren't looking for it. And even if they did catch on, they'd still have to eat it because there wouldn't be much else, and this would be cheaper. Grow different flavors, tasting like steak or hamburger or caviar. Maybe make it slightly habituating, the way cola is, so they don't want to stop. Mix it in with other foods, so they couldn't readily trace the reason for the declining birth rate. You know, this could work! What genius thought of it?"

Elmo, Nathan, and Natalie burst out laughing.

"I—I did," Lisa said faintly. "They—they thought it was a good idea. And if it wasn't, that maybe you could improve on it."

Martha shook her head. "Out of the mouths of babes," she muttered. "So you want me to stop breeding spiders and start breeding algae. And in return you'll keep your knowledge of my activities secret." She glanced sharply around. "Past, present, and future."

"Yes," Lisa said. "As long as you concentrate on positive, peaceful research and development. No more monsters. And we'll try to find a way to—to market the algae, so that some big company can get rich on it. Then it will never stop, any more than tobacco did, because there's money being made. And the human population will be controlled, because only by staying low enough so people don't have to eat the algae will they be able to have babies. The other creatures will have a chance."

Martha's brow furrowed. "I see you folk came prepared. It's not tight, but I could play with it and come up with a superior variant."

"For example, just as with the pycnos, you could genetically insert genes in the algae for biochemicals that would reduce a man's sperm count," Nathan said. "Weren't the Chinese working with an extract from cotton seeds called gossypol that reduced sperm viability?"

"I have a better idea," Martha said. "How about I insert a gene that produces a chemical that ages people prematurely? Imagine that. By the age of 13, humans would start dying of old age. Wouldn't it be fun to watch them all start dropping like flies with Alzheimer's disease just when they were becoming fertile! Wonder what effect that would have on the social security and Medicare system of the U.S.? Why I could bankrupt the U.S.!"

"Martha, we're trying to steer you on a more humane course," Lisa said angrily.

"And we'll be watching and checking on you from time to time," Nathan warned.

"I was just joking," Martha said. "Your algae idea sounds pretty good." She squinted at Lisa. "But you, girl—if it were up to you alone, what would you do?"

Lisa couldn't stop herself. "I'd give the police the evidence against you, and see you fry for murder. You killed Kalinda, and almost killed me."

Martha nodded. "But the others want to go for the big prize, the world. And they made you go along."

"Yes," Lisa said tersely. "You bitch."

Martha seemed satisfied rather than angry. "So you, too, are telling the truth. You will honor the deal."

"Yes."

"And I can't even fire you, because we'll be partners of a sort." Martha shook her head as if bemused. "Well, you've got me in check. I'll make the deal."

Lisa knew they had won, though for her it was a bitter victory. When she had learned Martha's role in Kalinda's death, she had wanted to kill the woman. But Natalie had made her face reality: she couldn't bring Kalinda back, but she could help see that no others died that way, and do the world a significant favor. So she had had to choke back her pain and rage and work with them to make it happen. And she knew that despite her anger, it was the right thing. It was a realistic compromise.

Slowly Lisa extended her hand. Martha took it and shook it once. Then Martha shook hands with the other three, concluding with her brother. This was the kind of agreement that could not be written. They all knew that.

Then Martha rose, walked to the edge of the stack, and disappeared over it. She was on her way back to her pet monster, but not to guide it to any more ships.

"It's better this way," Natalie said. The two men murmured agreement. And Lisa had to agree too.

"Who knows what scientifically valuable information she will discover," Nathan said, "if we can keep her in check and make sure she uses her apparent skills for the good of humanity."

"She might even be considered the new savior of humans and the earth," Natalie said wryly.

Elmo took Lisa's hand. "Next time you propose to me, I may accept," he said. She knew he was serious. She had proved to him that she had what it took.

They started down the steep slope.

Author's Note: Piers Anthony

MARCH 9, 1992, was an unusual day. I was in the middle of the editing of my fantasy novel *Demons Don't Dream,* and learned that Drew, a close acquaintance of my daughter Penny and the closest friend of Alan, my research assistant, had killed himself. Alan had been talking with Drew on the phone, and then there was silence. When other friends checked, they found that Drew had shot himself. I knew Drew, but wasn't close to him; my daughters have many acquaintances, and I try not to mess with their lives. Nevertheless it was a shock. My awareness had abruptly shifted from fun puns to death.

So I would hardly have noticed the letter I received that day from one Clifford A. Pickover of the IBM research center in New York, except that he enclosed one of his books: *Computers and the Imagination.* Now I use a computer, and I have dabbled with fractals, so have a certain layman's interest in such things. But it was evident that this man was into such matters in much the way I am into novels: compulsively. That book had colored fractal pictures resembling such things as an inner tube with heartworms, an ocean wave with pustules, the mountains of the moon overlooking the cataclysmic destruction of Planet Earth, skull-faces in an electrified pool of iridescent oil, and a knot-bodied red worm with eyeballs at either end. Strictly routine stuff, of course, but it showed that the man had imaginary aspirations. So I sent him a copy of my *Fractal Mode,* told him that I didn't much like IBM as a company, and wished him well.

But Cliff Pickover is not so lightly dismissed. He sent me others of his books, containing all manner of notions and illustrations: giant fractal sea shells, möbius-strip worms, a golden atom with two green electrons, a Mandelbrot set fissioning in the Pacific Ocean, a fractal Mexican hat, stones with indigestion, and kaleidoscopic rug patterns. Promising, but not exactly the magic of Xanth. His text showed a ubiquitous interest in things ranging from the Arabian Nights (me too: that's why I wrote *Hasan*) to computer generated poetry to prehistoric insects. I continued to brush him off politely, as I do with any routine fan. So then he upped the ante: "I've written a sci-fi novel . . ." After I recovered from my heartwormy inner-tube-sized wince at the bad word, I lectured him about the use of obscene terms like "sci-fi" in public, and read his novel. It was promising, but needed work. So . . .

So we collaborated, and this is the result. It gained 40,000 words, a new title, several bit players fractally merged and become major players, and the overall theme changed. Aside from such details, it's the same.

But I had my little adventures along the way. For example, the conversion from Cliff's ASCII mode to my word processor, Sprint, was imperfect; it left a number of midparagraph hard carriage returns in place. Rather than pick them all out individually, I devised a macro—that is, a combination of steps performed as one—to eliminate those annoying breaks in one swell foop. Only I neglected one minor aspect. I did a Find and Exchange, finding each carriage return [^J] that was followed by something other than a space [^]. You know, normally a paragraph ends, and the following paragraph is indented several spaces, so when there's one that has words instead of spaces, that's an error. I simply exchanged each [^J] for a space: that is, I got rid of it, leaving the paragraph whole, as it was supposed to be. I should have replaced it with a space question mark [?], meaning that whatever followed it remained as it was. A minor omission, of course, but with computers, little things can mean a lot.

What happened was that I did restore all those fragmented paragraphs—but with a few leading letters missing. Yes, I know, my collaborator would never have made such a mistake. But mistakes do make for some intriguing bypaths. Here are some samples:

> "I'll shoot it," heppard said and took a few hots at the creature from her position on deck.
>
> uddenly, Elmo let go of the blond girl or a second. "Help," he yelled as he ooked at his hand.
>
> Brenda creamed again.

Yes, yes, I know: many readers will say that it's more fun that way. But too much ooking and creaming makes editors nervous. So I tediously replaced the missing letters as I went through it, and as far as I know, none are issing ow.

Another thing I did was change the major characters from a last name to a first name basis. I like things personal. So, for example, I did a global exchange of Natalie for Sheppard. But sometimes the full names were given. Thus every so often I encountered Natalie Natalie. Once it came out "her frisky German Natalie dog."

I needed a new setting for a romantic scene, and I couldn't wait for my collaborator to work one up, so I drew on a personal resource. This requires a flashback:

Back in 1990 Alan's grandmother Dot McCulla visited us. She has always ranged around the world, collecting stones from many regions. But as she got older, she decided to give some of her collection to interested parties. Now I happen to be a reformed collector. I have collected a wide variety of things in my day, consistently—some would say compulsively. As a child I collected boxes, from matchboxes to crates, nesting them one inside the other so that they didn't take up too much room. I collected bottletops I found on the ground, noting their seemingly infinite variety, and played a homemade game with them that vaguely resembled the Chinese Go. As an adolescent I collected science-fiction magazines, cherishing each one. When I became a pro writer, and had children (no, the two aren't immutably connected), I could no longer devote a whole room to thousands of old magazines, so gave the collection to serious fans I knew would properly appreciate it. Something that precious can't be sold, after all. Now I collect one copy of each edition of the books I write—hardcover, softcover, American, British, German, etc.—and it keeps expanding beyond my shelving, being somewhere around five hundred now. But I don't think I'll give that away.

So I know the soul of collecting, and understand the importance of saving stones. So she gave several boxes of stones to me, and one day I hope to make a fancy rock garden with them, with sections for the stones from Texas, Cape Cod, Hawaii, Wales, Italy, France, or wherever. When she visited, we had her identify each stone by location, and we marked them. Thus we know that the igneous rock is from Hawaii, and that one stone is a fragment from an old Welsh castle. And some are from Newfoundland, including a little town she passed through called Come By Chance. At that point my ears perked, and I got an atlas and located it on the map. What an intriguing name and location!

So when I found myself amidst a novel set in Newfoundland, in need of a romantic setting, I remembered Come By Chance. I researched amidst the collection and located a stone from there. And that is the one Natalie found. Yes, it really does vaguely resemble that island.

So what other distinction does this novel have? Well, because of the luck of the draw that determines what is finished when, I am now working on three novels and an anthology, and this is the first of those to be completed, and so *Spider Legs* happens to be #100 in my cumulative total of books written. That doesn't necessarily mean it will be my hundredth published, but at least it's a personal marker of a sort. I hope you enjoy it.

Author's Note: Clifford A. Pickover

> *I am reminded of a French poet who, when asked why he took walks accompanied by a lobster with a blue ribbon around its neck, replied, "Because it does not bark, and because it knows the secret of the sea."*
>
> —Anonymous

I love to eat lobsters. I'm eating one right now, and I occasionally wipe my messy hands and return to typing on a laptop computer.

Lobsters *were* my favorite food before Piers and I finished *Spider Legs* this week. Now I'm less sure about my craving for lobster meat. In the past, I could get in the mood for writing this book by occasionally eating a lobster. As I would eat I examined the lobster's anatomy, the legs, the claws . . . People at the dinner table or restaurant often thought I was a bit odd.

My interest in lobsters, pycnogonids, and various strange creatures of the sea probably had its origin in an oceanology course I took during the summer of my junior year in high school. My specific fascination with pycnogonids peaked about the time I received my Ph.D. from Yale University, when I read about a 12-legged pycnogonid found near Antarctica of all places. Its proboscis was much longer than the rest of its body. Still, it would have been hard for me to predict that Pickover and Piers would be collaborating on pycnogonids several years later.

After I read about the antarctic sea spiders, a little time went by, and computer graphics and scientific visualization soon became two of my main interests. In the meantime, I published a number of popular books on the creative use of computers in art and science. (As Piers alluded to in his Author's Note, my books contain a weird collection of computer art, games, philosophies, and mind-expanding puzzles.) My Ph.D. is in molecular biophysics and biochemistry, but now I create computer art and write science fiction. Life is strange that way: it's largely unpredictable. So much of what we do seems to develop from chance meetings with people and what we are exposed to by our families and friends. Randomness plays such a great role.

Although my popular science/art books gave me a nice sense of accomplishment, my real dream was to publish a novel based on my interest in unusual biological creatures. Hence, this novel. *Spider Legs* is based on my explorations, on land and in the sea, into the rare and dangerous creature known as *Colossendeis.* Yes, the deep-sea *Colossendeis* is real! Pycnogonids are real. Various biological descriptions in the novel, such as the packing of the pycnogonid's digestive system into its legs, are based on scientific facts. However, the life cycles of the large, deep-sea forms, especially members of the genus *Colossendeis,* are still largely unknown to scientists. For a general background on the pycnogonid's life and behavior, see Lockwood's *Biology of the Invertebrates* (Wiley, NY, 1977).

How does Piers fit into all this? After completing a rough draft of the novel, I began to search for a collaborator to bring the book together and add material as needed. My first thought was Piers Anthony, science fiction and fantasy's most creative talent—and one of the most prolific. I had been reading his books for many years, but the idea for collaborating with Piers started when a colleague lent me a copy of Piers's fantastic novel *Virtual Mode,* which had just been published. I had spent some time working on *Spider Legs* and decided it would be beneficial to contact a real pro in the fiction business to develop the novel even further. To set the stage, I mailed Piers my book *Computers and the Imagination,* and I thought this would prepare him to receive further material from me. I waited a week or two. Then I followed up by sending him a draft of *Spider Legs.*

After some hesitation on Piers's part, it seemed like I soon hooked him on the idea of a collaboration, and what you see is the result. Collaborating turned out to be quite easy, and, oddly enough, choosing a title was one of our more difficult jobs. I had originally called the book *Phantom,* a title which we abandoned fairly quickly because the title had been used too many times before. Before we finally arrived at *Spider Legs,* we considered other titles: *PycnoPhantom, Legs, Killer Legs, Sea Legs, Pycnophobia, Fractal Phantoms, Spider Eating, Spider Hunter,* and even *20,000 Legs Under the Sea.*

Some of you may be interested in how I got the idea for Martha and Elmo's long teeth. It came from various children's stories I had read involving humans with large teeth. In fact these kinds of stories have had a long history. The scary story "The Teeth" in the children's book *In a Dark, Dark Room* by A. Schwartz (Harper-Trophy, 1985) is one good example. "The Teeth" is based on a story from Surinam (Dutch Guiana) collected in the 1920s by Melville and Frances Herskovitz. In the story, a boy continues to meet men on the street with large teeth. Each man he encounters seems to have bigger teeth than the previous. . . .

There is some precedent in the medical literature for a disease known as "vampire disease" which gives the impression of longer teeth because the gums recede. Other effects of this blood disorder disease include pale skin, sensitivity to sunlight, and partial relief by drinking blood. There's also a disease which causes long fingers: Marfan's syndrome. President Abe Lincoln is a suspected case, presently awaiting positive identification of the gene from his remains. People with Marfan's are also taller than average.

By now you have probably noticed that I love to collect quotations of all sorts. In *Spider Legs* you'll see a number of quotations by Robert Ingersoll. I found these in an old, tattered book at a local library book sale. The book was published in 1881 and is falling apart now, but hopefully I have preserved some of its wisdom here. For those of you who collect quotations, here are two favorites:

> You are so part of the world that your slightest action contributes to its reality. Your breath changes the atmosphere. Your encounters with others alter the fabrics of their lives and the lives of those who come in contact with them.—Jane Roberts

> If we wish to understand the nature of the Universe we have an inner hidden advantage: we are ourselves little portions of the universe and so carry the answer within us.—Jacques Boivin

You probably know all about Piers from his previous novels and Author's Note, but if you're interested in some of my hobbies, they include the practice of Ch'ang-Shih Tai-Chi Ch'uan and Shaolin Kung Fu, raising golden and green severums (large tropical fish found in the central Amazon basin), producing computer art, collecting prehistoric mammal skulls and carved African masks, playing piano, and working with the SETI League, a worldwide group of radioastronomers who scientifically search the heavens to detect evidence of extraterrestrial life.

My professional interest is finding new ways to continually expand creativity by melding art, science, mathematics, and other seemingly disparate areas of human endeavor; and some of my recent books include such titles as *The Alien IQ Test, The Loom of God, Keys to Infinity, Black Holes—A Traveler's Guide,* and *Chaos in Wonderland.* I also write the brain-boggler columns for *Discover* magazine, hold several U.S. patents, and am associate editor for various scientific journals. If you'd like to learn more about pycnogonids, see images of fossil pycnogonids, or learn more about Newfoundland, please feel free to visit my Internet web site, which has received over 100,000 visits: http://sprott.physics.wisc.edu/pickover/home.htm.

Enough about me. I'd like to hear from you readers. If you would like to send me your comments on this Anthony/Pickover collaboration, or obtain a photo of a real pycnogonid, or obtain more information and a complete list of my other popular science books, or send me your own favorite quotations, I can be reached at Dr. Cliff Pickover, P.O. Box 549, Millwood, New York 10546-0549 USA.

P.S. Although this Author's Note is finished, by now my lobster is cold. Shall I put it in the microwave to reheat it, or would the claws explode under the pressure of the warming fluid? Let's try the microwave. While we wait: Did you know this decapod (yes, that's its scientific order) has 19 pairs of legs. The eyes consist of a few elongated segments. The number of unfused ganglia (nerve tissue masses) posterior to the esophagael ganglion is five thoracic and six abdominal. I'm rambling. I know. I have a tendency to do that.

The microwave is beeping. The lobster is now warm, but I seem to have lost my appetite after thinking so much about its anatomy. I also keep thinking of the scene in the resturant where Martha Samules probes at the lobster to make it move. Perhaps if Martha were here, we could give her a chunk to devour.